Ransom's lips thinned. "Aside from the fact that we hardly know each other, I'm afraid I don't make a habit of deflowering virgins."

Persephone's cheeks grew hot. "But what if I said it did not matter?"

"Oh, I think it would matter very much—to your future husband."

"I plan to live the rest of my life as a spinster."

"Is that it, then?" His head lowered so that they were nearly nose to nose. "Lookin' for a bit o' rough before your parents send you off to the nunnery?"

"Would it be so bad?" He was close enough to her that she could see his eyes clearly even without her glasses, and they were mesmerizing; no matter how hard she tried, she could not look away. "Would I be so bad?"

"No, you would not." When he suddenly pulled away from her, she snapped back to reality. "But I would be bad. Bad for you. I'm far too selfish and wicked for you."

"Isn't that a good thing in this instance?"

Author Note

While most people might think making alcohol was purely a male-dominated space, women actually played a big part in starting this tradition, as well as helping it thrive.

The first-ever written record of a beer recipe was from ancient Mesopotamia, at around 1800 BCE. Sumerian priestesses would brew beer to celebrate the goddess Ninkasi.

In 1811, John Cumming started his own small distillery, which eventually became Cardhu Distillery, but the real hero(ine) of this story is his wife, Helen. Cunning and courageous, she found the most creative ways to evade alcohol taxation, such as walking twenty miles to the nearest township to sell bladders of whiskey she would hide under her skirts.

Bessie Williamson holds the distinguished honor of being the only woman to run and own a whiskey distillery in the twentieth century. She started working at Laphroaig Distillery in 1934, and when the owner died in 1954, he left the entire operation to her. Laphroaig flourished under her watch, but Bessie was also well respected for providing jobs for the local men, especially during tough times.

Believe it or not, a tale of forbidden love kick-started Japan's successful whiskey industry.

Taketsuru Masataka was in Scotland studying whiskey making when he met and fell in love with Jessie "Rita" Roberta Cowan. Despite their families' disapproval, Masataka and Rita married in 1920 and left for Japan, where Masataka established his own distillery, Nikka Whisky, in Yoichi. She is now known as the "mother of Japanese whiskey."

And so, ladies, in your honor, I raise a dram to you and your contributions!

PAULIA BELGADO

The Lady's Scandalous Proposition

Recycling programs for this product may not exist in your area.

ISBN-13: 978-1-335-59579-9

The Lady's Scandalous Proposition

Harlequin Enterprises ULC
22 Adelaide St. West, 41st Floor
Toronto, Ontario M5H 4E3, Canada
www.Harlequin.com

Printed in U.S.A.

Born and raised in the Philippines, **Paulia Belgado** has worn many hats over the years, from office assistant, flyer distributor, singer, nanny and farm worker. Now she's proud to add romance author to that list. After decades of dreaming of seeing her name on the shelves next to her favorite romance authors, she finally found the courage (and time— thanks, 2020!) to write her first book. Paulia lives in Malaysia with her husband, Jason, Jessie the poodle and an embarrassing amount of pens and stationery art supplies. Follow her on Twitter @pauliabelgado or on Facebook.com/pauliabelgado.

Books by Paulia Belgado

Harlequin Historical

May the Best Duke Win
Game of Courtship with the Earl
The Lady's Scandalous Proposition

Look out for more books from Paulia Belgado coming soon.

Visit the Author Profile page
at Harlequin.com.

They say siblings are your first friends, and I'm so lucky to have grown up with five of them.

So, to:

Tetil (#1)

Gella (#2)

Nell (#3)

Gen (#4)

Martin (#6)

—this book is for you!

With love forever,

#5

Chapter One

London, late 1842

Distillation, the process that turned mashed grain into fine whisky, was said to have been invented in the search for the water of life—*aqua vitae*—in hope of solving the puzzle that had plagued men for centuries: how to achieve eternal life.

Lady Persephone MacGregor, however, was trying to solve a different kind of puzzle. Not one as grand as cheating death.

No, this particular mystery was in the form of a small black card.

The card was so thick and expensive that despite having spent weeks in her possession, it remained unbent and pristine. On the card there was no name and no title. Instead, on one side, there was a single embossed stamp of a gold disc.

However, this card had led her to this precise moment, sitting in the back of a hackney cab in the middle of the night, on her way to a place no unmarried lady like her should ever be found.

How it had come into her hands was mere chance,

through a series of events that began when she left her home in the Scottish Highlands with her eldest brother Cameron, the Earl of Balfour. They had come to London so that Persephone could take part in the Season under the sponsorship of the Dowager Duchess of Mabury.

Sometime after they'd arrived, she'd gone to see Cam in his rooms but instead saw his valet, Murray, hurrying out the door. In his haste, something had fluttered off the silver tray he'd carried and landed right at Persephone's feet. At first she thought she had imagined it or perhaps her spectacles had failed her. But no, the ebony card had lain stark against the red carpet, the gold stamp glittering in the lamplight as if calling to her.

Whatever had possessed her to pick up the card and put it into her pocket, Persephone did not know; however, since she'd had it, the card had turned into an obsession, an itch she could not scratch. She had to find out what the card meant.

She had spent the last weeks gathering information and reading books in the library, trying to find answers, looking up the different organisations and groups in London and across England, searching through history books and bibles for answers. She even dared to write to well-known scholars to enquire if they had any knowledge of where the black card could have originated.

However, it was not in the library that Persephone discovered her first clue, but during an evening at the ballet, as she was in the crush of the crowds in the lobby at intermission. She was returning to the Dowager's private box after the interval when she overhead two men ahead of her talking about their plans for afterwards. It was then that she caught the two words that gave her the first real clue.

'The Underworld.'

Realisation struck Persephone like a bolt of lightning. The gold disc was a coin. The Greeks would bury their dead with a coin in their mouths. It was payment to the ferryman Charon, who helped those who had passed away to cross the River Styx and pass into the land of the dead.

It was then she knew that she would not solve this puzzle by consulting books or academics, but by listening to gossip from the sidelines of various balls and parties and reading gossip columns in the following days and weeks.

'...the black building located in St James's Street...'

A certain Mr R has been spotted about town...

'...can't get in without a membership or invitation...'

...a man of mythical proportions...

'...rules it like a kingdom...'

Persephone put all those pieces she gathered from various sources together and landed upon an answer. She knew where the black card came from, and no, it wasn't the Underworld of Ancient Greek myth, but rather the name of one of the most infamous gaming hells in London.

After days of preparation, Persephone put her plan into action. After her maid helped her to dress for the evening's activities—another ball at some important lord's house in Mayfair—she feigned a headache and begged to stay at home. Once everyone had left, she donned a black domino, sneaked out of Mabury Hall while the servants were having their supper and called a hackney cab.

As she sat in the back of the cab, Persephone's stomach roiled at the thought of what she was about to do, as well as the risk she was taking, not the mention the consequences she could face if she were caught.

The trip to England was their mother's dying wish, which was to have Persephone take part in the London Season. Their late mother's friend Miranda, Dowager Duchess of Mabury, offered to be their sponsor, and so Cam took Persephone aside and explained it all.

'It was the only thing Ma asked of us, Seph,' Cam said. *'She'd been planning it since you were born.'*

A small ache pricked Persephone's heart at the thought of her mother. Elaine had passed over seven years ago when she was twelve years old, but the pain returned every now and then. Her father had died not long after, in all likelihood because he couldn't bear to live without his beloved wife.

While Persephone had loved both her parents dearly and missed them every day, the truth was, had she been born a man, there would have been no need for her to come to England to find a titled husband; she could have stayed in Scotland with her other brothers. After all, by the time she was fifteen years old, she was helping run their family's business, Glenbaire Whisky Distillery.

So it was that while most young ladies learned to speak French or embroider pillows, Persephone was learning the fine art of making whisky. If she were a man, she could be a legitimate part of the business, not just a responsibility her brothers were burdened with. She could spend her days working in the fields or the granary with Lachlan and Finley or apprentice with Liam to become a master distiller.

Sadly, she'd been born a woman and her path in life was limited. However, it seemed, even with her sparse choices, she still could not find a future for herself, as after all these months in England, she was still without a suitor. While other ladies collected admirers and beaus, Persephone did not even have one gentleman interested in her.

Her nose twitched.

And whose fault was that?

'No one's but mine,' she replied to herself in a morose tone. Which was the truth, because she spent most balls and soirées hiding from eligible gentlemen. As soon as she arrived at any event, she sought out well-placed topiaries and marble statues, hoping that no one of the male sex would spot her.

Why?

Because the one thing they wanted from her was something she couldn't do.

Dance.

Unfortunately, that particular skill wasn't required in the distilling process, thus Persephone had never learned it. Well, she did have a lesson before coming to England, but that had been an utter disaster. Perhaps she should have tried harder to learn, but there was nothing she could do about it now. But with the English's obsession with dancing at balls, and attending such balls being one of the limited ways to meet gentlemen, it seemed she would not be able to find a husband at all.

'I would never force you to marry anyone you didn't want to,' Cam had assured her from the beginning. *'I will always take care of you.'*

When she remembered those words, she made a decision right there and then in the cab: when Cam and his wife, Maddie, returned to England in the summer, she would travel back to Scotland with them. Once there, she would convince them not to send her back. They had all, in a way, fulfilled their dear mother's dying wish—for Persephone to have a Season in London. It wasn't her fault no Englishman wanted her. How long was she supposed to wait?

Perhaps she'd live the rest of her life as a spinster, but then again, that would allow her to return home. It would not be so bad, she supposed. If no man would have her, she would always have herself. Her life would be much like it was before coming to England, with her days spent working at the distillery. She'd been fulfilled then, thrilled even, that she was able to use her skills, that she was useful, rather than a burden.

But now something did not quite feel the same.

Despite her resolve, doubt crept into her mind. Fleeting, but it was there: the uncertainty that she could leave England and be able to find contentment in a lonely life. While she had been happy back in Scotland, travelling to England had showed her that there was so much more to life, that there was a bigger world out there. And before she settled into a boring, quiet life, she wanted to experience more.

Excitement. Thrill. Adventure.

And passion.

Persephone was an innocent, but not ignorant in the ways of men and women. Plus, there was talk and gossip, and her own observations. How those married couples exchanged intimate glances; once or twice, she even caught a few of them whispering into each other's ears. How she longed for that closeness, that excitement. What would it be like to be in a man's embrace? To have a passionate love affair without consequences?

It was unfair that if she did not marry, her only options were to jump from debutante to spinster. Why could there be nothing in between? To feel that intimacy without having to go through the whole rigmarole of courtship and marriage?

Of course, that seemed impossible. How would she even find a man to have an affair with when she had barely interacted with anyone of the opposite sex?

The sharp tap that came from the roof followed by a gruff, 'We're 'ere, miss,' from the coachman jolted Persephone out of her reverie.

We're here?

She'd been so lost in her thoughts she'd hardly noticed the time. Taking a long, deep breath, she prepared herself. This moment could be the start of her last adventure before she went back to Scotland and settled into a life of spinsterhood.

Reaching for the handle, she stepped out of the cab. However, she misjudged the distance of the step to the pavement, causing her foot to slide forward. Thankfully she caught herself before she completely fell over.

'Och!'

Her vision blurred as her spectacles slipped down the bridge of her nose. She usually had a footman or her brother helping her down from carriages as she was always tripping over. Composing herself, she pushed her glasses back into place and blinked as she looked up.

Oh, my.

The imposing structure towering over her was entirely black, from the chimney stacks to the pediments over the windows, and even the numerous balustrades decorating the enormous property. And enormous it was, as it must have taken up the entire corner. Persephone could not even see where it ended from where she stood, as the black edifice melted into the dark night and thick fog where the illumination from the street lamps did not reach. There was no signage anywhere to indicate the name of the establishment, but Persephone knew this was it.

The Underworld.

After weeks of searching, she was finally here. A frisson of both excitement and fear shot up her spine. A tiny part of her wanted to turn and run to safety, but she didn't. After wondering and searching for so long, she had finally found the last piece of the puzzle. She only needed to find the courage to snap it into place.

With a determined intake of breath, Persephone pulled the hood of her cloak lower to cover more of her face, then marched towards the building and up the black marble steps. Raising her arm, she only hesitated for a second before her gloved knuckles rapped on the sturdy wooden door. A slot opened in the middle, the resounding snap of the wood making her jump.

'Password?' came the gruff voice from the other side of the door.

'P-password?' Persephone pushed herself up onto her tiptoes so that she could see through the slot; it didn't do much good as the opening was so small she could only see a pair of dark eyes peering out at her.

'Today's password,' the man repeated.

He must be the guard.

'I'm terribly sorry, sir, I don't know anything about a password. But I do have a ques—' The slot snapping shut made her start again. 'Hello? Sir? May I speak with you for a moment? I only wish to ask a question.' A few seconds passed, but there was no answer.

Persephone stared at the door, her shoulders slumped. How was she supposed to know the password? The card didn't have—

The card.

With an excited squeak, she retrieved the black card from her pocket, then knocked again. The slot opened and the menacing eyes locked on Persephone. 'Can't let you in without the password.'

'Wait!' she shouted before he could shut the window, then held up the card. 'What about this?'

Unblinking, the guard's glowering stare fixed on the gold-embossed circle. The slot snapped shut again. Persephone's heart sank.

Oh, fiddlesticks.

Maybe she'd been wrong about the card and this place. *Perhaps—*

'Crivvens!' she exclaimed as the door swung open and what was possibly the largest man she'd ever seen appeared before her.

He was tall—even taller than Cam, and perhaps twice as wide. His shoulders reminded Persephone of the cliffs back home and his arms were like tree trunks. Most of his face was covered by a thick white beard and bushy eyebrows, and all she could make out of his face was his ominous gaze.

Persephone swallowed hard. 'I…uhm…'

The giant stepped aside. 'Enter.'

Afraid to disobey him, she scuttled into the foyer. Directly across from the front door was another entryway, though vastly different. This one was much taller, occupying the space from ceiling to floor. It was made entirely of gold.

'Is that real?' she asked the guard. 'I mean, the go—'

He held up a hand, so she clamped her mouth shut. Then, he put two fingers to his lips, sending out a piercing whistle. Moments later, a tall, lanky boy appeared on her left, seemingly from thin air.

She started, stumbling back. 'Where did you come from?'

'Thomas,' the giant boomed. 'Take 'er to the office.'

'This lady here?' Thomas eyed Persephone suspiciously.

'Aye.' Bushy white eyebrows knitted together. 'Ye know where it is, eh, boy?'

His head bobbed up and down.

'That's right. Run along, then.'

Persephone raised a hand. 'Er, excuse me? Sir?'

The giant's massive head swung towards her, but he remained silent.

'Where am I going, exactly?'

He let out a snort, then turned his back to her.

'Harrumph.'

Why, I never—

'This way, miss.' Thomas jerked a thumb behind him, then spun on his heel and placed his palm against the wall. He gave a push and a panel slid away, revealing an entryway.

'How marvellous!' Persephone scrambled towards the wall to examine it. 'How does it work? Is there a—'

'You must follow me, milady. The master don't like to be kept waitin'.'

'The master?'

'Come on, now,' he said, gesturing with his hand. 'Let's get goin'.'

Shrugging, she answered, 'All right.'

The boy was quick and light on his feet, yet purposeful for a boy his age, which she guessed was about twelve or thirteen. Persephone didn't spend much time around children, though she had observed many of them in the village surrounding Kinlaly Castle, her Scottish home. They were often carefree, running and shouting as they played. Thomas, however, had the serious air of a man four times his age as he led her through a maze-like series of hallways and staircases where the unadorned walls were lined with panels of thick, dark wood. The silence inside was deafening, and for a moment, fear gripped Persephone as she wondered if anyone would be able to hear her scream from in here.

'Oomph!' She collided with Thomas, not realising he'd stopped. 'My apologies, I didn't realise we were here.'

Wherever here *was*.

'Right through there, milady.' He jutted his chin down the hallway.

'In there?' She eyed the ominous lone door at the end. What was behind it? With a name like The Underworld, her imagination filled the space with horrific objects like skulls and dead animals, spider-webs and black curtains, perhaps even torture devices and manacles on the wall.

'Yeah. Master sent ye the invitation, didn't he?'

'Invit—?' *The card.* 'Right. I mean, yes. Yes, he did.'

'Go on then.'

She straightened her shoulders. 'I will. Thank you, Thomas.'

The boy tipped his hat, then sidestepped around her before scampering off.

Persephone pushed her glasses further up her nose, then planted her hands on her hips. Part of her hesitated— this invitation had not been sent to her personally and so she was not supposed to be here. But then again, she'd come this far. Why turn back now?

Carefully, she approached the door and knocked. There was no answer, so she tried a second time. Supposing that the office was empty, she turned the knob and stepped inside.

Hmm.

The office was, well…an office. In fact it reminded her of Cam's study back at Kinlaly Castle. Curious, she walked inside for a closer inspection. The furniture was made of heavy polished wood and rich leather; there was a large desk and chair occupying the majority of the space, while a large carpet covered most of the floor. The walls were lined with paintings depicting landscapes and houses, except for one wall that had an enormous window looking out onto the street. Behind the desk was a set of shelves, filled with leather books and various other objects—small figures made of marble and ivory, an ornate clock and a few exotic pieces Persephone could only suppose were Egyptian and Far-Eastern in origin.

No skulls or torture devices.

A giggle bubbled from within her. How silly she was. Of course a business like this had to have an office. There was nothing disconcerting about this place.

'Tell me who you are and what you're doing here right now.'

The low, sinister the voice that came from behind her froze the blood in Persephone's veins. Her body refused to move, even though her mind screamed at her to leave. But how could she? There was only one exit, and she could only suppose that whoever had caught her was blocking it.

Footsteps padded across the floor as the man drew closer. 'I said, tell me who you are and what you're doing here.'

Speaking proved difficult; her throat was dry as a bone. However, Persephone had managed to regain control of her body, and she turned around slowly, so that the hood of her cloak did not slip off. Her chest tightened as she peered up at the man who had caught her snooping.

Oh.

Taller than most Englishmen she'd encountered— though not as tall as Cam—the man towered over her, his chiselled jaw set hard. His thick mahogany hair was neatly combed back, save for a stray lock that lay across his fore-head. The firm mouth, high cheekbones and straight aquiline nose could have been carved by an Italian master.

But what unsettled and thrilled her the most were those eyes. One green, the other brown. Both glaring down at her with a stare that could rival a thousand suns.

He was the most beautiful and dangerous man Persephone had ever seen.

Ransom could not remember the last time he had had to repeat himself. Whenever he gave anyone a command, they complied without hesitation. However, in this instance, he found himself saying his words a third time to the diminutive trespasser.

'I said, tell me who you are and what you're doing in my office.'

Once again the stranger didn't answer and so with one last step, he closed the distance between them, then pushed back the hood that kept the stranger's face hidden. From behind gold-rimmed spectacles, a pair of emerald eyes blinked up at him.

Eyes set on a very feminine face.

Very few things unsettled Ransom. As the owner of one of London's largest gaming hells, he had to be prepared for anything and everything. The heady mixture of money, liquor, and power brought out the worst in people, so control was essential lest chaos and pandemonium overrun The Underworld. In his nearly twenty years in this business, he thought he had seen, heard, and tried everything.

Finding a young woman snooping in his office, however, was certainly something he had yet to encounter. It was unnerving to say the least, and being caught off guard was an experience he did not care for. A man like himself could not afford to give even a hint of being rattled.

Thankfully he regained his composure in no time. 'Do not make me repeat myself a fourth time.'

'I... I was invited.'

'I highly doubt that.' Crossing his arms, Ransom leaned forward. While he meant to be intimidating, he instead received a whiff of a clean, floral scent, with a touch of citrus and spice. 'How the devil did you get past Charon?'

'Charon?' A bemused grin set upon her plump pink lips. 'The man at the door's name is really Charon?'

Actually, it was Toby, but that hardly sounded intimidating for a door guard. It was one of those things about The Underworld that started as a myth and grew out of proportion; Ransom thought it only added to his business's reputation.

In any case, he would be having a stern word with Toby/Charon before the night was over. But first, he needed to get rid of this woman. 'A lady like you should not be in a place like this.'

'A lady? What makes you think I'm a lady? Nay, I'm not even from London.'

Ransom had detected a slight Scottish burr in her accent earlier, but it sounded exaggerated now. 'Your cloak is made of thick velvet, and from what I can see of your dress—' he nodded at where the black fabric had parted '—your gown's fine embroidery tells me it's made by some expensive dressmaker down on Bond Street.'

'I could have stolen both,' she replied quickly.

'These as well?' He plucked the gold spectacles perched on top her pert little nose. 'Fine gold, lightweight. Very good craftsmanship.' When her right hand shot up to retrieve them, he pulled them out of her reach.

'I need those,' she stated. 'Please give them back.'

'Need them? So these are yours?'

Her nostrils flared, but she gave a sharp nod, then held her hand out.

For a moment, Ransom considered holding on to the spectacles in exchange for information, but saw the flash of anxiety on her face.

She would make a terrible poker player.

Carefully, he placed the glasses into her outstretched palm.

'Thank you,' she said as she put them back on. 'And apologies for the…misunderstanding.'

'You still haven't answered my question. How did you get in here?'

'I—I told you. I was invited.'

'And I said I did not believe you.' Ransom knew every single soul who entered The Underworld, who they were, what they were doing, and where they were at all times. Anyone who got through the doors couldn't so much as breathe without him knowing it.

'Here.' She waved something at his face.

The obol.

The card was the only way to get inside The Underworld without a membership. Ransom gave gold-embossed cards to anyone being considered for membership, those he wanted to do business with, or as a favour to certain members who wanted to bring guests. He was certain he hadn't given one to this woman, as he kept track of every single obol card. He would have to check his records to find out who had not used theirs yet.

'So this is an invitation?' Her emerald eyes gleaned hopefully, seemingly encouraged by his stunned silence.

'Did you steal it?'

Colour bloomed in her cheeks. 'No.'

'You lie.' How unfortunate that she wasn't being considered for membership. She was a terrible bluffer; The Underworld would make a fortune. 'Did you steal it from your father? Brother? Husband?' The last word stuck in his throat like a fishbone.

She shook her head, and the lamplight in the office sent shocks of gold through her fiery hair. He'd been so unnerved by her presence in his private office that he hadn't noticed her red hair or how the light made her rosy cheeks glow. She wrinkled her nose, which Ransom discovered was smattered with freckles. 'I did not steal it.'

He raised an eyebrow at her, noting how she emphasised the word *steal*.

'I merely…found it.'

'Then you are aware it was not meant for you.'

'I didn't know who it was meant for when I picked it up from the ground,' she reasoned. 'If someone were careless enough to lose it, that's not my fault, is it?'

'It was not given to you and yet you took it.'

'Or perhaps I found it, and now it is mine,' she said smugly. 'That's some kind of law, isn't it?'

'You mean the old proverb? "He that finds, keeps, and he that loses, seeks."'

She clapped her hands together. 'Exactly. We agree to disagree then.'

'That's not how this works.' The urge to rake his hands through his hair was strong, but Ransom refused to show his frustration.

'In any case, sir,' she continued. 'My curiosity has been satisfied. I shall be on my way.'

When she attempted to sidestep him, he blocked her way. 'I don't think so.' Unfortunately for her, Ransom's curiosity was far from sated and the fastest way for him to find out how the card came into her possession would be from her own lips. Once he discovered who she'd got it from, he would find the scoundrel that dared misplace—or give away—his precious obol, and mete out the corresponding punishment.

'I beg your pardon?'

He plucked the card from her fingers. 'The obol has earned you a tour of The Underworld.' Her eyes widened. 'That's why you're here, aren't you?'

A myriad of expressions crossed her face, as if she were contemplating his words. She pressed her lips together, then said, 'I look forward to it.'

And so for the second time that evening, Ransom found himself unsettled. He had fully expected her to demand that he let her leave or worse—start screaming. She had called his bluff, something few people had ever done.

Who was this bold chit?

'Before we begin, how may I address you, Miss—'

'C-Cora.'

'Miss Cora.' Her answer came far too quickly, but he had already supposed that she would give him a fake name.

'And you are?'

'Ransom,' he replied curtly.

'Mr Ransom—'

'Just Ransom,' he interrupted.

'Ransom.' The way her *R*s rolled caused a curious, pleasurable tingle in his ears. 'Where are we going first? The gaming floor? The card rooms?'

There was no way he was going to parade her out in the main gaming floor or to the card rooms where everyone would see her. Though her accent confirmed she was not part of the English aristocracy, she had obviously been brought up in a genteel manner. Perhaps she was the daughter of some wealthy Scottish merchant who had hoped to foist her off on an impoverished titled lord in need of a dowry in exchange for raising their social status? Whoever she was, he could not allow someone like her to be so publicly exposed in one of London's most notorious gaming hells.

'No, we're not going anywhere near the floor.'

'But this is a gambling den.'

'Gentleman's club,' he corrected. Well, that was what was listed in the business registry's office anyway. Ransom did what was necessary to keep up appearances. There were full-time kitchen staff to serve meals, a few rooms for members to stay overnight, a fully stocked library, a sporting club with boxing ring in the basement, and of course, 'gifts' to the right people in government.

She snorted. 'That's not what I heard.'

'Oh? And what have you heard about us?'

Her mouth snapped shut.

'In any case, Miss Cora, as this is a gentleman's club, women are not allowed inside.' At least, not women like her. 'The gaming—*entertainment* areas, card rooms, billiard rooms, smoking rooms, and the sporting club are off-limits.'

'Then where will you tour me? The bookkeeper's offices? The kitchens?' she asked pertly. 'How exactly are you going to show me your gambling den—'

'Gentleman's club.'

She rolled her eyes. 'Gentleman's club, without showing me where the gentlemen gamble—er, are located?'

She was correct, but there was no bloody way he was going to expose her to the members of The Underworld. However, an idea came upon him. There was one way for her to observe the activities without being seen herself. 'Come with me.'

'Where are we going?'

'Do you want a tour or not?' He walked over to the door and opened it. 'Shall we be on our way? Or have you changed your mind?'

'Of course not.'

'Let us begin then. Just follow me.'

Ransom led her down the hall, away from his office, then down the staircase to the second level. This was the one level inside The Underworld that had a guard standing outside the entrance, and no one except Ransom and the people who worked in there were allowed inside. He nodded at the burly bald man—Norris—who stepped aside. He didn't meet Ransom's eye, nor did he react to Miss Cora's presence.

'Where are we going?' she asked in a rather loud voice.

'Shush. You must keep your voice quiet in here.' He gestured to the doorway 'After you.'

Her hands balled at her side, Ransom observed the hesitation on her face. Nonetheless, she appeared to screw up her courage and crossed the threshold. Strangely, he felt a modicum of pride at her bravery.

'Wh-what's going on here?' she whispered as she glanced around, confusion now painting her pretty face. 'Who are these people? And what are they doing?'

The sizeable room resembled an attic, and in fact when Graham Hale owned the place, it had been used for storage and served as a sound buffer between the main gaming floor and the private rooms above. However, when Ransom bought out Old Man Hale, he found a more effective use for the space. 'Those are my most valuable employees.'

About a dozen men lay face-down on the floor in neat rows on top of fabric-covered pallets, hands cupped around their temples. None of them lifted their heads or even acknowledged their presence, just as they had been trained. 'I call them my eyes in the sky.'

'Eyes in the sky?' she echoed. 'What are they looking at?'

'Why, the gaming floor, of course. From here, they can see everything that's happening downstairs.'

Her head tilted to the side. 'Whatever for?'

'Anyone who walks into The Underworld thinks they can win,' he began. 'Some nights they do, which is why they keep coming back, but most often, they don't. And when they don't, they might get desperate and resort to other means to win.'

'You mean cheating.'

'Clever one, aren't you?' Ransom couldn't stop the corner of his mouth from tugging upwards. 'And my eyes in the sky can spot almost all cheaters.'

'How do they know if someone's cheating?' she asked. 'Couldn't someone simply be skilled? Or perhaps lucky?'

'True, but there are some games that are pure chance and if someone's on an extraordinary winning streak, then one of my men will spot them.'

'And the games of skill, like cards?'

'Some men may try to smuggle in good cards and switch them. Or some men work in teams, trying to signal to each other. However, if someone has the natural ability to win, I don't begrudge them. Besides, it is not possible to keep winning eternally. A player might get hungry or tired or simply careless. If they keep playing long enough, they eventually lose.'

'So, the real skill is learning when to stop.'

Ransom narrowed his eyes at her, surprised by her astuteness and insight.

'How do they learn to spot cheaters? Are they taught?'

'In a way,' he said. 'They used to be cheats themselves.

Tossed out of the lower gaming hells. I recruit them my-self.'

'Do you test them yourself too?' Emerald eyes spar-kled with mirth. 'Do you cheat, Mr Ransom?'

'Ransom,' he corrected. 'And I never cheat.'

'Truly? But you run a gambling hall.'

'We do not cheat in The Underworld. Anyone with even the slightest knowledge of numbers and gaming knows that there is only one truth in gambling: the house always wins. I merely…take advantage of weaknesses.' And for a moment he wondered what her weakness was.

'Some might say this is cheating.' She motioned to the men on the floor. 'You could use your "eyes in the sky" to look at players' cards, for example, and ensure your dealers always have the better chance of winning.'

'But how would this information be relayed to the dealers downstairs? By the time they run down to inform them, the hands would have been played.'

'True.'

Ransom could practically hear her thinking as her brows furrowed together. Before she could go on any further, he said, 'Would you like to see for yourself?'

'S-see? You mean, be one of your eyes in the sky?'

'For a few minutes, at least, until you get bored.'

Her eyes lit up. 'I'm not sure I'll be bored for at least… an hour,' she guessed. 'But…aye. I would love to see it for myself.'

Glancing around, he guided her towards an empty pallet. 'Here you go.'

She looked down. 'Must I lie down?'

He nodded. 'That is the only way to look through the ceiling.'

'I… All right.' With a determined shrug, she sank

down to her knees on the pallet. 'It's quite soft.' She bent down to sniff at the pallet. 'And the linens are fresh.'

'Of course. My men often have to stay up here for hours and so they must be comfortable.'

'Hmm…yes, comfortable indeed.' Positioning herself, she lay down prone on the pallet. 'And I look through this?' She tapped her fingers on the rectangular hole on the floor.

'Yes.'

She frowned sceptically, but peered forward. 'Oh… everything looks distorted.'

'I had spyglasses—similar to opera lenses—installed so everything is magnified. Perhaps your spectacles are in the way.'

'Oh.' She lifted her head up. 'Perhaps so.'

Getting down onto his knees beside her, he extended his hand. 'May I?'

She nodded, and he plucked the glasses off her nose and placed them into his front coat pocket. Before he could get a good look at her face, however, she once again turned to the spy hole. 'Oh, I see,' she squeaked. 'I see everything. Oh! It's marvellous. Beautiful. The décor, I mean. The lights…the furniture…the artwork.'

'Not what you expected?' he asked wryly.

'Not in a place called The Underworld.' He could practically hear her smile. 'And so many people. Do you really mean to say that not one of them has ever looked up and caught a glimpse of your spies?'

'We are high up, hence the need for the spyglasses. That, and the ceiling is made of mirror shards,' he explained. 'Anyone who looks up and sees a pair of eyes could easily think that it is their own staring back at them. But, no, no one has ever looked up, not when their attention is fixed on the game and money is at stake.' Gamblers paid attention to little else but the turn of the roulette wheel, the roll of the dice, or the flipping of cards.

'How many—' She halted abruptly, then let out a huff.

'What's wrong?'

'You said women weren't allowed on the gaming floor.' Craning her neck up, she glared at him. 'There are definitely women there.'

'Are there now?'

'Yes.'

When she turned back to the spy hole, he quietly lay down next to her. 'What do you see?'

'Women. Several of them.'

'And?'

Just a little closer, he told himself as he leaned towards her. Just so he could take in another whiff of her clean floral and citrus scent.

'What are they doing?'

'Well…one woman, she's leaning over the roulette wheel and…'

He waited a stretch before saying, 'And?' A stray wisp of red hair tickled his cheek as he whispered into her ear. 'What else?'

'She's…bent down so low and her dress…'

'What about her dress?'

'It's…well, I think she should have a word with her modiste. It seems to be missing a few key pieces of fabric.'

Ransom bit his tongue to stop himself from laughing aloud. 'And? Is she with anyone?'

'I… The gentleman next to her, I suppose. And…' She took in a sharp intake of breath.

'Yes?'

She swallowed audibly. 'She sat herself on his lap.'

'And what's he doing?'

'He's touching her.'

He was so close now that he could feel the warmth of her skin. His lips were but a hair's breadth from her cheek. 'Where?'

'I…would rather not say.' She pulled away from the spy hole and when she turned her head towards him, their lips nearly brushed. 'I… Oh.'

Quickly, she scrambled up to her knees and pressed a hand to her chest. Even in the dim light, Ransom could see the flush on her cheeks. 'Those women…'

'I should have clarified.' Calmly, Ransom stood up and brushed some imaginary lint from his trousers. '*Ladies* are not allowed on the gaming floor. But women are.'

Most other gaming hells had women at the ready for their patrons, but Ransom had no stomach for the flesh trade. However, he understood that it was a necessary evil in this business, and banning the working women of London from The Underworld would be bad for profits. So, he struck up an agreement of sorts with a few nearby reputable brothels to allow some of their workers to ply their trade here, though Ransom forbade his employees from interacting with the women. It was a rule he himself also observed.

'Do you understand the difference?'

She nodded, the colour from her face abating, though her eyes remained glazed.

'Perhaps the excitement has worn out your nerves, Miss Cora.' He offered her his hand. 'Shall we continue on?'

She didn't answer or take his hand, and instead attempted to stand up on her own. In doing so, she must have stepped on her own skirts and tripped forward, her hands landing squarely on Ransom's chest. Though the impulse to wrap his arms around her was strong, he raised his hands high up away from her to avoid temptation. Nevertheless, she slammed against him. Her fingers gripped the lapel of his coat and she lifted her head up to meet his eyes, her lips parting.

Ransom, being only human, gave in to the urge to stare at those luscious lips and imagine what they might taste like. His mind continued down this dangerous path, picturing himself kissing her freckled nose, smooth skin, and cheeks. When he met her naked emerald gaze straight on, however, the orbs turned dark, and to his consternation, he saw a flare of desire in them—one that mirrored his own. His cock twitched involuntarily as breathless longing filled his body.

This was absolutely unacceptable.

'Miss Cora?'

'Yes?' she breathed, her pupils widening.

'Would you be so kind as to release me?'

She gasped, then shook her head. 'I… Of course.' Swiftly, she let go of his lapel and took a step back, but refused to release her gaze on him.

When he put his arms down, the numbness from holding them up dissipated, only to be replaced by an ache. The twinging pain was welcome, as it distracted him from the other feelings coming from his nether regions. 'Perhaps it's best we conclude our tour.' Without another word, he walked towards the exit. He didn't hear her reply, but the footsteps behind him told him she was following.

Good.

She had no business being here in the first place, and he had no business being aroused by some slip of a girl.

Yanking the door open, he allowed her to exit first. He closed the door behind him and turned to her. 'Shall I have someone call you a hackney cab?'

'Yes. I mean no.'

'No?'

'I…that is…' She fiddled her fingers together, her head shying away from him. 'I don't want that.'

'And you think you have a choice?'

'No… I mean…there is one more thing I want.' Slowly, she put her hands to her side, then lifted her head. 'What I came here for.'

Exasperated, he said, 'And what, pray tell, is that?'

'An adventure,' she stated.

'An adventure.' He crossed his arms over his chest and leaned back on the door. 'Wasn't tonight enough of an adventure?'

'No.' She held his gaze steadily. 'It was not.'

'What more could a girl like you want?'

'I would like to start an affair.'

A pulse pounded in Ransom's temple.

What the—?

'If you think I'd let you go downstairs and pick out some random man to sleep with—'

'No, no.' She shook her head vigorously. 'I do not want to s-sleep—have an affair with a man from your club.'

'Then who the hell do you mean to start your affair with?'

Her mouth opened and once again, a pretty blush bloomed on her delicate cheeks. 'You. I would like to have an affair with you, please.'

Had Ransom not been leaning back on the door, his knees would have given way.

He was not merely unsettled this time. He was damn well disarmed and rattled.

Bloody. Hell.

Chapter Two

Persephone wasn't sure exactly why she said those words to him, but they stumbled out of her mouth before she could stop them.

Well, she did know why she said those words. It was because she wanted to. Of course she knew that a lady was not supposed to say such things to a man, but she was so tired of always having to do things that were expected of her. If she were to have any kind of adventure before she went back to Scotland, she would have to start doing things her way. And when she had seen what that man was doing to the woman down at the gaming floor, she couldn't help but imagine being in her place, but with Ransom's firm lips on her neck and his hand under her skirt as he—

He cleared his throat. 'Perhaps I did not hear you correctly—'

'Oh, yes, you did,' she insisted. 'I would like us to—'

'Why?'

'Why?' she repeated.

'Why me? Why an affair?'

'Why not?'

'One does not simply walk up to a man and propose to have an affair.'

'And how does one propose an affair?'

His frowned. 'Are you being glib?'

'No, I genuinely want to know.' She gnawed at her lip. 'Is there some kind of secret method or manner for asking of such a thing?'

'The fact that you have to ask tells me that you've never had an affair before.'

She threw her hands up. 'Well, obviously. Otherwise, I wouldn't be asking.'

His bi-coloured eyes darkened. 'Tell me, Miss Cora.' He took a step forward, looming over her. 'Have you ever been kissed?'

Heat curled in her belly as his rough, low voice caressed her like velvet on her skin. 'I… Yes, I've been kissed before.' One boy back in Scotland had been bold enough to try, but thankfully it had been quick and rather forgettable.

'Truly? Really been kissed? Not just by some fumbling lad brushing his lips on yours?'

'He… It's not…' Her tongue suddenly became as clumsy as her feet. Why was this so difficult? From what she'd been warned all her life about men and their lusty appetites—not to mention all the rules of society meant to keep unmarried men and women apart—she thought he would have jumped at the chance for an easy tumble.

Unless of course he had a different reason for hesitating.

'Am I not pleasing to you?' Her stomach clenched. 'Do you find me unattractive?'

'What kind of question is that?'

'A serious one.' The fact that he answered her question with a question told Persephone that he didn't want her to hear the truth. Her heart dropped to her stomach. 'It's all right if you say you do not.'

His lips thinned. 'Miss Cora, aside from the fact that we hardly know each other, I'm afraid I don't make a habit of deflowering virgins.'

'Would it make a difference if I said I was not a virgin?'

'I would bet The Underworld that you are.'

Her cheeks grew hot. 'But what if I said it did not matter?'

'Oh, I think it would matter very much—to your future husband.'

'You think wrongly then,' she declared. 'I do not want to be married.'

'All women like you want to be married,' he countered.

She straightened her shoulders. 'I assure you, I do not.'

'But you have no choice in the matter.'

'I plan to live the rest of my life as a spinster.'

'Is that it then?' His head lowered so that they were nearly nose to nose. 'Lookin' for a bit o' rough before your parents send you off to the nunnery, then, eh?'

'Would it be so bad?' He was close enough to her that she could see his eyes clearly even without her glasses, and they were mesmerising; no matter how hard she tried, she could not look away. 'Would I be so bad?'

'No, Miss Cora, you would not.' When he suddenly pulled back from her, she snapped back to reality. 'But I would be bad. Bad for you. I'm far too selfish and wicked for you.'

'Isn't that a good thing, in this instance?'

A small smile formed on his lips. 'Not for you. I am a soulless cad who would bring nothing good into your life.' Reaching for her hood, he pulled it over her head.

'If you're looking for an exciting liaison, I suggest you find some randy young buck who would no doubt be more than happy to oblige. There are many of them around.'

Persephone found herself suddenly turned around, a gentle hand pushing on her lower back as she was quickly guided down the stairs to where she began the evening—at the threshold to The Underworld.

'Charon,' Ransom called. 'Have Thomas or one of the men call a hackney cab for the lady. A decent one. And put in on my personal account.'

'Will do, Ransom,' the burly man replied.

Before she could say another word, Ransom disappeared into the hidden entryway, the hidden panel sliding back into place with an audible click.

'I— Wait!' She'd been so preoccupied during the entire exchange that she'd forgotten to ask him for her spectacles back.

Oh, fiddlesticks.

She considered banging on the wall and attempting to retrieve them, but remembered that she carried an extra pair in her reticule, since she'd managed to break three pairs in the last five years. This was the first time she was thankful for her clumsy nature, as the thought of facing Ransom again after he'd dismissed her so coldly left a bitter taste in her mouth.

She fumbled for the spectacles, put them on, then blinked until Charon's blurry figure came into focus. When the burly guard placed two fingers into this mouth to whistle for the boy once more, Persephone raised a hand to stop him. 'No, thank you.'

'The master—'

'I said no, thank you, Charon,' she repeated firmly. 'I can find and pay for my own cab, thank you very much.' She strode over to the door, but he blocked her way. Mustering up her courage, she glared at him. 'Please move out of the way and then I can be out of your hair.'

The guard remained silent for a moment, then stepped aside and opened the door. She muttered her thanks and hurried out.

The rush of cold air was a welcome balm against her flushed skin. A plethora of emotions passed through her—mostly embarrassment, but also shame and disappointment.

And then there was that lingering heat deep and low in her belly. Was this what desire felt like? Persephone curled her fingers into her palms.

Curse him for being so attractive.

Mostly, though, she was vexed at herself, because despite the things he'd said, she still had the urge to run back and see him again.

I shouldn't have come here.

It was much too late for regret, of course. For now, she only had to think of one thing—getting back to Mabury House and sneaking in undetected. With a deep sigh, she strode away from the gloomy black building, quashing the urge to look back.

'Lady Persephone, dear, are you quite all right?'

'Huh? What?' Persephone's head snapped up so quickly it dislodged her spectacles. 'Uhm, yes, Your Grace,' she murmured as she righted the frames.

The Dowager Duchess's gaze narrowed on her, her intelligent dark eyes probing Persephone's face. While Persephone had thought her ethereally beautiful when she first met the Dowager, she quickly realised that behind the attractive façade was a sharp mind. 'Are you sure? There are smudges under your eyes and you look like you're nearly ready to fall asleep into your toast and eggs. Did you not sleep well?'

'I slept enough, Your Grace.' No, actually, she hadn't, as it had taken her another hour to find a hackney cab to bring her back to Mabury House. Then, after she had crept back inside, she had tossed and turned in bed. Despite his sound rejection of her, Persephone couldn't help but think of Ransom until the wee hours of the morning. He had haunted her all night, and when she had finally managed to fall asleep, he appeared in her dreams. Those eyes…that arrogant, handsome face…the warmth of his breath on her cheek…

The temptation to sneak back to The Underworld was strong. Did he leave his club at all? Were there places where she could possibly run into him?

Perhaps I could search for another invitation.

Or forge one. Maybe she could even find a way to obtain the password so Charon would let her in. She groaned inwardly at the silly thoughts that had kept her awake.

I've turned into an infatuated fool.

'Is your headache returning?' asked Miss Merton. The Honourable Miss Harriet Merton served as a chaperone and companion for all the young misses under the Dowager's sponsorship. 'Should we send for a doctor?'

'There's no need to be concerned over me,' Persephone assured them.

The Dowager placed her teacup back on her saucer. 'Lady Persephone, as you know, your brother left you in our care when he went back to Scotland with Maddie and your mother was a dear friend of mine. Thus I take my role as your sponsor and guardian seriously.' Her tone turned sombre. 'I've given it much thought and Miss

Merton agrees with me. I think it's time we speak plainly about certain matters, particularly about last night.'

The fog of fatigue lifted from her mind. As the two older women looked at each other, then at Persephone, she found herself unable to speak or move, pinned to the spot like a hare caught in a trap.

Oh, Lord, she knows I sneaked away.

'Y-Your Grace, allow me to explain—'

'There's no need.' The Dowager gave a graceful wave of her hand. 'I'd rather like to give you the benefit of the doubt and believe that you were, indeed, feeling unwell. However, I think I know why you chose to stay here instead of attending the ball.'

Crivvens, it's worse than I thought.

How much did the Dowager know? Had she somehow found out that she had propositioned Ransom? Could he have discovered who she was and sent word to the Dowager?

Mortification filled her. Cam was going to be furious when he found out.

'It's nothing to be ashamed of, my dear,' Miss Merton assured her. 'Sometimes…things just don't turn out the way we planned.'

Persephone didn't know whether to laugh or cry. Though right now, all she wanted was for the earth to open up and swallow her whole.

The cherubic-faced chaperone patted her hand and continued. 'The important thing is that you don't give up, and try again.'

'I beg your pardon?' Persephone yelped, then gasped at her own outburst. 'I mean, I'm sorry…what exactly are we talking about?'

'Y-your Season, dear.' Miss Merton's brows drew together. 'What did you think we were talking about?'

'Oh!' A laugh burst out of her, and she coughed in a poor attempt to cover it up. 'M-my S-Season.' Mother of mercy, they didn't know anything about where she had been and what she had been doing last night. Waves of relief crashed through her. Her secret was safe.

'You haven't danced a single dance since you arrived here,' the Dowager said.

'And whenever a gentleman approaches you, you find some excuse to hurry away,' Miss Merton added. 'Or else you avoid balls entirely.'

Persephone swallowed hard. She thought she'd been clever, but perhaps she'd been too confident that no one would notice her antics. 'I'm sorry.'

'Oh, no, dear, do not be sorry.' The Dowager flashed her a faint smile. 'If anyone is at fault it should be me. I was so thrilled that you were coming here and that I would be able to do this last favour for my dear friend. I was so determined to make your Season a success, one that would have made Elaine so proud, that I failed to see to your needs.' Reaching over, she covered Persephone's hand with hers. 'Perhaps you are just not ready for the Season. Or we have not prepared you properly. I know you're already nineteen, but you've never been exposed to London society before. It was unfair of your brother and I to ask so much of you.'

Persephone had never thought of it that way. 'I don't know what to say, Your Grace.'

'There is no need to say anything.' The Dowager gave her hand a firm squeeze. 'I have decided that we will take up residence in Highfield Park for the next few months.'

Highfield Park was the Duke of Mabury's magnificent estate in Surrey. 'I do have a few things to settle at the Dower house, but I'll visit and stay over at the main residence as needed.'

'It will give you some more time to mature,' Miss Merton interjected. 'And become more acclimated to England.'

Persephone couldn't believe what she was hearing. 'Does that mean we won't have to attend balls? Or go to dinner parties or teas? Or attend the opera?'

'Yes,' the Dowager said with a laugh. 'But not for ever.'

'And we may plan a few soirées here and there,' Miss Merton said. 'With eligible gentlemen who are of the proper social status.'

With the mention of gentlemen, Persephone couldn't help but think of a certain man with green and brown eyes.

'Would that be amenable to you, dear?'

She'd only been to Highfield Park once, during Cam and Maddie's wedding, but she had loved the Surrey estate. 'Yes, Your Grace. I would definitely be amenable to staying in Highfield Park.'

'Excellent.' The Dowager beamed and picked up her teacup. 'I'll write to your brother today and explain our plan, though I'm sure he'll agree.'

'Thank you, Your Grace, for being so considerate.'

And saving me the trouble of having to come up with more excuses to avoid dancing.

'Do not worry, dear,' Miss Merton said. 'This is only temporary. Once you've found your bearings, we'll come back to London.'

'It's how we prepared my previous protégées after all,' the Dowager added. 'And they both found success.'

Hooray.

'That sounds…er…wonderful.' Of course, Persephone wasn't going to mention her plan of retuning to Scotland and becoming a spinster. But then again—oh, how excellent that this was all working in her favour. She wouldn't have to attend any more balls for a while.

And there was another bright side to all this—she wouldn't be tempted to go back to The Underworld or see Ransom ever again.

Chapter Three

Like clockwork every morning for the past five years, Ransom began his day on the club's main gaming floor. At this time of day, The Underworld seemed like an entirely different place—empty, quiet, and clean. As soon as the last guest left in the wee hours of the morning, the efficient housekeeping crew would sweep in, cleaning, dusting, mopping, and scrubbing every surface free of grime and dirt from the night before. And as was his standing order, all the heavy velvet curtains were to be drawn back, windows opened, and fresh air allowed to circulate. Light and air were cleansing, especially in places where these were precious commodities.

'Clyde, come here,' Ransom called to his right-hand man, who followed him around every morning as he did his daily inspection.

Clyde quickly appeared beside him. 'Yes, Ransom?'

'See this?' He rubbed a finger on one of the mouldings on the mantel above the fireplace. 'It's dusty. Have Hastings and her crew come back and give everything a once-over.'

'I'll go find her now. What else?'

'My nine o'clock appointment—'

'Charon's expectin' them and he'll alert me as soon as they arrive.'

That was why Clyde was the highest-paid employee on staff—because he knew exactly what Ransom wanted and anticipated his every need. 'Excellent.'

'Anythin' else?'

'Nothing at the moment.' Ransom dismissed him with a curt nod, then went up to his private gallery that over-looked the main gaming floor, where he could look down and observe the activity below every evening.

No one else was allowed here, and Ransom never mixed with the crowds downstairs. Few people ever saw him while they were at the club. He never met with members personally and if he did, it did not bode well for them.

No, he was not the type of gaming club owner who wooed and fawned over his clients. He certainly enjoyed taking their money, but after years on the floor and bend-ing over backwards for these fine gentlemen of the ton, he'd grown sick of them. And if keeping his distance gave him an air of mystery, then all the better.

A bright flicker blinded him temporarily as the mir-rored ceiling overhead reflected the morning light. At this time, the light and air streaming through the large open windows gave the room a calming quality.

In the evenings, however, once the curtains were drawn and only the five crystal chandeliers provided illumina-tion, the room transformed into a completely different world. The smell was different too. There was something intoxicating about the atmosphere in The Underworld at night when it was full to bursting with clients—perhaps it was the thrill and excitement mixed with desperation and misery that gave the place such a heady perfume. It was also this time when the tables churned money, where fortunes were made and lost at the turn of a card or spin of a wheel. But no matter which way Lady Luck's whims turned, she always blessed the house, and of course, Ransom's vast personal fortune, allowing him to buy anything and everything he could ever want.

Not bad for a man who had grown up in London's most hellish rookery.

Once he saw Clyde return with the head housekeeper, Hastings, Ransom gave them a nod before heading back upstairs to his office. As he sat down on his leather chair, his attention was drawn to the right-hand drawer underneath his desk. Before he knew it, his hand was already reaching towards it.

No.

He drew his hand away and pushed his chair back as far as he could, ensuring the drawer remained out of his reach. The temptation was strong, and in the last six months, he had given in a few times, opening the drawer to look at what he kept inside. Perhaps one day he'd forget about it and the memory of that night would eventually fade, instead of haunting his dreams.

Ransom shot to his feet and circled the desk. He looked around him, admiring the exotic objects displayed on the shelf behind his desk, as well as the paintings hanging on the wall. These things he kept on display not because he was interested in them. In fact, he had no idea where half of the items had come from or who'd crafted them. The paintings themselves were mostly worthless, though they did depict the various homes and tracts of land he'd purchased over the last five years.

All these items were here for him to view every single day because they had one thing in common: another man—a particular man—wanted them, and Ransom had the means and the money to ensure that this other person could not have them.

''Scuse me, Ransom?' Clyde's head popped in through the open entryway. 'They're at the door.'

Just in time.

If things went well—and Ransom was confident that they would—he would soon gain another painting to hang on the wall.

'Good morning,' came the cheerful greeting from the visitor. 'My, my, I never thought I'd ever see this place.'

Ransom clasped his hands behind him and turned to the man standing in the doorway. 'My lord.' He bowed his head low, leaning forward as far as his posture would allow, a bitter taste brewing in his mouth. He could own the entire world, and yet thanks to pure chance, he had no choice but to show deference to this man who was born to the right parents. 'Good morning, and thank you for coming today.'

Devon St James, Marquess of Ashbrooke, flashed him a bright smile, his blue eyes twinkling. 'How could I possibly say no to Ransom, proprietor of my favourite gentleman's club? As per your request, I've brought along a guest this morning.' Ashbrooke stepped aside, allowing a second man to enter the office. 'May I present His Grace, Sebastian, the Duke of Mabury.'

'Your Grace.' Ransom's bow was even lower and deeper this time. 'Welcome.' As he straightened up, the dark-haired man's onyx eyes fixed on him.

'Mr Ransom,' the Duke greeted him.

'Ransom,' he corrected. 'Just Ransom.' The man who had taken him in had not given Ransom permission to use his last name, and so even after the drunken sod died he never thought to use it or invent one for himself. And as for the man who'd sired him? Well, that was one name he had no right to.

'Ransom, then.'

'It's a pleasure and honour to meet you, Your Grace.'

'I wish I could say the same, Ransom, and that we could continue with these little pleasantries, but do you think we could skip all that so you can tell me why I'm here?'

So, Mabury preferred to get straight to the point.

Ransom was beginning to like this man. 'Of course, Your Grace. First, allow me to thank you for coming on such short notice.'

Mabury's mouth twisted wryly as he glanced at Ashbrooke. 'You have Ash to thank for that. He wouldn't leave me alone until I agreed to come here. Like a dog with a bone.'

The other man simply grinned. 'I like to think of myself as tenacious. A good quality in a man, is it not?'

Mabury rolled his eyes, a gesture Ransom supposed he made often when he was around the Marquess. 'I hope whatever bribe you paid for getting his cooperation was worth it, Ransom.'

'There was no money involved, I assure you.' The Marquess of Ashbrooke was not only blessed with a title, wealth, and charm, but had the luck of the devil himself, so Ransom could not pay him off nor hang any debts over his head. However, once he offered the Marquess the promise of a future favour, Ashbrooke immediately agreed to bring the Duke in for a meeting. While he did not yet know what this would cost him, Ransom knew it would be worth it.

'Please, take a seat, Your Grace, and I promise I'll get right to the point.' He gestured to one of the chairs in front of his desk, then took his own seat on the other side.

The Duke sat down on one of the chairs, while Ashbrooke took the other. 'You don't mind my staying, do you? I'm rather curious what it is you want from Sebastian.'

'If His Grace doesn't mind, I don't.' Ransom looked at Mabury, who shrugged.

'You know,' Ashbrooke continued. 'I thought you wanted to meet Sebastian because you're approving him for a membership. Damn lucky man.' He slapped his hand on his thigh. 'The waiting list is a mile long and I myself was only approved last year. But to my surprise, he's never even sent in an application.'

Indeed, if Mabury had a pending application for membership, Ransom would have gone to him directly, rather than having to contact him through Ashbrooke. 'You do not play, Your Grace?'

'I did.' Mabury leaned forward, fixing him with his dark eyes. 'In fact, in our younger years, Ash and I used to frequent this very club. What was it called then…?'

'Hale's,' Ashbrooke offered. 'And you're right.' He laughed. 'Was that back when we were at university? I don't even remember…though God knows, I hardly remember anything of those days.'

Mabury continued. 'I do recall the previous owner. Graham Hale, wasn't it? What happened to him?'

'Still alive and healthy, and enjoying the attentions of his newest wife,' Ransom answered. 'He moved to a country estate in Essex after I bought him out.'

'And you renamed his club The Underworld.'

'Actually, it's still called Hale's. But…' Ransom clasped his hands together. 'We're not here to discuss my club, are we?'

'No, we are not,' Mabury said. 'So, why are we here?'

And so it begins. 'Your Grace, you have a piece of unentailed land on the southwest corner of your estate.'

'And how did you come to know this information?'

'I have my ways.' Actually, what he had was a team of private investigators at his beck and call. 'But it's come to my attention that your neighbour would like to purchase it.'

'Asking you how you also knew that would be fruitless, as would denying it, so yes, as it happens I have been offered a generous amount for the land.'

'I would like to purchase it,' Ransom stated. 'At double whatever your neighbour is offering.'

'Double?' Mabury's eyebrows shot up. 'For a tiny strip of land that borders two estates? What would you do with it?'

'Whatever I please.' Razing it down sounded like a good idea. Or perhaps he'd start a pig farm; the stench would be unbearable for miles around.

'But it's useless. There's nothing on it and from what my tenants have told me, the soil's not rich enough to grow anything.'

'It can't be useless if your neighbour wants it,' Ashbrooke interjected.

'Only because he's tired of taking the long way around to get to his estate,' the Duke replied. 'He says his old bones need a rest from all the jostling when he takes his carriage in from town.'

'Old bones—you mean to tell me that old codger is still around?' The Marquess tapped a finger on his chin. 'What was his name again?'

'Winford,' Mabury supplied. 'The Duke of Winford.'

From a very young age, Ransom had learned to never show his emotions. Any hint of them would allow other people to exploit him, or worse. However, hearing that name released a floodgate of one specific emotion.

Pure, unadulterated hate.

'How about I triple his offer? Or you could name your price, Your Grace.' He was like one of his patrons, stalking the tables, eager and greedy for a win, placing all his bets on one card. He couldn't help it; hearing that scoundrel's name made Ransom abandon all reason.

'Perhaps you should give this some thought.' Mabury sized him up, his intense stare nearly boring a hole in him. 'I understand you're a very rich man. I've heard all about your investments in various businesses around town.'

'And I have heard of yours.' Of course he had. Ransom didn't meet with anyone without having them thoroughly investigated first. 'Congratulations on the opening of your new locomotives factory, by the way. You must have put a lot of work into it.'

'I wish I could take all the credit.' A small smile appeared on Mabury's lips. 'But anyway, about the land, I've already promised Winford I would sell it. What am I supposed to tell him?'

Ransom had a few choice words for Winford, but none of them were fit to say in polite company. 'You haven't signed a contract yet, have you?'

'No.'

'Then you don't owe him any explanation. Just tell him you have a better offer.'

Mabury remained silent as he clasped his fingers together and rested his chin on them. 'I'll tell you what, Ransom. If you come see the land first, I shall consider it.'

'See the land?' Ransom had expected an outright refusal or perhaps an exorbitant price.

'Yes. You're an intelligent businessman; you don't invest in something without knowing its worth, do you?'

'Of course not.' But oh, he knew the value of the land. It just wasn't monetary.

'Then come as my guest to Highfield Park,' Mabury

said. 'Next week. My wife has finally agreed to a much-needed break and thus we are holding a few events there.'

'You want me to visit your home? As a guest?' Ransom shook his head. 'No, thank you. I shall stay at an inn nearby or better yet, I'll come in the morning and head right back to London afterwards.'

'Not if you want that land,' Mabury said firmly.

'Would your wife not object to the presence of someone like myself?' Ransom countered. 'You do know who I am and what I do?'

'I know more than you think.' Mabury's face turned calm and that's when it hit Ransom.

He knows.

Of course he knew. Anyone with eyes and acquainted with Winford would have instantly guessed.

'Well, Ransom?'

'I…accept your generous invitation.' *Bugger.*

'Wonderful, you'll stay the week then?'

Though posed as a question, it was not a request.

A whole damned week in the countryside.

'I look forward to it.'

Mabury stood up, and Ransom and Ashbrooke followed suit. 'Don't bother,' Mabury said, waving his hand as Ransom began to walk with them to the door. 'We shall see ourselves out. I shall have my man of business send you the details.'

'Your Grace. My lord.' Ransom bowed his head low once again. He didn't raise it until the two men left.

I shouldn't have agreed.

In a split second he was at the door, ready to chase after Mabury, but the murmurs outside made him halt. He leaned forward, trying to listen through the gap.

'…so it's true then, what they say about him?' Ashbrooke was saying.

'Yes. At least, the connection is there. It's hard not to see it, once you've met them both.'

'Now it makes sense, the reason that he wants the land so much.' The Marquess let out a breath. 'He really is the old codger's bastard.'

Not quite.

Ransom gritted his teeth.

'I thought it was just gossip,' Ashbrooke continued. 'But you're right, it's hard to deny it when they both have the same unusual eyes.'

'You know how these things are, Ash,' Mabury said. 'Gossip is just that—gossip. But there is usually a grain of truth to it.'

'So, will you sell?'

The Duke paused. 'I'm not sure. It depends on how the week goes.'

Ransom had heard enough and took a step back from the door, then strode towards the glass cabinet in the corner of his office. Taking out the glass decanter from inside, he poured himself a measure of brandy before sitting back down at his desk. He took a long sip, allowing the warm, smooth liquor to settle into his stomach as he welcomed the numbness.

Damned Winford. The scoundrel didn't even have to be here and yet he rattled Ransom like no one else could.

Old beast.

A tough one too, seeing as the man outlived all his relatives and wives.

And his only child.

When Ransom was growing up in the rookeries, he'd learned a trick that perhaps had saved his sanity and his life. Whenever something bad happened—like when his adoptive father came home stinking of alcohol and beat Mum black and blue—he would take all of his feelings—

his anger, despair, horror—put them in a box and lock them away. That way, he didn't have to feel anything at all. It allowed him to function, to make it through hellish day after hellish day. It was also the only way he found the will and strength even at the tender age of nine to leave that drunk old bastard once he lost everything and everyone he cared about.

Ransom hurled the glass at the wall, the crystal breaking with an audible crash. The brandy ran down the wall in rivulets. The anger and resentment he'd learned to box up over the years threatened to bubble over. He rarely unleashed the fury, and when he did, it broke him into a million pieces like the brandy glass.

Bastard.

Ransom shook his head. No, he was the bastard. The illegitimate son of Winford's only child.

He slumped back into his chair, closing his eyes as he raised a metaphorical glass to the man who had destroyed his life.

Here's to you, Grandfather.

Though he knew he'd been adopted, Ransom had never cared about who his real family were, especially after he'd built his empire. He didn't usually put much stock in rumours either, but one day, he'd seen it himself. He'd looked the old bastard in the face and saw his own bi-coloured eyes staring right back at him. The old man had gone pale, then turned around and walked the other way.

Ransom had sent his private investigators to sniff out the truth. And he did learn it, though some days, he wished he hadn't. He confronted Winford one day, and that went about as well as anyone would have imagined.

Since then, Ransom had made it his life's mission to thwart Winford in every way. He had discovered that the man loved art and collecting foreign objects, so he out-bid him at every auction, paying thousands of pounds for various pieces that he knew nothing about except that Winford wanted them. If he found out that Winford wanted a particular piece of property, Ransom was there, snatching every house and patch of land from under his nose. Even Mabury's worthless piece of land that would do nothing but give the old louse comfort, he would not allow Winford to have.

Ransom very much looked forward to the day when the old sod finally took his last breath. Winford had married twice after his only son died, but produced no more children, nor did he have any other family or presumptive heirs. He would die alone, his title would go extinct, and Ransom would never have to think about the name Winford ever again.

Until then, the drive to bring as much misery as possible to Winford was a burning need Ransom could not quench, and each acquisition only fuelled his rage.

'Ransom?'

Starting, Ransom's eyes flew open.

'I knocked a few times, ye didn't answer,' Clyde said as he cautiously crept into the office. His eyes were drawn briefly on the broken glass, before turning back to Ransom. 'Hastings is done, if you'd like to check again.'

'In a moment,' he said, then dismissed Clyde with a curt nod. As soon as he left, Ransom sank back into his chair. Once again, his attention drifted back to the right-hand drawer on his desk.

Just this once, he told himself.

Then perhaps after this, he'd smash it and throw it into the rubbish, so he'd never have to see the damned thing again.

He grabbed the knob and pulled the drawer open, then

peeked in as if he didn't already know what was inside. The gold frame glinted as the glass surface of the spectacles reflected his face back at him.

His rage from earlier dissipated, replaced by a different emotion, one he could not name. All he knew was that whenever he looked at the spectacles, he would replay the events of that night in his mind.

The way her red locks glinted in the lamplight.

The blush on her cheeks.

Her sweet, clean scent and the warmth of her skin.

He quickly shut the drawer with a loud slam that echoed through the room.

There had been so many times since that night that he'd threatened to throw the spectacles away. He hadn't even realised that he had them until the following day when his valet had found them in his coat. Filled with dread, he thought, what if she was completely blind without them? Had she even made it home? Charon had said that she'd declined the offer of payment for a hackney cab, but he did have young Thomas trail her until she found a coach.

There had also been numerous instances when he'd been tempted to find her. He could easily pinpoint whose obol she had found, or even use his investigators to ferret out her real identity. However, he knew that whoever she was, there was one thing for sure: he would never be able to have her. He was a lowborn bastard raised in the rookeries. The spit and polish of money could never erase his past.

You could have had her, you fool.

She'd wanted him. Why he had said no to her that night, he wasn't sure. It was true, he didn't make a habit of deflowering virgins, but he wanted her too—it just hadn't felt right.

Despite the fact that she'd only offered use of her sweet

body, he could see that in her emerald eyes, she'd offered something more. Softness, warmth, tenderness—all the things a selfish, soulless bastard like him didn't deserve.

Think of something else!

Because each time he did think of her and how he'd turned down her proposition, he'd eventually begin wondering if she'd asked any other man after him. And if she had succeeded in finding her affair.

It was a good thing he didn't have another brandy glass in his hand or else it would have joined its twin in shards on the floor.

He could not—would not—be waylaid from his life's mission to destroy Winford. Nothing stopped him from achieving his goals, and a girl would certainly not be the first thing to make him forget who and what he was.

Rising to his feet, Ransom loosened his ascot tie as the atmosphere in the room turned stuffy. He'd have Hastings come and clean up the mess of brandy and glass, and in the meantime, he'd find some other place to work for the rest of the day.

Having never been invited to spend a week in the country by any member of the ton, Ransom wasn't sure what to expect and, more importantly, what to pack for such a trip. Thankfully, his trusty valet, Jones, knew exactly what to do.

'Leave it to me, Master Ransom.' The man was positively giddy at the thought that they'd be going to a fine country estate—and that of a Duke, no less. 'Once the Duke's man of business sends the invitation and details, I'll take care of everything.'

'I shall leave it to your capable hands,' Ransom said.

'I swear, he's walkin' on clouds,' Clyde remarked with a shake of his head as the valet left the dining room. Since yesterday, Ransom decided he'd conduct his business at home, so he had Clyde over for a late luncheon to discuss important matters before The Underworld opened later that afternoon.

'I suppose you can't blame him that he's creamin' his britches at the thought of stayin' at a fancy duke's house,' Clyde added as he slurped a spoonful of cucumber soup.

'You mean because he has to work for me now?' Ransom asked wryly.

Clyde stopped halfway through his second spoonful. 'No offence.'

'None taken.' Ransom truly didn't take offence at the idea that being in his employ was a step down—from a valet no less. But he understood and respected male pride, and the dignity of one's work. Jones had been in the employ of a viscount before coming to work for Ransom, so in his world, working for a gaming hell owner was indeed a demotion. Still, Ransom liked the man well enough. Jones kept all his clothes laundered and was an authority in all the latest in male fashion. Thanks to him, Ransom didn't have to think about putting together outfits for important events, which freed up his time and energy for more important matters.

'Yer really going to be gone the week?' Clyde asked.

'I'm afraid so.'

'You ain't never gone on holiday before, Ransom.'

'It's not a holiday.' He didn't know what it was, exactly, as he still could not figure out Mabury's reason for inviting him.

'Now, can we get to business? We will need to plan ahead so you can keep things running smoothly while I'm away. I'll still be working and I expect daily reports to be sent to Surrey for the entire time I'm away.'

It took another few days for Ransom to prepare for

the trip; then he was on his way to Surrey in his luxurious carriage. Jones had ridden ahead to prepare his rooms and wardrobe at Highfield Park. Unfortunately, on the way there, there had been a huge accident involving three carriages, and no one could pass for hours. Thus, instead of arriving before luncheon, it was six o'clock by the time Ransom's carriage pulled up the driveway at Highfield Park.

'Oh, dear, Master Ransom, where have you been?' Jones met him at the door as the butler, who had introduced himself as Eames, let him in.

'There was an accident; nobody could get past,' he said as the valet quickly ushered him upstairs and into his rooms.

'We only have a few minutes to get you ready for dinner.' Jones clucked his tongue as he took in Ransom's dishevelled state. Having been stuck inside the stuffy carriage for hours, he'd long since discarded his coat and cravat, and a layer of travel dust had settled over his hair and the rest of his clothing. 'Goodness, we won't even have time for a bath. There's water in the pitcher.' He gestured to the washstand by the bed. 'Master, please do refresh yourself as best as you can while I get your clothes ready.'

Ransom did as he was told without protest as Jones hovered over him like a mother hen, while giving a rapid-fire summary of the evening's activities. Despite Ransom's protests at being treated like a baby chick, he could not deny that the man was a miracle worker; in twenty-seven minutes flat, he had managed to get Ransom ready for a formal dinner.

'You look magnificent.' Jones beamed before sending him on his way.

Ransom retraced his steps as best he could recall, but

the manor was huge and he was forced to double back a few times. Finally, he recognised the main hallway that would lead him to the staircase. According to Jones, all the occupants would gather in the foyer before dinner. He took the steps two at a time and reached the bottom quickly, and thankfully, a familiar face greeted him there.

'You've made it.' The Duke of Mabury flashed him a wry grin. 'I was waiting for word of your arrival.'

'I was merely delayed, Your Grace.' Ransom bowed his head low. 'Did you think I wouldn't show up?'

'I would have been disappointed if you hadn't.' Mabury turned to the two women who flanked him, one older, who had the Duke's dark hair and eyes, and the other a pretty, petite brunette. 'Forgive my rudeness, Mother, Kate. Allow me to introduce—'

'Och!'

The loud yelp that came from behind him made Ransom whirl around. Before he could act further, a green mass of fabric came hurtling towards him and, having no other choice, he opened his arms and caught the ball of silk and taffeta.

'Oh, dear,' sighed a feminine voice which sounded as if it came from somewhere inside the mass. 'Forgive me, my lord, I must have tripped over my skirts.'

Ransom's entire body froze at the sound of the familiar Scottish burr.

It can't be.

As the bundle of fabric in his arms wiggled, a whiff of a familiar floral scent tinged with citrus tickled his nose. He immediately dropped his hands to his sides.

No, this couldn't be happening.

'I'm terribly sorry. I'm so clumsy and this is a new dress.' The woman inside the fabric raised her head and emerald eyes blinked owlishly at him from behind a pair of gold-rimmed spectacles 'I didn't—*eep!*'

Ransom's chest squeezed every bit of air from his body as he came face to face with the woman who had haunted both his dreams and waking hours for the last six months.

What in God's name was she doing here?

Chapter Four

What on God's green earth was he doing here?

Persephone moved to adjust her spectacles, just to ensure it was really him, but her arms wouldn't move. But no, even through her blurry vision, there was no mistaking the man before her. The knot in her belly tightened.

Ransom.

Six blissful months she'd spent at Highfield Park, away from the noisy, crowded city and more importantly, the dreadful balls and soirées of the ton. Out here she could breathe—not just because of the fresh air, but because she'd found a purpose.

A few weeks after Persephone had arrived, the Dowager noticed that she'd grown melancholic; when questioned, Persephone confessed that she was bored. After a lengthy conversation, the two women came up with a special project to occupy her time. The project had been diverting her attention for the past months, allowing her to put her mind to good use. Being so preoccupied, The Underworld had faded from her memory.

But now, Ransom was here and she had to face the reality of what happened that night.

'Lady Persephone, are you quite all right?' Miss Merton cried as she made her way down the stairs. 'I was just behind you when you fell.'

Kate, the Duchess of Mabury, rushed to her side, her hands patting Persephone's shoulders and arm. 'Are you hurt? That looked like a nasty tumble.'

'It would have been, had Ransom not been there,' the Duke of Mabury said. 'Thank you for catching her.'

Ransom did not reply, but gave the Duke a nod.

'What happened, dear?' Miss Merton asked, concern still marring her face. 'I thought Mrs Ellesmore fixed that hem earlier today.'

It was my clumsy feet, that's what happened.

'I…uhm…wasn't paying attention and my slipper must have caught on something. Apologies, I'll take more care in the future.'

'Not to worry at all, dear, I'm just glad you weren't hurt.' The Dowager turned to Ransom. 'Apologies, sir, and welcome to Highfield Park.'

Mabury cleared his throat. 'Allow me to continue introductions…'

Persephone's heart hammered as the Duke introduced Ransom to the three women.

'And finally, this young lady is Lady Persephone Mac-Gregor.'

'Lady Persephone.' There was no hint of recognition in his voice as he said her name, but the green and brown eyes boring into her told otherwise. 'A pleasure to meet you, my lady.' He bowed his head.

'The pleasure is all mine, Ransom,' she replied.

'Your name is truly just Ransom?' Kate asked. Being a duchess—and American—she tended to be direct and always spoke her mind. Aside from her brilliance with locomotive engines, it was what Persephone loved most about the young duchess, and hence they became fast friends over the last few months.

'Yes, Your Grace,' he replied, without giving an explanation.

'It provides an air of mystery, I think,' the Dowager said. 'Adding to the myth of the man.'

'The Duke has told you who I am and what I do? You truly don't object to my presence here?' Ransom asked the women.

'This is Sebastian's home, he may invite who he pleases,' the Dowager said.

Kate shrugged. 'I'm much too busy to care about what the ton think. And like my husband, I judge people by their character, and not their occupation.'

For a second, Ransom looked taken aback. 'Then allow me to thank you for inviting me here.'

'Now that we are all acquainted, shall we proceed with our evening?' the Duke suggested.

'Yes, I'm quite famished,' Kate declared. 'I'm looking forward to what Pierre has prepared for us tonight.'

The Duke gestured towards the dining room. Persephone followed behind the Dowager, moving swiftly so she could avoid Ransom. So, he'd been invited here by the Duke. But why?

The reason, of course, was no concern of hers. As the Dowager said, it was Mabury's home so he could invite anyone he pleased. Persephone could only pray that Ransom wasn't intending to stay long.

A series of dreadful thoughts entered her head—was he going to say anything about that night? Did the Duke already know about her little adventure, and about how she had propositioned Ransom? No, he wouldn't have said anything. If he had, Persephone hardly thought he'd have been invited to dinner at Highfield Park.

I'll just have to avoid him.

Unfortunately, since there were very few of them at dinner, Persephone was seated directly across from him.

Blast it.

'Tell me, Mr Ransom,' Miss Merton began as the footmen finished ladling their soups for the first course. 'How long are you staying at Highfield Park?'

'It's just Ransom,' he reminded her. 'And I will be here for the week.'

Persephone groaned inwardly.

A whole week?

She had hoped he was just there for dinner.

'How fortuitous,' the Dowager said. 'Perhaps you could join us for next week's festivities.'

'I'm afraid I'm here on business, Your Grace,' Ransom replied politely. 'The Duke and I will be extremely busy.'

Business?

Persephone glanced at Ransom, but he kept his gaze on his soup as he took a spoonful in his mouth.

'What festivities are you speaking of, Mama?' Mabury asked. 'It's too late for May Day, isn't it? Why, it's already June.'

'I know, darling, but you and Kate missed out because you were so busy with the factory,' the Dowager began. 'I thought, well, why not have another festival in the village so that we can celebrate together? Besides, we haven't sponsored a festival in years, not since…' Her voice trailed off and she cleared her throat. 'In any case, it's just for a few days. There will be entertainers, peddlers selling their wares, and games and prizes. I've invited all our neighbours and friends.'

'How wonderful.' Kate clapped her hands together. 'I would very much like to help, Mama. I'm afraid I've been remiss in my duties as Duchess, and I should like to get to know our tenants and the villagers better.'

'Lady Persephone and I shall be helping as well,' Miss Merton said. 'We're in charge of the games and prizes.'

'That sounds like a wonderful idea.' The Duke turned to Ransom. 'Looks like the ladies will be preoccupied while we conduct our business.'

'Indeed.'

'But you still must take part somehow, Sebastian,' the Dowager said.

'Of course, Mama.'

'And you, Ransom?' the Dowager asked. 'Surely you could spare a few hours of your time this week?'

'That will be up to the Duke, ma'am,' he replied politely. 'Assuming we can conduct our business and get it out of the way.'

'We'll try our best to conclude it as soon as possible,' the Duke replied.

Persephone did her best to act normally throughout the next two courses. Ransom was polite throughout, answering questions when someone asked them, but never asking them himself. When he spoke, Persephone kept her head down, pretending to concentrate on her food. When there was a lull in conversation, however, she did her best to avoid his gaze.

Don't look at him.

Don't.

Look.

At—

She lifted her head, and sure enough, those green and brown eyes were staring back at her. Heat crept into her cheeks, and the tightness in her stomach intensified.

He was still the most beautiful man she'd ever seen,

and even more dangerous now that he could reveal her secret at any moment.

Yet, she still wanted to know what it would be like to kiss him.

Persephone Anne MacGregor, you idiot.

Dear Lord, she'd spent months trying to forget her infatuation with this man, and he had just walked in and destroyed all her hard work. How truly unfair.

'Lady Persephone? Did you hear what I said?'

She nearly jumped out of her chair at the Dowager's question. 'I beg your pardon, Your Grace, my mind was elsewhere.'

'I asked if you had any news of your brother and Maddie?'

'Oh, yes.' Persephone wiped her mouth with her napkin. 'I received a letter from Maddie just this morning.'

'How are the Earl and Maddie?' Miss Merton enquired.

'They're both keeping well,' Persephone continued. 'Maddie adores Scotland.'

'That's good to hear,' Kate remarked. 'I know she's been missing her work at the forge. She'll be so happy when they come back later this summer and she sees their brand-new ironworks factory for herself.'

'She's actually with my other brothers at the distillery most days, learning all about the fine art of whisky making.' Persephone envied her friend. Though being at Highfield Park was a respite from London, she still wished she was back at home, working in the distillery. How she missed the smell of the grain, the heat of the copper pots, and the sound of the liquid in the still as it churned.

'And very fine whisky it is, one of the best I've ever had,' the Duke said, raising his glass at her. 'Your family is truly talented. I have never tasted a whisky as smooth as Glenbaire.'

'Thank you, Your—'

'Glenbaire?'

All eyes turned to Ransom, who went still, lips pressed together, eyes like a stormy sea.

Persephone frowned. *What was wrong with him?*

'Yes, that's the distillery owned by the MacGregors,' Mabury explained. 'Lady Persephone's family. Her brother is the Earl of Balfour.'

Ransom's gaze briefly touched on Persephone, before his expression turned neutral. 'I see,' he said, before turning back to his roasted pheasant.

Persephone wasn't sure why, but she had a feeling that something was amiss. She was already waiting for the axe to fall, but now it was as if she was waiting to see if the entire sky would crash down on her. She could only pray that Ransom would conduct his business quickly and leave Highfield Park before the week was up. In the meantime, she would avoid him.

Yes, that was it.

She needed to keep well away from him. She would find excuses not to be in his presence.

And definitely don't seek him out.

Chapter Five

Glenbaire Distillery.

The name shot through him like lightning.

Cameron, Earl of Balfour. Lord Balfour.

And brother to one Lady Persephone MacGregor.

That's how she found the obol.

A few months ago, Balfour's man of business in London, George Atwell, had sent over a bottle of fine Scotch whisky for Ransom to sample. Mabury was right—it was one of the best he had ever tasted. Ransom wanted to stock it at The Underworld, but would only do so if he met with the owner first. As it happened, Atwell said the Earl was due to be in town on personal matters, and so Ransom had sent him the obol.

In all honesty, he'd forgotten about it. Many people sought to do business with him, but most were too intimated to come to The Underworld after receiving the obol—or perhaps too stupid to discern its meaning. In a way, it helped to weed out the people who were not serious enough to engage in business with. Balfour was just one of many recipients of his invitations. And *Miss Cora* had said she'd found it.

Of course a woman named after the queen of the Underworld from ancient Greek myths would figure out its meaning. The irony was not lost on Ransom.

That answered the question of how the obol came into her possession. However, he still didn't know what she was doing here, at Mabury's ducal estate.

Ransom pushed the thought away. No, it didn't matter. She didn't matter. She was just some girl who meant nothing to him, who had charmed him in a moment of weakness. Besides, he had business to attend to. One way or another, he had to convince the Duke to sell the land to him and not to Winford. He would not be distracted by her or her emerald eyes. He would not think about her proposition or whether the invitation was still open.

The rest of the dinner was tedious and seemed to go on for ever. Ransom did his best to ignore Lady Persephone. He wished he could look at her, not because she was stunning, but so he could try to discern what she was thinking and feeling. However, her eyes remained downcast for most of the meal. She wouldn't even look at him, perhaps ashamed of what had passed between them. Ransom supposed he should be used to it by now. After all, ladies of the ton were only interested in him for one reason.

Lord knew, he was no innocent himself. Many women came to him—most of them members of the ton looking for a thrill, something different from their humdrum lives. In the early days when he was beginning to build his empire, he enjoyed himself, taking part in various illicit affairs, meeting women in secret love nests; many of the women had husbands who were members of The Underworld. But as time went on and he jumped from one woman's bed to another, he began to realise how these ladies of the ton truly viewed him: he was good enough to bed, but not good enough for anything else.

Lady Persephone was just like those women.

Course after tortuous course came and went, and when the liveried footmen set the plate of vanilla pudding in front of him, Ransom sent a prayer of thanks to heaven that the meal was almost over.

Once the plates were cleared, Mabury stood up, and everyone followed suit. 'Shall we head to the library for some after-dinner refreshments? We have port for myself and Ransom, and sherry for the ladies.'

'If you'll forgive me, Your Grace, I wish to retire early,' Ransom said, mustering up all the politeness he could. 'I'm afraid my journey here has been long.'

'That's a shame, Ransom,' the Duke said. 'But I understand. We can begin our business tomorrow. Will you meet me in the foyer after breakfast? We'll ride out before the weather gets too hot.'

'Of course, Your Grace.' Ransom bowed his head. 'Now, if you'll excuse me, I shall head back to my rooms. Good evening, everyone.' Without another word, he left the dining room, the tightness growing in his chest as a quiet rage brewed beneath. Despite himself, he itched to know if Persephone had propositioned anyone else. Wondered if those lips had finally been kissed. Or if another man had had the pleasure of seeing her naked skin.

His footsteps faltered at the thought as he was making his way up the staircase. He grabbed the banister to stop himself from falling backwards. God, he wanted to punch something at the thought of another man touching her.

'Ransom, wait!'

No. Not now. 'What are you doing here?' he hissed as he spun around to face Lady Persephone. 'You shouldn't be here.'

'Please… I…' She took deep breaths as she nearly caught up to him halfway up the staircase. The cut of her dress was modest, but since he was two steps above her, he had a good view of her heaving bosoms as they threatened to burst out of her bodice. His cock stirred.

'Ransom, I just…want to explain.'

He folded his arms and looked directly at her. 'Glenbaire,' he said. 'That's how you got the obol.'

She nodded. 'Cam's valet, Murray…he dropped it. And I picked it up. As far as I know, Cam never tried to look for it. If he had asked me about it, I would have given it to him.'

'What do you want from me now, *Lady Persephone*?'

'Are you going to tell the Duke? Or my brother?'

'About what?'

'You know.' She shifted her weight from one foot to another. 'About me and…you.'

He paused for a moment, enjoying the way she squirmed. Finally, he decided to grant her relief. 'Of course not.'

'Thank you.'

'My business with the Duke is far too important for me to compromise it over something so trivial and unremarkable.' Persephone flinched visibly, and for some reason, his gut clenched. He tamped down the urge to take back his words. 'Will that be all, my lady?'

She nodded wordlessly.

'Then I bid you good-night.' Turning around, he marched up the stairs to his room. Jones was already there, waiting to help him undress.

'Did the dinner go well, Master Ransom?' he asked eagerly.

'Yes,' he lied. 'Jones, I'll be leaving with the Duke early tomorrow morning for a ride. Please have breakfast sent up to me and make sure to make the necessary preparations.'

'Of course, Master Ransom.'

As he undressed to get ready for bed, he could not help but feel remorse at his quick dismissal of Persephone. His words had been harsh, but the truth often was.

Perhaps part of him had hoped that her offer of an affair was still on the table. But seeing her—the real Lady Persephone and not Miss Cora—had dashed all hopes of that.

What did you think? She was never within your reach.

Not that he ever allowed himself to think that he would be anything but a willing body should he have accepted her proposition. Nor could he think that the affair could have been anything more. He did not deserve what she offered behind those warm emerald eyes.

Ransom pushed aside all thoughts of Lady Persephone MacGregor. Stealing that land from right under Winford's nose was the most important thing in the world to him; he needed to remember that. He could not let himself be distracted by anything or anyone else.

Chapter Six

'Here it is, Ransom.' Mabury slid off the saddle of his large black stallion in one smooth motion, then gestured around him. 'A little less than an acre of rock, sand, and pebbles. Wonderful, isn't it? Just think of all the things you can't do with it.'

Ransom dismounted from his own horse. 'Lovely,' he said, his voice dripping with as much sarcasm as the Duke's. 'A little patch of heaven.' He kicked a large stone with the tip of his Hessian boot, sending it skidding across the bare, dry soil.

Mabury pointed to a spot in the distance. 'Those trees are where Winford's property begins. It's about a mile out to his home, Hollylane Manor. On the south side is the main road that leads to London. He means to connect them via this land.'

Ransom stared at the line of trees, then spun on his heel to face the Duke. 'How much do you want for it?'

'You truly want this land?' Mabury said in an exasperated voice. 'There is nothing I can do or say to dissuade you?'

'Absolutely not. Name your price, Your Grace.'

'What if I go too high?'

'I assure you, you cannot.' Ransom's patience was wearing thin. 'How. Much?'

The Duke let out an audible sigh. 'I have no need of money.'

'And neither do you have need of this land, otherwise you would have done something with it by now.' Ransom gritted his teeth. 'Why don't you just sell it to me, damn you?'

The Duke did not flinch. In fact, his face, his very presence exuded an eerie calm Ransom had never encountered before. Heaven help The Underworld if the Duke ever decided to play cards there.

The silence between the two men stretched on, until Mabury finally spoke. 'Why do you want it?'

'Why do you care?'

'I need to know the truth.'

Ah, so that was why he was making this difficult. 'The truth? You've seen it yourself.' He gestured to his eyes. 'Do you want me to confirm it? So you can run to your friends from the ton and create more gossip?'

'I don't give a whit about the ton, Ransom, they can hang for all I care.' The Duke's nostrils flared, his lips pulling back. 'I just do not want any trouble. If this land means what I think it means to you, then I want no part in this. I will not be used in your little game of revenge.'

'This is not a little game, Your Grace,' Ransom sneered. 'If I tell you the truth of my parentage, will you sell to me?'

'That is not what I'm asking, Ransom. You do not have to bare your soul to me, I have not earned that right.' Mabury's expression softened. 'Peace is what I truly want.'

'Peace?'

'Yes. I will not have this pile of earth used to cause grief—to anyone. I do not know what you are planning, but I can bet that you're doing this to provoke Winford.' He scrubbed a hand down his face. 'But then again, if I handed it over to Winford instead, you'd go after me, wouldn't you?'

'I would not do that to you.'

'Viscount Keller would say otherwise.'

Ransom narrowed his gaze at him. 'You know about that?'

'Everyone knows about that. You made the man a pauper when he would not sell you that building down by the docks Winford wanted. You got what you wanted in the end anyway.'

It had cost Ransom a great deal of money and effort to buy out Keller's debts from all over town so that he could call them in at the same time, but it had been worth it. He had never thought it would cost him this deal, though.

Forget about the land, he told himself.

Winford wouldn't even make anything on his investment on it. As Mabury said, it was a useless pile of rocks.

He turned back towards the line of trees, imagining the old codger sitting inside his luxurious manor all warm and cosy these past thirty years. Never giving a thought to anyone but himself, especially not the illegitimate grandchild he'd sent away to live in squalor and dirt and hunger.

'What if I swear to you that I won't do anything to provoke Winford? I won't even touch the land.'

'How can I be sure? Once I sign over the title to you, you can do with it as you please.'

'You'll have to trust me.'

'Trust is earned,' the Duke shot back.

'Is that why you invited me here then? To see if you can trust me?'

'Perhaps. I don't know.' Mabury shrugged. 'All I know

is that I've found peace in the last year, and I just want to live my life, protect my tenants, and watch my children grow in a world that's better than ours was.'

So, the Duke of Mabury was an idealist.

Ransom stifled a laugh. Who could blame him? The man had everything—a title, wealth, not to mention a family who adored him. He never had to feel guilt or loss, or the burning need for revenge. 'Then we are at an impasse. Perhaps I should head home tonight.'

'If you wish.'

Neither spoke as they mounted their horses. 'If you don't mind, Ransom, I need to stop by the village to see one of my tenants. Will you be able to make it back to the house by yourself?'

Ransom glanced around. 'Apologies, Your Grace, I did not think to remember the way.'

The Duke *tsked*. 'It's my fault, I should have told you before we left or had one of the stable-hands escort us. But, if you don't mind coming with me, I promise I shan't be long.'

Seeing as he had no choice, Ransom nodded. 'Of course, Your Grace.'

They didn't ride too far and soon they were entering a fairly large and bustling village, much bigger than Ransom had imagined. He followed Mabury down the main road, then stopped outside The White Horse Inn.

'I'm meeting John here,' the Duke informed him as he dismounted and tied his horse to one of the hitching posts. 'Why don't you come in and have an ale? They've recently started selling their own brew, and I've heard good things.'

'Why not?' Ransom slid off his mount and tied the reins to the post next to the Duke's. They were about to enter the tavern when the door opened and a small figure burst out.

'Yer Grace.' A young boy, about twelve years old, stopped in front of Mabury and Ransom, then bowed.

'Michael,' Mabury greeted. 'Is that you? My, you've grown taller.'

'Thank you, Yer Grace.'

'Did you come here with your father? Is he inside?'

'N-no, Yer Grace.' The boy shook his head vigorously. 'Da sent me here to tell you he can't meet with you today. Sheep got through a hole in the fence, and he's out looking for a couple of strays. He says sorry, Yer Grace, and he can meet you here again tomorrow at the same time?'

'All right, but make it the day after.'

'Yes, Yer Grace.'

'And thank you for informing me, Michael. Does your father need help rounding up the sheep?'

'Joseph and Franklin are out lookin' for them as well, Yer Grace. He said for you not to bother.'

'All right then. If anything changes, send word to Highfield Park.' He ruffled the boy's hair affectionately. 'Run along now, and give my regards to your mother.'

'Yes, Yer Grace.' The boy grinned at him, then turned and scampered away.

'You really would have gone out to look for sheep with your tenant?' Ransom asked.

'Of course. Someone very intelligent once told me that you should never give anyone work you wouldn't do yourself.' A small smile tinged his lips. 'Anyway, it seems we can head back to the house now—'

'Sebastian! Sebastian!'

Both men turned in the direction of the voice. Coming down the main road was the Duchess, walking along with a large basket on her arm. She wasn't alone. The Dowager and Lady Persephone were with her.

Ransom tensed as the women drew closer. His eyes were trained on Lady Persephone, who looked especially lovely in a cream-coloured walking dress, her hair tucked into a bonnet, her complexion pink and healthy. Her steps faltered when their eyes met, but she quickly collected herself.

'Kate? What are you doing here?' The Duke's smile widened. Anyone could tell he was thoroughly pleased to see his Duchess, though his elation faded when he saw the basket. 'Should you be carrying that?' He immediately grabbed it from her. 'That's much too heavy for someone—' He cleared his throat. 'I mean, I don't want to you to strain your arm.'

Kate gestured to the Dowager. 'Mama wanted to visit a few families this morning.'

'Jeremy David broke his leg when he fell off a ladder the other day, and Mrs Finley has had her baby,' the Dowager explained. 'Also, Mrs Jenkins's husband passed away last month, and I heard from one of the footmen that she's been having an awful time seeing as she has two children to raise. I thought we'd bring them some food and medicine.'

'Excellent idea, Mama,' the Duke said.

'And what about you? I thought you were conducting some business with Ransom?'

'Yes, but we had to cut our tour short. I was supposed to meet John here, but he's currently indisposed. We were about to head back to Highfield Park.'

'Why don't you come with us?' the Dowager suggested. 'I'm sure the villagers would appreciate seeing you around, especially since you've spent most of the year in London.'

'I suppose I could. But Ransom wanted to head back as well, and he doesn't know the way.'

'Oh.' The Dowager flashed Ransom a disappointed look, then sighed. 'That's unfortunate. Couldn't you come with us, Ransom? You could spare one morning to help those in need.'

'I—' Ransom clamped his lips shut. The last thing he wanted was to traipse around a village giving alms to the needy. And he especially didn't want to do it with Persephone. However, even thinking of denying the Dowager—especially when she trained those big dark eyes on him and smiled so expectantly—made him feel like a villain. 'Of course, Your Grace, I would be happy to.'

'Excellent.' The Dowager raised an elegant eyebrow at him and cleared her throat delicately, glancing at the basket Persephone carried.

Taking the hint, he said, 'Allow me, Your Grace.'

'Thank you.' Persephone allowed him to take the basket.

Out of politeness, Ransom offered the Dowager his arm and she took it. He had meant to offer his other arm to Persephone, but she had already trudged on ahead.

The group continued down the road, with the Duke ahead and the Duchess on his arm, Lady Persephone behind them, and Ransom and the Dowager bringing up the rear. They stopped at two houses, visiting briefly with each family.

'Mrs Jenkins lives further out,' the Duchess said. 'It's quite a walk.'

'Perhaps we can take a short rest,' the Dowager suggested. 'Mrs Grover has also packed a few refreshments for us. Why don't we have a small picnic?'

Mabury nodded to the huge gnarled oak tree up just

off the road ahead of them. 'There. We can take shelter from the sun under the branches and sit on the roots.'

They walked on, following the Duke as he led them to the great oak tree. They all found comfortable spots, and the Dowager motioned for Ransom to come over to help her unpack one of the baskets. From the corner of his eye, he thought he spied Lady Persephone staring at him, but when he turned his head, she quickly looked away.

'How goes your business this morning, Sebastian?' the Dowager asked as she handed out bottles of lemonade and sandwiches wrapped in cloth. 'Did you finish it?'

'Not quite.' The Duke unwrapped one of the cloths and handed his wife a delicate square of bread. 'Ransom and I are still thrashing out the details.'

'I thought we had reached an agreement. You said I should return home,' Ransom replied curtly.

'I said, if you wish,' he clarified. 'I didn't tell you to pack your bags.'

Ransom eyed the Duke carefully. Did this mean that he was willing to negotiate further?

'Then you're staying longer?' the Dowager exclaimed. 'How wonderful.'

'Wonderful?' Ransom frowned.

'Yes. Surely you won't be working the entire time you're here? Sebastian promised he'd lend us a hand with the festival, and now you can too. We need all the help we can get.'

'Ma'am, I'm afraid there's nothing I could possibly contribute to your efforts.' Ransom wasn't exactly the charitable kind.

'Nonsense.' She waved away his objections. 'Besides, doing something that benefits others does wonders for the soul.'

He guffawed. 'Ma'am, I don't think anything can help my soul.'

'True, he's far too selfish and wicked,' Lady Persephone interjected.

Ransom's head snapped towards her, causing her to blink twice. She inhaled sharply and placed a hand over her mouth as her face turned the same shade of red as her hair. 'I…uh…'

The Dowager was aghast. 'My dear, I don't think… Perhaps you are too harsh with your assessment of our guest. You hardly know him.'

Persephone swallowed hard. 'Apologies—'

She was interrupted by the audible pop of Ransom opening his lemonade bottle. 'There is no need for apologies.' He threw his head back and took a healthy swig. 'Your assessment, Lady Persephone, is on the mark. I couldn't have said it better myself.'

Her blush deepened.

'Ransom, my mother is a wise woman, one of the wisest I know.' Mabury grinned at the Dowager before continuing. 'And you might want to consider her advice.'

Ransom did not miss the pointed look Mabury gave him. Was he trying to manipulate him into participating in this festival? And if he did, would he sell the land to him?

Carefully, he weighed his options. 'Ma'am, I would be happy to provide prizes for your festival,' he said. 'What would you like? A horse? Some livestock? How about a hundred pounds or perhaps a gold trophy for the winners?'

'No, no,' the Dowager laughed. 'The point is not for you to write a bank draft and be done with it. Your time and presence are what's required.'

Did this woman have any idea how much his time and

presence was worth? Each evening he was away from
The Underworld could mean thousands of pounds of lost
revenue. Ransom opened his mouth to object, but once
again, one glare from the Duke had him tempering his
thoughts, reminding himself of the land and Winford.

'Assuming His Grace and I are not occupied with business, I would be happy to assist.'

*How much effort could organising and running some
games take?*

Besides, it would be worth it if it allowed him to gain
the Duke's trust and obtain the land.

'Excellent. You can assist Miss Merton and Lady Persephone with the games.'

Damn. He would have to spend more time with her
this week.

Perhaps the cost of the land was too high.

'M-me?' Lady Persephone gasped. 'I mean… Your
Grace, Miss Merton and I are perfectly capable of doing
this ourselves.'

'Really? You just told me this morning that there was
so much to do and not enough time in which to do it.'

Lady Persephone's expression turned dark. 'Right,'
she muttered. Putting down the bottle of lemonade, she
brushed her hands on her skirts. 'I'm feeling quite re-
freshed now. I would like to walk ahead.' She flattened
her hands on her knees and pushed herself up. 'Perhaps—
och!'

Her hands flailed in the air as she fell forward. Ransom sprang into action, catching her before she hit the
ground. 'Ouch!' she cried out when he tried to lift her.
'My leg!'

'Persephone!' Kate cried. 'What happened?'

'I… It hurts.' Persephone's face twisted in pain.

'Easy now,' he said. 'Here, let me.' Gently, he helped her sit back down on the branch.

'Did you twist your ankle?' the Dowager asked, concerned. 'Should we fetch a doctor?'

'No, I'm fine.' Persephone winced. 'It's just a leg cramp. It happens if I sit too long in an uncomfortable position.'

'If you were not comfortable, you should have said something,' Ransom admonished.

'I didn't think we would be staying long,' she shot back.

'Perhaps we should all head back to Highfield Park,' the Duke suggested.

'Please don't make a fuss,' Persephone pleaded. 'I'm fine. I just need to rest for bit until this cramp goes away. I'll wait here so you all may continue on to see Mrs Jenkins.'

The Dowager patted her hand. 'We can't just leave you here, dear. I'll fetch Higgins and have him bring the carriage round so you don't have to walk all the way back.'

'I'll stay with Persephone,' the Duchess offered. 'Sebastian and Ransom can deliver the basket to Mrs Jenkins.'

'Unfortunately I don't know where she lives,' the Duke pointed out. 'And I'll not let you go on your own, Kate.'

'I'll stay with the lady,' Ransom found himself saying. Before the women could object, he added, 'We're out in the open, still well within sight of the village. Lady Persephone's virtue and reputation shall remain safe.'

The Dowager pressed her lips together. 'I suppose you're right.'

'We will be fine, ma'am,' he assured her.

'He's right, Mama,' the Duchess said. 'Mrs Jenkins's house isn't much farther, and we'll be back in fifteen minutes at most. You'll be able to fetch the carriage and bring it here in less time than that.' She gave a little laugh. 'That's hardly enough time for Ransom to ravish Lady Persephone.'

Indeed, he would need much more time than that. He could spend hours in bed, exploring every inch of her. He especially wanted to find out if she had freckles elsewhere on her body. Then he would—

'It's settled then,' Mabury said. 'Kate and I will deliver the basket to Mrs Jenkins and come back.' He gave Ransom one last warning glance before he led his wife away.

'I'll be right back with the carriage, dear, don't fret.' The Dowager flashed Persephone a reassuring smile before she too left.

Ransom fumed silently. This was the last place he should be, alone with Lady Persephone MacGregor. Not knowing where to direct his frustration, he turned it on her. 'Confound it, woman, are you always this clumsy?'

'No, I'm usually even more so.' Her lopsided smile and the spectacles askew on her nose made his heart thump in an unnatural rhythm. 'And I told you, I had a cramp.'

With a deep sigh he reached over to straighten the gold frames on her face. 'You must be more careful or one day you'll seriously hurt yourself. I can't always be there to catch you when you fall, you know.' His hand moved lower, meaning to brush a stray lock of hair away from her face. However, he paused as his fingers cupped her jaw, this thumb lingering on her cheek.

She gasped. 'Ransom?'

Quickly, he tucked the hair into her bonnet. 'Hmm?'

'I… Nothing. I mean.' She sat up straight. 'I just want to apologise.'

'Apologise? For lying to me?'

'I did not lie to you,' she said, indignant.

'Really? What about your name, *Miss Cora*?'

'Oh, well…' She wrung her hands. 'That is my name. I mean, that's what my mother used to call me when she was alive. She said it meant "heart" in Latin, because she truly believed I was the heart of our family.'

The sadness in her eyes made his chest ache. *Damn.* 'And what about the nunnery?'

'Nunnery?'

'You know, the reason you propositioned me? You were running off to a nunnery to become a spinster, remember?'

'I never said anything about a nunnery. You did,' she reminded him.

He blew out a breath. 'Then what exactly are you apologising for?'

'For making things awkward. I didn't know you'd be here or that you were even acquainted with the Duke. Otherwise I wouldn't have asked you…what I asked you that night…'

'You mean, for an affair,' he finished. 'Why ever would you ask that of anyone?'

Colour heightened in her cheeks. 'I'm not going to a nunnery, but I am leaving England to go back home.' She bit her lip. 'I was sent here for the Season and the Dowager is my sponsor.'

'In hopes of finding a husband.'

'Yes. And, well, I've been here so long and I still haven't found anyone. I just don't think London is the place for me. I want to go back to Scotland. I was happy there, working with my brothers at our distillery. My brother, the Earl, is returning to England at the end of the summer to fetch me for a visit home, then I'm supposed to return to London for the next Season. But, once we're back home, I'm going to convince him to let me stay.'

'And so you wanted one last adventure before you left London for good.'

'Yes.'

An ache grew in Ransom's throat as though he'd swallowed nails, but he had to ask. 'When I turned down your proposition, did you find an acceptance elsewhere?'

Persephone shook her head.

'Good.' The pain dissipated and Ransom could breathe again.

'Good?' She cocked her head to the side. 'Why so?'

'Because you shouldn't give your virtue away to just any man.' He fixed his gaze on her, looking deep into her emerald eyes. 'You need someone tender and gentle, who will show you the respect you deserve.'

'And love?'

'Yes. Perhaps that too.' A bitter taste pooled in his mouth. Not everyone deserved love; he certainly did not. But someone as sweet and innocent as Persephone should know about love and tenderness.

'Do you think I would find such qualities in one man?'

'I don't know.' They certainly were not in him.

'Ransom…' Her eyes darkened. 'You never answered my question.'

'Your question?'

'From that night.' She leaned so close that he knew if he took a deep breath, he would be able to smell her intoxicating perfume. 'If you found me unattractive.'

His throat went dry. When she had posed that question, it had taken all his strength not to show her exactly how attractive he found her.

'The Dowager is lovely, isn't she?'

Her words took him by surprise. 'I beg your pardon? Why ask me such a question?'

Persephone bit her lip. 'She is, isn't she? So graceful and beautiful and charming. Do you think—'

The sound of hooves and carriage wheels interrupted her. Springing up to his feet, Ransom saw the carriage with a team of four horses thundering towards them.

'I'm here,' the Dowager announced as she alighted from the carriage. 'How are you feeling, dear?'

'Much better, I think. I can wiggle my toes and the pain is gone.'

'Allow me, my lady.' Persephone's fingers grasped Ransom's, and he gently pulled her up.

'Yes, I believe I'm fully recovered,' she declared. 'Thank you, Ransom.'

'You're welcome.' He turned to the Dowager. 'Ma'am, I almost forgot, the Duke and I left our horses back in the village. I shall retrieve them and wait for him here. You don't need to wait for us.'

'Why, of course. And by the way, Ransom,' the Dowager said. 'Miss Merton, Lady Persephone, and I will be expecting you at the library tomorrow morning at half past ten to plan for the festival. Don't be late.'

'I wouldn't dream of it, ma'am.' He bowed low to both ladies and turned on his heel. Once he was far enough away, he flexed his hand and took a deep breath to calm himself.

That was much too close.

He couldn't be alone with Persephone. *Ever.* He had nearly lost control, touching her like that. Still, he was glad to at least have found out the truth from her. And though he told himself that it was none of his concern, he was relieved that she hadn't slept with anyone else.

He raked a hand through his hair. Unfortunately, he would not be able to avoid her this week, not after his promise to the Dowager. Ransom told himself that the torture of being near her would be worth it; there was no price too high when it came to taking something Winford wanted. But whatever happened, he could not let himself give in to temptation, for if he did, it wouldn't just be him who had to pay the price.

Chapter Seven

Persephone told herself she was not looking forward to spending the morning with Ransom. She certainly did not ask her maid to prepare her favourite morning dress for him, nor did she wear her green shawl because it matched her eyes. And if her step had a spring in it as she sprinted towards the library, it was only because her hearty breakfast had given her extra energy.

No, she was not looking forward to seeing him at all. *Oh, bother.*

Halting just as she was about to enter the library, Persephone slapped a hand on her forehead. How could this have happened? The six months of trying to temper her infatuation had evaporated with just one touch. Her hand slid down to her cheek where she swore the brand of his fingers remained.

When she first came to Highfield Park, all she could think of was that night and Ransom. If it hadn't been for the Dowager and her help in coming up with the project to distract herself, she would have ended up like some heroine of a gothic novel, roaming the halls in despair, longing for her lost love.

Infatuation, she reminded herself. *That's all it is.*

She was older and wiser now, having had her twentieth birthday four months ago. Surely, she could put aside these girlish emotions for another few days until he left.

With a determined shrug, she walked into the library. She had made a point of arriving fifteen minutes early, hoping to have some time alone to compose herself so she would not look foolish when Ransom arrived.

'Good morning, Lady Persephone.'

The low baritone aroused a pleasurable, warm feeling in her belly. Turning around, she faced Ransom. 'Good morning. I, uh, seem to be early.'

'As am I.'

How could it be possible he looked even more handsome today? Yesterday, she thought he had achieved peak attractiveness, with his hair windswept, his riding clothes fitted closely to his trim body, and those shiny boots clinging to his strong calves. Today, however, his clean-shaven jaw and combed mahogany hair showed off the healthy, sun-kissed skin of his face. Her eyes lingered on his firm lips, wondering if she'd got closer to him yesterday, would he have kissed her?

Mother of mercy, if anyone could hear her thoughts, she really would be hied off to a nunnery.

'I should g-go,' she stammered, glancing around for an exit. Unfortunately, he blocked the door behind her.

'Go?' His eyebrows drew together. 'Why? Her Grace and Miss Merton should be arriving soon. There's no reason for you to leave, only to come back again.'

'I—I suppose so.' She glanced at the clock on the mantel. Twelve minutes. She took a deep breath. Just twelve minutes alone with him. She could not possibly embarrass herself in that short amount of time.

'In the meantime, perhaps you could tell me how far

you've got in terms of planning for this festival and what other matters need to be settled?'

'Excellent idea.' That should provide enough of a distraction and make the time pass more quickly.

She led him to the large table in the centre of the room, then sat in one of the chairs. He followed suit, taking the seat opposite her.

'So, what have you done so far?'

Retrieving the small notebook and pen from her pockets, she lay it flat on the table and flipped through the first few pages in search of her notes on the festival.

'What's that?'

'What?'

He pointed to the sketches on the page. 'That?'

My project!

'Nothing.' She snatched the book away and began to thumb through it, hoping he wouldn't ask any more questions. It wasn't that she was ashamed of her project—she just didn't want him to find out how unusual and unladylike she was.

How unlike the Dowager she was.

Now that she had some time to think, Persephone admitted that it had been silly to feel jealous of the Dowager receiving attention from Ransom during yesterday's outing. He was just being polite, and the Dowager was old enough to be his mother, even if she did look a great deal younger than her actual age. Still, standing next to such an exquisite lady as the Dowager made Persephone feel so…lacking.

'Have you found it?' he asked, one eyebrow raised.

'One moment.' Flipping back, Persephone found the correct pages, then placed the notebook down on the table once more. 'We've made a list of games for the children, like a three-legged race, blind man's bluff, and so on.' She pointed at one section of the page where she had written down a list. 'And there will be the usual competitions, such as best pies, fattest pigs, prettiest sheep...'

'A prettiest sheep competition? There's such a thing?'

'Aye. The farmers pick out their sheep and dress them up in ribbons and flowers... Have you never heard of these growing up?'

'I'm afraid not. I was raised in London.'

'Oh? Which part?'

'Nowhere you would care to know,' he said brusquely.

She was taken aback by his answer, but continued. 'Anyway, Miss Merton and I will be in charge of the children's games, and we've asked a few of the tenants to run the competitions, but we need someone to judge them.'

'You should have the Duke judge the sheep one.'

'The Duke?'

'Yes, I think His Grace would enjoy having to look at sheep for a good part of the day.' A wry smile played on his lips, and the chill in the air between them dissipated.

'You jest,' Persephone said.

'Not at all, it would be a truly fitting job for him.' His grin grew wider.

She chuckled. 'I'll note that down then. Now, we don't have much planned for the young men of the village.'

'The men?'

'Yes. It would be good to give them a chance to compete with each other and win some prizes. So far, we only have a tug-of-war and a two-man wagon race.'

'Hmm.' Ransom rubbed his thumb and forefinger on his chin. 'Do you have similar festivals or fairs back home in Scotland?'

'We do.'

'And do the young men there compete in games and such?'

'Aye, we have quite a lot, actually. There's drumming and dancing, and of course they compete in various events like hammer throwing, running, jumping, caber tossing—'

'Caber tossing?'

'It's a game where you hold a large beam of wood—the caber—and throw it into the air so that it flips over completely.' Using her pen, she re-created the ideal trajectory of the caber.

'Ah, I see. Why did you not suggest these games?'

'I never thought to,' she said. 'I shall certainly ask the Dowager for her opinion. Of course, we might have to choose the easiest ones to modify and re-create. We might not have time to craft a caber.'

'Did you watch these games back home?'

'Aye, and my brothers competed in them too. Cam's pretty good at the caber tossing, and Lachlan's decent with the hammer throw. It's exciting to watch and there's the music and the dancing…' Had it been less than a year since she'd been home? It seemed as though she'd been here for ever.

'You miss your home, don't you?'

Persephone closed her eyes. 'I do.'

'Then why did you come to England? It sounds as if Scotland has many of these big, strapping young men who easily could catch a young lady's attention.'

Her eyes flew open. 'It wasn't my idea to come. The truth is, I'm here to fulfil my mother's dream of giving me a proper London Season. She was English, you see.'

'And how did she happen to marry a Scottish earl?'

'My father wasn't always an earl. I mean, he didn't grow up with the title. The previous earl had been a distant relative who'd had no sons of his own. Good thing too, as my mother's parents would not have allowed her to marry Pa if he had not had a title. But my mother was happy with Pa, and she adjusted well to life in Scotland.'

'If she was happy enough with a Scottish gentleman, why would she wish for you to have an English husband?'

'It's not quite that simple. You see, my father's branch of the family were all merchants; we've owned the distillery for generations. When he inherited the title, we were no longer part of the merchant class, but Scottish high society wouldn't accept us. However, my mother reasoned that if I were to have a proper Season in England, we could somehow bridge that gap. It would be a way for us to show high society that we were ready to take our place in the world.'

'But you don't agree.'

Persephone shrugged. 'It's simply the way things are. But so far, my Season has been a disaster.' Planting her elbows on the table, she rested her chin on her palms. 'I haven't met any eligible gentlemen, and no one has yet offered for me.'

He frowned. 'Why not?'

Lifting her head, she met his intense stare. She supposed it wouldn't hurt to tell him the truth. She would never see him again after this week was over. 'I can't dance.'

His stare did not waver. 'What does that have to do with anything?'

'Apparently, everything,' she said with a nervous laugh. 'Balls are the arena of the Season, and dancing is the weapon of choice. And I'm afraid I'm woefully under-armed.'

'Isn't dancing a part of any young lady's education?'

He had no idea, of course, of Persephone's unusual upbringing.

He probably wouldn't approve.

While he wasn't a gentleman, he was rich and powerful. One day he would want a wife, and with his fortune, he could find a beautiful, genteel woman who could do all the ladylike things Persephone could not and give him a crowd of green-and-brown-eyed children. That jealous feeling from yesterday returned, intensifying as she thought of the fictional woman who might one day be Ransom's wife.

'Well? Could your brother not find someone to give you dance lessons?'

'I did. One.'

'One? And?'

'It was a complete and utter disaster.' She sighed. 'I just couldn't remember the steps or which foot to start with for which dance. I kept treading on my dance master's feet and nearly broke his toes.' She cringed, remembering that day. 'He said I was too dim-witted to learn how to dance, and a clumsy cow to boot.'

He muttered something under his breath.

'I beg your pardon? What did——'

'Oh, you're here already?'

Persephone's spine stiffened at the sound of the familiar feminine lilt. As the Dowager entered the library, looking fresh and lovely in her violet morning gown, whatever was left of Persephone's confidence deflated.

Oh, why did I tell him about that awful dance lesson?

Now he could confirm she'd been a clumsy cow for most of her life.

'Your Grace.' Ransom got to his feet and she followed suit, curtseying as the Dowager Duchess and Miss Merton drew closer to them. 'I was unsure of where the library was and so I thought I'd give myself time to find it. Lady Persephone arrived but a few moments ago.'

'Excellent.' The Dowager took the seat at the head of the table, and Miss Merton sat beside Persephone. 'Now, shall we begin?'

The next two hours were devoted purely to festival planning. The Dowager was delighted at Persephone's suggestion to include some Scottish games, and they decided they could feasibly incorporate some of them, including a stone put, weight throw, hammer throw, and a hill race for the younger boys.

'I think we have most of the games settled, as well as the judging,' the Dowager declared. 'I'll make a list of the things we need to prepare and have my staff and a few of the tenants help secure them. You'll write down the rules and such, Lady Persephone?'

'I will, Your Grace.'

'Excellent. Now, shall we have some luncheon? All this work has me famished.' The Dowager stood up from her chair, and everyone else rose to their feet. But before they could leave, Ransom spoke.

'Your Grace, if you don't mind, I have some correspondence to attend to.'

'You won't be joining us for luncheon then? What will you eat?'

He shook his head. 'My valet will bring me a tray while I conduct my business. The Duke has been gracious enough to allow me some privacy in the smoking room.'

'Of course. I understand that you are a busy man. Thank you again, Ransom, for your assistance in this matter.'

'My pleasure, ma'am.' He gave a low bow, and a curt nod to Miss Merton and Persephone before he left.

Persephone ignored the way her heart sank at the loss

of his presence. Besides, thinking about how she had re-layed the embarrassing dance lesson made her cringe.

He must think me such a silly girl.

The three women headed to the dining room for an informal meal of ham, bread, cheese, and some warm soup, chatting amiably about their plans for the festival.

'If you'll excuse me, I shall return to the Dower house and start on the preparations,' the Dowager declared once they had finished.

'And I will retire for a rest in my rooms,' Miss Merton said.

'Lady Persephone, how do you plan to spend the rest of the afternoon?'

Persephone patted the notebook in her skirt pockets. 'I'm working on a few things, Your Grace.'

'Ah.' The Dowager's eyes sparkled. 'And how is your project coming along?'

'Quite well. In fact, I have to go to the village tomorrow to make sure everything's ready for the festival.'

'Excellent, I shall have my carriage and a footman ready at your disposal.'

'Thank you, Your Grace.' She truly was grateful for the Dowager's support all these months.

Persephone and Miss Merton walked the Dowager out to the foyer and said their goodbyes. Miss Merton returned to her rooms, and Persephone found herself alone.

Perhaps I'll take a quick walk in the gardens.

She turned towards the staircase, but before she could take a step, a footman blocked her way.

'Excuse me, Your Ladyship.' He bowed low, then handed her a slip of paper. 'This is for you.'

'For me? From whom?'

'I don't know, my lady.'

But the look on his face told her that he did know, he

just wasn't going to tell her. She unfolded the paper and read its contents.

Come to the library.

'The library?' she said aloud. Who could have sent her this? Perhaps it was Kate, already back from her excursion with the Duke. They'd left early this morning for some appointment in town and were not due to return until the next day. Maybe their appointment had been cancelled.

Intrigued, she made her way to the library once more. 'Kate?' she called as she entered. 'Are you in here?' Her steps faltered when she saw the tall figure waiting inside, casually leaning against the mantel. 'Ransom?'

'Lady Persephone,' he greeted. 'Thank you for coming.'

'Wait, you sent me this note?' She strode towards him. 'Why?'

The expression on his face shifted, as if he too were wondering the same thing. 'It's about your dance master.'

'My dance master?'

What on earth was he talking about?

'What about him?'

His mouth turned into a grim line. 'What he said about you was unacceptable and deplorable.'

'I was a terrible student,' she said with a forced laugh.

'Or he was a terrible teacher. And an ass.' His jaw hardened. 'If a student cannot learn a lesson, then it is the teacher's duty to tailor his methods to the student. It is not your fault you didn't learn from him, Persephone.'

The way he said her name made her heart flip. 'I... It's very kind of you to say, even if it's not true.'

'But it is. It's not that you can't dance. Anyone can learn to dance, they just need the right teacher.'

'Maybe the right teacher for me doesn't exist,' she said with a sigh. 'It doesn't matter anyway, I've two left feet and no sense of rhythm either.'

'You can learn.' He stretched out his arm towards her. 'Let me prove it to you.'

She eyed his open palm. 'Wait…do you mean to teach me to dance?'

He nodded.

'You truly think you can teach someone as hopeless as I am?'

'Ten minutes. That's all I need to make a start.' He offered his hand to her. 'Please?'

Persephone's heart leapt. Before she knew it, she was placing her hand in his. The most curious, pleasurable sensation tingled along her spine as their bare fingers touched.

He pulled her away from the mantel. 'Give me your other hand.'

Persephone did as he asked, then glanced around them, noticing that two of the wingback chairs that had originally been by the fireplace were now pushed to the side to leave an open space. 'Wait.'

'Yes?'

'Should I take my spectacles off?'

'Take them off?'

'Yes. My dance master—Mr Murphy—said I shouldn't wear them as it "destroys my overall form."'

'Then how are you supposed to see where you're going?' he asked, his tone incredulous.

'My partner is supposed to take the lead. I follow.' Scrunching up her face, she tried to recall Mr Murphy's tone. '"The woman is like a silk scarf in the wind, beautiful, dainty, and ornamental, while the man is the master."'

'He was an idiot then,' Ransom fumed. 'First of all, your spectacles not only allow you to see what's around you, but they prevent you from becoming too dizzy. Next, your partner is not the master—he's just that, a partner.' His fingers gripped hers tighter, and he raised their hands up. 'While he may "lead" the dance, the two of you are equals on the ballroom floor, working together towards one goal.'

'One goal—you mean trying not to look foolish?'

A small smile graced his lips. 'I suppose. Now, while the man does lead, the woman must also do her part. Dancing requires quick thinking and sensitivity.' He took a step to the right. 'You didn't follow me.'

'Because you didn't tell me to,' she pointed out.

'Yes, but on the dance floor, your partner will not call out the steps to you. You must be able to read his cues so that the dance becomes seamless. Now, focus on my hand.'

She glanced at his right hand, the fingers long and elegant as they covered hers. 'Yes?'

'Feel the subtle movement it makes.' He tugged slightly. 'See?'

'Why, yes.'

Why didn't I feel that earlier?

The answer to that, of course, was that she had been too busy focusing on the way his smile made him even more handsome and on the warmth building low in her belly at their close proximity.

He took another step to the right, and this time, she followed suit. When he nudged with his other hand, she moved with him to the left. He repeated the movements twice more, then by the third time, they moved in sync.

'Now you're doing it,' he said, as they continued the side-to-side motions.

'But we're not dancing.'

'Aren't we?' He added a little swing to their movements. 'And...' His fingers pulled at hers, so she took a step forward just as he moved back, then to the left, then he pushed forward. 'A basic box step,' he declared as they repeated the move. 'We're practically waltzing.'

'We are, aren't we?' she said, delighted. Following the subtle movements of his hands felt natural to her; if only Mr Murphy had explained it this way, she would have been dancing all this time.

But they weren't *really* dancing.

'Why are you frowning?'

Persephone lifted her head to meet Ransom's fierce stare. 'This isn't really waltzing, is it? This is just moving in a square. To truly dance, we must—' A gasp escaped her lips as he pulled her closer, his left hand sliding down to her waist.

'Now we are truly dancing.'

He whirled her about, and though it took her a few tries, she eventually learned to read his cues and translate the subtle messages the pressure of his fingers conveyed.

Turn this way. Go faster. Move here.

It was as if she really could understand this wordless language.

'There,' he said when he slowed them down to a stop. 'How was that?'

'It was wonderful,' she said, sounding surprised. It hadn't been a real waltz, and she knew they didn't have the grace that most dancers had on the ballroom floor. No, she needed much more practice to match the elegance of the other ladies who had been dancing Season after Season. But it was a start nonetheless, and she had learned an important lesson. 'I see it now.'

'See what?'

'What you were talking about. Dancing requires a solid partnership. Two dancers must complement each other—a good lead must have confidence and skill to inspire trust in the other, but in turn, a good follower is an active participant so the partnership remains strong and cohesive.'

'Exactly,' Ransom said. 'When we work together, we become as one.'

The grip of his fingers on her waist tightened. What that meant, Persephone didn't know, but a current of warmth coursed through her veins, as if she'd swallowed a whole measure of whisky in one gulp.

He released her without warning. 'I should leave.'

'How is it you know how to dance?' she burst out, not wanting him to go yet.

'I taught myself. When I was younger.' An inscrutable expression passed briefly across his face.

'Oh.' A thought popped into her head. 'It's probably a good skill for a young man to learn, especially if he wants to impress ladies.' The thought of other women in his arms sent jealousy slithering through her stomach. 'With your skills you must have been very popular.'

'No, not like that.' Ransom shook his head vigorously. 'My sisters wanted to learn, and I promised to teach them some day when we were older.'

'Sisters? You have sis—'

'Ten minutes,' he said, his tone clipped and brusque. 'Our ten minutes are done and as I promised, I have taught you to dance, my lady.' He bowed, turned on his heel, and marched away.

Persephone stared after him, and when the door slammed, she winced.

What was that about?

Amelia.

Carrie.

Dorothy.

Over the years, most days came and went without Ransom reciting those names to himself. Sometimes, he couldn't even picture their faces.

But this was not one of those times.

Ransom blinked through bleary, tired eyes. The clock on the wall indicated that it was five o'clock, and the crick in his neck said he had slept upright on the leather chair in the cigar room of Highfield Park.

If one could call it sleeping.

Slumber escaped him, as he attempted to flee from his own dreams and memories. Tried to keep that box locked up tight so he wouldn't have to feel the despair threatening to overpower him.

'Some day I'm going to dance at a ball,' seven-year-old Dorothy declared as she twirled about barefoot on *the dirty floor of the tiny single room they called a home. 'I'll be pretty as a princess.'*

'Yes, you will,' Ransom, all of eight years old, as*sured her.*

'But how?' six-year-old Carrie asked. *'We're too poor to get lessons.'*

'I'll learn,' he promised. *'And then I'll teach you.'*

'Me too! Teach me!' tiny Amelia cried. *'Please, Ransom?'*

'Of course,' he said, confident. *'I'll teach all of you.'*

They'd been so young when the illness took them. Ransom didn't even know how they got sick; there was no money to summon a doctor, after all. All he knew was that it was swift, taking the youngest, Amelia, first, then Carrie and Dorothy, until finally it took Mum. Ransom and that bloody drunken bastard had been spared.

And once again, opening the box of emotions he'd kept locked up threatened to shatter him into pieces. A white-hot sliver of pain threatened to break his chest open. Their faces swirled in his mind, turning into a dark pool of despair. As quickly as he could, he pushed those emotions back into the box, locking them away.

'Master Ransom?' Jones's voice drifted through the haze of his mind.

'What is it?' The clock's short hand was now on seven and the long one on fifteen.

The valet crept into the room with careful steps, a tray in his hands. 'Master Ransom, I know you said you were not to be disturbed, but that was yesterday afternoon.' Disapproval and disappointment marred his face briefly.

Ransom rubbed at his eyes and scrubbed his fingers on his scruffy jaw. After he left the library yesterday, he locked himself up in the smoking room, diving deep into his correspondence and business at the club. There were piles of letters, not to mention pages and pages of reports from Clyde detailing everything that'd happened at the club, an hour-by-hour report for each of the days Ransom had been at Highfield Park. It had kept him busy for hours and when Jones came to remind him it was time to dress for dinner, he nearly bit the man's head off and told him he was not to be disturbed for any reason.

'Since you missed dinner, I thought to bring you breakfast and coffee.' The valet raised the tray in his hands.

Ransom gestured to the table in front of him, and Jones placed the tray down before pouring steaming black liquid from the silver pot into a delicate china cup.

'Thank you, Jones,' Ransom said, accepting the cup. He inhaled the steam, the scent slowly awakening his senses. He took a sip. 'Did the other guests ask about me?'

'The Duke and Duchess spent the night in London and the Dowager stayed at home. From what I heard from the staff, it was only Miss Merton and Lady Persephone who dined last night.'

Lady Persephone.

Teaching her to dance had been a mistake.

Holding her so close was an even bigger one.

I shouldn't have done it.

But he just couldn't stand it, seeing her so glum. And that dance master of hers, calling her dim-witted and that ugly name—Ransom wished he could hunt him down and string him up from a tree. But since he couldn't, he decided to teach her how to dance instead. To show her that she wasn't clumsy.

And for a brief moment, nothing outside that room, outside the two of them, had existed. They were the only two people in the world. A thought—a delusion—had entered his mind, that perhaps there could be something more between them. That maybe he deserved a smidge of the tenderness in her eyes, and maybe she could re-place whatever soul he had lost when his mother and sisters died.

But that delusion that there could be more between him and Persephone was just that—a figment of his imagina-tion, something his mind conjured up to make him be-lieve his wicked, selfish, soulless self could deserve more.

And now he was paying for it.

'Is she—? I mean, are the ladies having their break-fast?'

'Chef Pierre did not prepare a buffet nor did the footmen set the dining table, so I assume they chose to have trays sent up to them.'

Taking a healthy swig of coffee, then scarfing down a slice of toast, Ransom turned to the valet. 'Jones, please have a bath prepared. I'd like to shave as well.'

'Of course, Master. Will you be heading out for the day?'

He rubbed a thumb and forefinger on his chin. 'Yes, I think I'll head down to the village.' Perhaps some fresh air, maybe an ale at the inn, might do him some good.

Ransom finished the toast, swallowed the last of the coffee, and once again packed away the emotions and his past into the box before locking it up.

The White Horse Inn was much larger and cleaner than similar establishments in London Ransom had been in. But there was a familiarity about it that soothed him, from the sturdy, well-worn tables and benches, to the smell of sweat hanging in the humid air, and even the din of laughter and clinking and slamming of mugs. Before he became owner of The Underworld, it hadn't been unusual for him to spend time in places like this, rubbing elbows with other working men as they bolted down their meals during the scarce breaks their employers granted them. Far from the crystal chandeliers and spinning roulette wheels of The Underworld and the quiet civility of Highfield Park, Ransom felt at home in this place.

'What can I get ye?' the barkeep asked as Ransom approached him. 'Some food, milord? Drink?'

'Just an ale. And I'm not a lord.'

The man rubbed his beard as he looked Ransom up and down. 'Coulda fooled me.'

Reaching into his pocket, Ransom placed a twopence coin on the counter and pushed it towards him. 'One pint.'

The barkeep retrieved a mug from a hook above him, then placed it under one of the swan-necked nozzles protruding from the counter before giving the porcelain handle a pull. 'Here ye go.' He slid the mug filled with amber liquid towards Ransom.

'Thanks.' He took a sip. 'That's quite fresh. And delicious.' Perhaps it had been a while since he'd had a pint in a public house, but still, the brew was not too bitter, and even slightly fruity.

The barkeep jerked a thumb behind him. 'Just got our brewery workin'.'

'You didn't have one before?' Ransom asked. Parliament had passed the Beerhouse Act well over ten years ago, making it cheap for anyone to brew their own beer. Since then, ale and public houses had opened on just about every street corner in London.

'Too expensive and we're mainly a coachin' inn so didn't see the need to. But got me a good loan so couldn't say no. Mind you, buildin' the damn thing was a pain in the arse, but worth it. Got people comin' in now for a pint just 'cause.'

Ransom took another sip. 'I understand.' He had contemplated building a brewery in The Underworld, but the sporting club took up most of the basement and a renovation would have meant shutting down the club for a time. Besides, his members preferred fine liquor and wine. He had a few barrels in stock, of course, but mostly bought from nearby breweries. Still, if he had something of this calibre, he was sure he could convince his clients to start drinking ale. 'I'd like another one, when I'm done. I'll be in the corner.'

Ransom took his mug and sat himself in the far, darkened corner, away from the other patrons. He sipped on his ale, content to watch people go about their business.

When he finished his ale, he raised a hand to the bar-keep, trying to flag him down so he could get his second ale, but the man's attention was turned towards the entrance, his face lighting up with a smile as he waved someone over.

'Yer Ladyship!'

A sense of dread came over Ransom.

But it couldn't be.

Slowly, he swung his head in the direction of the newcomer.

What the hell is she doing here?

Ransom fumed, his eyes tracking Lady Persephone as she breezed into the inn, all smiles as she greeted the young barkeep. He wanted nothing more than to run over there and drag her out of this place, but he was frozen to his seat, unable to move.

Perhaps she's just got lost. Or she's with the Dowager and she just went ahead inside.

He decided to be patient, lest he make a fool of himself by acting like a jealous husband. He hunched further over his mug, watching. Waiting.

Lady Persephone leaned over the bar and laughed at something the barkeep said. As they continued their conversation, Ransom kept a watchful eye on the door, but there no sign of the Dowager or Miss Merton or indeed anyone else from Highfield Park. But they still could arrive.

Any moment now.

He let out a relieved breath when the barkeep walked away from her, all the way to the other end of the counter. However, the man lifted a section of the wooden top upwards, then stepped out, before making his way back to Lady Persephone. He opened a door to the right of the bar, and she disappeared through it, the man following behind her. Ransom shot to his feet, the table nearly turning over.

I'll kill him if he touches her.

He crossed the room with purposeful strides, his vision growing red as his imagination filled in the gaps of what they could be doing in the back. Had she found the adventure she was searching for? How long had she been coming here? And to think just the other day she had said she'd remained untouched. A horrible thought burrowed into his head—had his curt dismissal yesterday pushed her into the arms of this new lover?

Curling his hands into fists, Ransom burst through the door. 'Get your hands off her you—' He skidded to a stop, eyes growing wide at the sight before him. 'Lady Persephone?'

Lady Persephone and the barkeep—as well as three other employees—gaped at him. They were all standing in front of three massive barrels, and what appeared to be a giant furnace blazing away in the corner. There was a strong stench in the air and he struggled to take a breath.

'R-Ransom?' Persephone's mouth formed a perfect O. 'What are you doing here?'

'Customers aren't allowed here.' The barkeep cracked his knuckles. 'Should I show you out or do ye know the way?'

'It's all right, Grant,' she soothed. 'He's a guest of the Duke of Mabury.'

Grant eyed him warily. 'If ye say so, Yer Ladyship.'

'Where is your chaperone, Lady Persephone?' Ransom strode towards her. 'You should not be in here alone.'

'It's a small village, and everyone knows everyone,' she replied. 'The Dowager's carriage took me here so I have the footman waiting outside and—' she gestured to one of the female employees wearing an apron and cap '—Grant's wife is here.'

Ransom scrubbed a hand down his jaw. 'What in God's name is this place anyway? And why are you here?'

'It's a brewery,' she said matter-of-factly. 'That's the furnace. It heats up the brew kettle upstairs and—'

'I know what a furnace and brewery are,' Ransom interrupted. 'But why are you here?'

'Why wouldn't she be?' Grant let out a guffaw. 'She built it.'

Ransom wasn't quite sure he'd heard the man correctly. 'You…built it?'

A pretty blush covered Persephone's cheeks and the bridge of her freckled nose. 'Yes.'

'Why? How?' And those were just the first two questions on his mind.

'Because I was bored,' she said. 'I was sitting around Highfield Park doing nothing with my time.'

'And the Dowager let you come here and build this?' Persephone chuckled. 'It was her idea.'

Ransom wondered if he was going insane. Or perhaps he was still back in the chair in the smoking room, trapped in a dream. 'So you did this? Everything?'

'*Pfft*. I mean, obviously I didn't build the barrels or fit the pipes or install the pumps.'

'*Pfft*. Obviously,' Grant echoed.

'But I came up with the plans. It's really not much different to our distillery back home. Brewing ales is basically the same process as distilling whisky at the start. I've never built a brewery from scratch, though, so I took a few trips to London and Kate and I visited a few breweries and ale houses.'

'Ka— The Duchess of Mabury toured breweries with you?'

'She helped me to source the materials and assisted me in building the pump.'

'What did the Duke have to say?'

'I don't remember exactly what he said, but he was quite impressed.'

'You mean to tell me, the Duke knew about your plan to tour breweries and went along with it.'

'Obviously.'

'Obvious—'

Ransom glared at the barkeep, who clamped his mouth shut.

She frowned. 'What's all this fuss about then, Ransom?'

'I…' He scrambled for a coherent thought.

Lady Persephone did all this.

She had thought of it, planned it and then made it happen. Was it possible to be awed and aroused at the same time?

You incredible woman.

He cleared his throat. 'Would you give me a tour?'

Her wide smile lit up the room. 'Of course.'

They started upstairs, as Lady Persephone said that was where the process began. There were more workers there, and they all seemed to know Lady Persephone as they greeted her enthusiastically.

As she explained each step to him, Ransom listened intently, though he didn't understand half the words and terms she used. He had a rudimentary knowledge of how ale was made from when he investigated having a brewery built at the club, but that had been some years ago and he hadn't delved into the finer details. But it was obvious that Lady Persephone knew the process inside and out. He followed her like a lovesick puppy, listening eagerly as she explained the mashing and fermentation processes.

They ended the tour in the room with the three barrels where he'd burst in on them, where, he learned, the ale passes through twice—first as grain and hot water in the mash tun, then during its first fermentation in open barrels, which was why the air had that strong stench.

'Isn't it marvellous?' Persephone exclaimed. 'The whole process, I mean.'

You're marvellous.

'It is.'

'But what are you doing here?' Her delicate brows drew towards each other in a frown, causing a line to appear between them. 'I mean, I didn't see you at all yesterday, after…after…'

'I was busy with club business.' Ransom's chest ached as he sensed her confusion and hurt. 'I asked not to be disturbed and I lost track of time. I came here for a drink and then I saw you.'

'You seemed terribly upset to see me here today.' She pursed her lips. 'Did I do anything wrong? You left the library so abruptly yesterday.'

'No, not at all.' He ached to touch her cheek again. Or any part of her. Maybe even hold her in his arms.

''Scuse me, Yer Ladyship, Mr Ransom.' Grant appeared in the doorway. 'His Grace and the Duchess are here.'

'Kate's here? Do send them in, Grant.'

The barkeep stuck his head back to the main room and seconds later, the Duchess of Mabury entered. 'Persephone, is this it?' Her neck craned up at the barrels. 'I can't believe it. It's really here.'

'Aye, I'm so glad you can finally see it.' She strode over to her friend and clasped her hands. 'This is all thanks to you, the Dowager, and the Duke.'

'We merely provided encouragement and resources.'

'Your brilliant mind is a terrific resource,' Lady Persephone said warmly.

'I— Ransom?' The Duchess gave a start when she noticed his presence. 'What are you doing here?'

'He happened to be having a pint when I arrived,' Lady Persephone explained. 'Then I gave him a tour.'

The petite brunette eyed him. 'Is that so?'

'It is, Your Grace.'

'Hmm.' She turned to Lady Persephone. 'I know you've just finished a tour, but would it be an imposition to request another one?'

'Not at all.'

'Excellent. Scbastian's outside meeting with John, but he says he should be done soon. I'm sure he'd like to come along as well.'

As the Duchess predicted, the Duke soon joined them. He didn't comment on Ransom's presence, but he did give him a strange look. During the tour, the two men straggled behind while the women chatted excitedly as they wound up and down the three levels of the brewery.

They had reached the basement when the Duke asked, 'What do you think of her?'

'Brilliant. Amazing. Talented.'

And very, very irresistible.

His eyes might as well be glued onto her, as he couldn't tear his gaze away.

'I beg your pardon? Talented?'

'Yes, why—' He faltered as he saw the Duke's amused expression. 'Wait, what are we talking about?'

'The brewery, of course.' Mabury slapped his palm on one of the enormous barrels where the ale was kept during the final stage of fermentation. 'This grand lady will be a fine addition to the village. What did you think I was referring to?' The corner of the Duke's mouth tugged upwards as he nodded in the direction of Lady Persephone. 'But I agree. She is.'

'Definitely.'

'Most men wouldn't think so. They might say she's strange.'

'I am not most men, Your Grace.'

'So, you're telling me you're not the least bit intimidated by her intelligence and capabilities?'

'Of course I am.' Ransom wasn't just intimidated, he was bloody well terrified. Because it was one more reason she was far above him. In fact, she was so out of his reach, she might as well have lived on the moon. 'As I should be. Women like Lady Persephone may one day rule the world and the female sex may realise that they don't need us menfolk. But you already know that.' He nodded at the Duchess, who was deep in conversation with Lady Persephone as the latter showed her the underback barrel, which collected the wort from the mash tun upstairs.

The Duke lifted an eyebrow at him. 'Indeed.' They watched the women some more, then headed upstairs to conclude the tour with a pint of ale each in the main room of the inn. When Mabury attempted to pay when they had finished, Grant waved them away.

'Yer money's no good here, Yer Grace. I wouldn't be able to pay for the brewery if it weren't fer yer business loan. And of course, none of it woulda been built without Her Grace and Her Ladyship.' He snorted at Ransom. 'Ye owe me for that second one, though.'

Ransom produced another coin from his pocket with a laugh. 'Here you go, my good man.'

'We should head home,' the Duchess said. 'Mama will be waiting for us.'

Mabury groaned. 'Could we not have one more pint? I'm not exactly looking forward to finding out what task I have been assigned for this festival.'

Ransom could barely stop himself from snickering as he caught Lady Persephone's amused smirk. 'I'm sure it's something gravely important, Your Grace.'

Chapter Eight

'I know the day isn't over yet, but I think it's safe to say that our festival is a success,' the Dowager declared.

'And none of it would have happened if it weren't for you, Mama,' Kate said. 'This is all your work.'

'Indeed,' Persephone agreed.

The festival had started early in the morning, and by noon, the crowds were teeming. It was now late afternoon and the number of people in attendance had doubled when news spread of the festivities, bringing in people from the village and beyond who wanted to enjoy the summer sun and amusements.

Sellers and peddlers from near and far set up tables, hawking their wares: fine pottery, ribbons, knives, combs, toys, and the like. There were also booths that offered food and treats, including pies, jellied eels, pickled whelks, brandy balls, hot buns, and cakes, as well as refreshments such as lemonade, ginger beer, and of course The White Horse Inn's brand-new ale.

Persephone had passed by the inn several times to check on Grant, but he was too busy slinging mugs of fresh ale to entertain her, which Persephone took as a good sign. Initially, he'd been reluctant about having her build the brewery; in fact, he'd been downright suspicious. However, thanks to the Dowager's persuasive nature—and the Duke's generous loan—he had eventually agreed.

'I'm absolutely exhausted,' Miss Merton moaned, then snapped her fan open. 'And this heat.'

'Aye.' Persephone wiped the sweat from her neck with her handkerchief. 'Running around after all those children wore me out.' She had spent most of the day supervising the children's games, and while she had had a grand time laughing and chasing them about, she was glad it was over and she could now enjoy the rest of the festival at her leisure.

'How about a cold ginger beer?' the Dowager suggested. All four women agreed, so they made their way to the seller's booth.

Despite the heat and fatigue, Persephone couldn't be any happier, and not just because of the festival. After she and Ransom had run into each other at The White Horse Inn two days ago, he'd seemed less agitated and reticent. In fact, he'd almost been downright cheerful, albeit in his own way.

What had caused this change in him she did not know, nor did she have the chance to ask because they had yet to find themselves alone since that day at the brewery. The only thing she could be certain of was that something had shifted in him—and between them. In fact, just this morning, as she was guiding the children through their game of blind man's bluff, she'd caught him watching her from the sidelines. When she waved at him, he returned the gesture, along with a smile.

'Is that pretty blush due to the heat?' Kate whispered, a wry smile touching her lips. Miss Merton had slowed down due to the heat, so she and the Dowager trailed behind.

'Definitely,' Persephone replied.

'Are you sure it's not because of a certain handsome businessman?'

'I beg your pardon?'

Kate's voice lowered in volume a notch. 'You and Ransom.'

Persephone stumbled forward, but Kate caught her arm before she fell. 'R-Ransom and I?'

'Yes. I've seen the way you look at him when you think no one is watching,' Kate said. 'And I can tell you that he looks at you the same way.' She nudged her. 'Would it be so bad?'

'Would what be so bad?'

'He's unmarried, rich, and more importantly, he knows the value of a hard day's work.'

'He's not a gentleman,' Persephone pointed out.

The corner of the young duchess's mouth curled up. 'But you don't give a whit about that, now, do you, Persephone?'

No, she did not. But her and Ransom…married? She didn't dare allow herself to imagine it.

'Would Cam object?' Kate asked.

'I don't know. He's said from the beginning that he wouldn't force me to marry anyone I didn't want to.' Cam would certainly admire a self-made man like Ransom. She contemplated telling Kate the truth about her plan to remain in Scotland rather than attending any more Seasons, and about her troubling infatuation with Ransom. 'I…'

The sound of a horn blasted across the festival grounds, and Persephone sent a prayer of thanks to the heavens for the distraction. 'That's the horn for the wagon race.'

The two-man wagon race was one of the day's main events. A track was mapped out along a two-mile stretch of road that ran around the village where six teams of two people would race to the finish line for the grand prize of ten pounds.

Taking their ginger beer with them, the women made their way to the starting line, where the race would end as well. The crowds were starting to gather around the track, eager to watch the action.

'There's Sebastian and Ransom,' the Dowager said.

Persephone's head immediately swung to where the Dowager pointed, her heartbeat stuttering as she saw Ransom's tall frame.

'Is the prettiest sheep contest finished?' Kate asked, her grin reaching from ear to ear. Though he hadn't complained, the Duke wasn't terribly happy about his assignment. 'Wait, what's happening? Why are they all gathered around that one cart?'

'Let's find out, shall we?'

They followed behind the Dowager as she led them to the small group forming by the starting line, the Duke and Ransom right in the thick of it. As they drew closer, Persephone couldn't take her eyes off Ransom. Like most of the men, he'd removed his coat due to the heat, as well as rolled up his sleeves, showing off the dark tan of his sinewy, muscled forearms. She hadn't thought it possible, but her body's temperature rose a few more degrees.

'I'm sorry, boy, rules are rules,' Mr John Lawrence, one of the Duke's tenants who was in charge of the race, said.

'But Pa just broke his arm,' a young boy of about ten or eleven years old pleaded. 'I can still drive the cart.'

'Sorry, Alby, we need to be fair.'

'What's happening, Sebastian?' the Dowager asked. 'Why aren't you starting yet?'

Persephone sidled up beside the Dowager, trying not to stare at Ransom, who stood just a few feet away from her.

'I'm afraid we have a last-minute disqualification.' Mabury gave the boy a consoling smile. 'Alby and his father were supposed to join the race, but his father injured his arm in the hammer toss.'

'Oh, dear.' Persephone worried at her lip. While she hadn't actually handed the man the hammer, a small part of her felt responsible for the injury and now Alby's disqualification. She had suggested the game, after all.

'I told him he shouldn't have done it,' Alby pouted. 'But he's a stubborn old git—er, man. Beggin' your pardon, Your Grace,' he said sheepishly to the Dowager. 'But I can still drive. I've been drivin' our wagon since I was eight.'

'It's a two-man race, Alby,' Mr Lawrence gently pointed out. 'Each team has to have about the same weight, to balance out the wagon so the race is fair.'

'Couldn't he find someone to ride with him?' Kate asked. 'Someone roughly the size of the boy's father?'

The boy's expression turned stricken. 'No one'll want to ride wit' me. Everyone thinks I'm just a silly boy.'

'There, there, Alby.' Mr Lawrence squeezed his shoulder. 'Why doncha you go over there with my boys?' He pointed to the two children playing under a tree. 'We'll sort this out.'

'All right, Mr Lawrence,' the boy said, then dashed off in the direction of the boys.

Mr Lawrence gestured to the five other wagons waiting at the starting line. 'Almost everyone else who can drive a wagon and is brave enough to race is already competing.'

'I'll do it,' the Duke volunteered. 'I'll ride with the boy.'

'Beggin' your pardon, Your Grace, but it might not be

a fair race with you in it. Not when the other riders see their landlord racin' against them.'

'True. They might try to let you win, Sebastian,' the Dowager added. 'And—wait, I have an idea. Ransom, couldn't you take the place of the boy's father?'

'Me, ma'am?' Ransom shook his head. 'I don't know the first thing about driving a wagon.'

'You wouldn't have to. All you would need to do is sit next to the boy.'

'Or I could just give him the ten pounds,' Ransom countered. 'Or how about fifteen?'

'That's not the point, now, is it?' The Dowager chuckled. 'The boy needs to win the money fairly.'

'You think he'd choose the risk of losing over fifteen pounds?' Ransom crossed his arms over his chest. 'Isn't there anyone else? An uncle or a neighbour?'

'No one.' Mr Lawrence clucked his tongue and shook his head. 'The boy and his father came down here from Bedfordshire last year. Havin' a bad time of it because the other families haven't warmed up to 'em yet. My boys say the older ones give Alby trouble.'

Persephone noticed a tick in Ransom's jaw, but he remained silent.

The Dowager *tsked*. 'Is the father all right after injuring himself? Is he at home with his wife?'

'Ain't got no wife,' Mr Lawrence said. 'From what I heard, his wife and daughter died of scarlet fever. That's why they moved here, for a new start.'

Persephone gasped. 'That poor child.'

Ransom grumbled. 'Fine. I'll ride with him. Call the boy.'

'Really?' the Duke exclaimed in an incredulous tone.

'Yes. Don't ask again or I might change my mind.'

'Wonderful.' The Dowager clapped her hands together. 'Thank you so much, Ransom.'

He yanked at his collar to loosen it, exposing a patch of skin. 'I just hope I won't regret this.'

The Duke clapped him on the shoulder. 'If I see you fall off that wagon, consider us even for that sheep stunt you pulled.'

Fall? Persephone clutched at her chest. While she was happy that Alby would be racing, she didn't even think of the possibility that Ransom could be hurt.

Her nerves rattled, she considered not watching the race. Perhaps she could sit in the inn or shop for a trinket to distract herself. However, if anything happened to him—

Swift as she could without tripping over her toes, she rushed over to Ransom, who was now standing by the wagon, Alby at his side.

'...I'm the best driver my age, milord!'

'I'm sure you are, Alby.' Ransom patted the boy on the shoulder. 'And it's just Ransom.'

'Uh, hello,' Persephone greeted them. 'Ransom, would you kindly introduce me to your new friend?'

'Of course. Lady Persephone MacGregor, this is Albion Johnson.'

Alby's big blue eyes widened, then his cheeks turned scarlet. 'H-how do you do, milady?'

'It's a pleasure to meet you.' Persephone retrieved her handkerchief and then tied it around his neck. 'Here you go, laddie. My favour.'

'A favour?'

'Mmm-hmm.' She straightened the kerchief. 'In the olden days, during jousting tournaments, a lady would award her chosen knight her favour to show her support. I hope it brings you good luck.'

The boy beamed. 'I know it will. We're going to win this, you see?' He looked up at Ransom. 'Right, Mr Ransom?'

'Right. Looks like the race is about to start. Why don't you get ready and I'll join you in the wagon in a moment. And it's just Ransom,' he repeated, though he didn't seem annoyed.

'Yes, Ransom!' he said enthusiastically, then scrambled up to the driver's seat.

Persephone turned to Ransom. 'Are you sure about this?'

'Not really,' he muttered in a low voice, leaning close so only she could hear.

'Then why do this? You said no at first.' She frowned. 'You're looking a little green around the gills. What's the matter?'

'I... I...' He puffed out his cheeks. 'That—that thing—' he pointed to the wagon '—makes me nervous, all right? Any kind of fast-moving transport does.'

'Nervous?' Her voice came out a little higher than she wanted. 'But you made it all the way here from London.'

'In a carriage,' he qualified. 'A closed carriage with a comfortable, velvet-covered seat. Not a rickety, rolling death coach.'

'You've never ridden in an open wagon before? I've been riding in one since I was a child. We use several to transport our grain back in Scotland.' She narrowed her eyes at him.

He really was scared.

Poor dear.

'It's not too late,' she said. 'You can still say no. The race hasn't started.'

'Are you mad? I have to do this now.' His jaw clenched and a sheen of sweat appeared on his brow. 'I can't disappoint the boy. He'll be a laughingstock. No, I must do this.'

A warmth that had nothing to do with the weather spread through her. 'You're not so selfish and wicked after all,' she teased.

Before he could say anything, the horn blew once again, indicating that the competitors had to line up. 'I should go.'

'Stay safe and good luck, Ransom.'

'Thank you.' He glanced up at Alby, whose cheeks were flushed with excitement. 'Do you have any advice?'

'Hold on tight?'

He chuckled with a nervous energy and shook his head. 'I shall see you at the finish line,' he said, then added, 'Hopefully.'

Persephone watched him climb into the wagon and then waved at them. The boy waved back and snapped the reins, directing the horses expertly in the direction of the other wagons. She then trudged over to where Kate and the others waited, and they had a good view of the starting/finish line.

'How exciting,' the Dowager exclaimed. 'I'm so glad Ransom decided to join after all.'

'That poor boy… I had no idea,' Kate said. 'Sebastian, we should do something for them.'

'This is a start.' The Duke nodded his head to where Alby and Ransom were pulling up to the starting line. 'He's the youngest competitor out there and he's driving to boot. The other boys will think him the village hero when he comes across the finish line. Unless he breaks Ransom's neck.'

Persephone's heart leapt into her throat.

Hold on tight, indeed.

The crack of the starting pistol made Persephone jump,

and the wagons sped away. The thunderous sound of the hooves deafened her and the cloud of dust the wagons left in their wake had the spectators coughing. When the dust cleared, her heart sank as she saw Ransom and Alby trailing at the back.

Please, be safe, she prayed. *Oh, Lord...*

Wiping the dust from her spectacles, she squinted at the competitors. They were much too far away for anyone to see now, and soon they disappeared around the bend.

'Now we wait,' Mabury said.

And Lord, did they wait. To Persephone, time stretched on. She couldn't help but think of all the terrible scenarios, the awful possibilities. What if their wagon overturned and they were crushed? Or they lost a wheel and crashed into a tree?

A hand gave hers a reassuring squeeze. 'They'll be fine,' Kate said.

A million years seemingly passed before the telltale sound of hooves in the distance told Persephone they were coming around the last bend.

'Oh, I can't look.' She gripped Kate's shoulders and closed her eyes. 'Please...tell me, are they there?'

'I... Yes, I see six of them.'

'Thanks goodness,' she cried in relief.

'They're coming closer...closer,' Kate narrated. 'Is that...? No, I think it is! Oh, Persephone!'

'What is it?'

'Open your eyes!' Kate urged.

And so she did. After blinking away the blurriness, she gasped. 'I can't believe it!'

Two wagons led the pack and one was Alby and Ransom's. The crowd cheered as they hurtled towards the finish line. Alby drove the horses hard as Ransom shouted his encouragement. Persephone felt nauseous and excited at the same time.

They could really win it.

They were nearly there, at the final stretch. Ransom let out a loud *huzzah* as they pulled ahead of the other wagon and broke the ribbon strung across the finish line.

'Yes!' Persephone raised a fist in the air. 'They did it!'

The spectators went wild as they crowded around the wagon, cheering Alby's name. When Ransom stood and lifted the boy up on his shoulders, they hollered even louder.

Persephone and Kate hugged each other tight. 'They won!' they cried, jumping in happiness.

'He actually did it,' the Duke said with a chuckle. 'Luck of the devil himself.'

They stayed back, allowing the two winners to bask in the adoration of the crowd. Mr Lawrence hurried over to them, and invited the Duke and Duchess to award the prize. The crowd parted as the couple wound their way to the wagon; Mabury helped Kate up so that they stood in the back of the cart, then handed the boy the prize money.

Persephone noticed Ransom glancing around, then stopping when their eyes met. Despite the distance, she could nearly feel the intensity of his stare and her heart thudded madly against her chest.

Once the crowds began to disperse, Ransom helped Alby down from the wagon, knelt down to his level, and said a few words. The boy nodded eagerly, gave him a hug, then scampered off. Rising to his feet, Ransom's gaze fixed on Persephone once again.

Her feet propelled her towards him as if they had a life of their own. He strode towards her too, meeting her halfway. 'Ransom, I'm so glad— Oh!'

She found herself engulfed in his strong arms. It felt

so natural to melt into them, and she didn't care if anyone was watching. The embrace was over in a second, however, as he stepped back.

'Persephone.' A hand cupped her jaw, his thumb stroking her cheek. 'I thought I was going to die.'

So did I.

And she was still so overcome with all the emotion—fear, excitement, happiness—that she couldn't bring herself to care that it looked inappropriate for him to touch her so intimately. Besides, everyone was celebrating around them and no one seemed to take notice.

Trying to lighten the mood, she laughed aloud. 'You took my advice then?'

'I did.' His other hand landed on her waist. 'But the entire time, I had this thought. What if I died and I never got the chance to tell you something.'

'Tell me what?' She was on tenterhooks, waiting for him to finish. 'What, Ransom?'

'My, isn't this a sight?'

They broke apart. 'I…' She swung around to face the newcomer. 'I beg your pardon, sir?'

The older man smiled, causing the wrinkles on his face to deepen. 'Don't let me interrupt your sweet reunion.'

She cocked her head to the side. The man's hair was pure white, and his frame slight but tall. From the cut of his expensive clothes, she could tell he was wealthy and supposed he must be older than seventy years of age. Behind him was a manservant of some sort holding a cane and a hat, and watching vigilantly over his master as if the older man could fall at any moment and he would have to sacrifice himself to break his fall.

There was something about him that was familiar, but what, she couldn't quite deduce.

'Allow me to introduce myself.' The man moved closer, leaning down to her face. 'Leopold, Duke of Winford.'

Persephone could not stop the gasp escaping from her mouth as different-coloured eyes—one green, one brown—stared back at her. She whirled around. Ransom stood there, unmoving, teeth gritted, hands clenched into fists. His body was so rigid she feared he would break in two, while his contemptuous stare was directed at Winford.

'Ransom? Do you know this man?'

He didn't answer her as he continued to glare at Winford. The Duke, on the other hand, only smiled smugly.

'Ransom?' she prompted.

'You should leave.'

His words hit her like cold water to the face. 'I beg your pardon?'

'Go back to the Duchess and the Dowager,' he ordered, his tone glacial. 'Now.'

'No, absolutely not.' She flexed her toes, as if planting herself on the ground like a tree. There was no chance she was leaving him alone, not when he was acting like this.

'Fine, we'll leave then.'

'You—what?'

Ransom nodded at the old man. 'Shall we, Your Grace?'

The man's thin, cracked lips spread into a smirk. 'A walk then? The fresh air will do us some good.' He nodded at his servant. 'Finch, stay here. We do not want to be disturbed.'

'Yes, Your Grace,' he said with a low bow.

Ransom walked ahead and the old man followed. When Persephone attempted to trail them, Finch stood in her path.

'Get out of my way,' she ordered.

The man's faced remained stony and he did not meet

her eyes. Her next few attempts were thwarted as each time she sidestepped him, he blocked her way.

Blasted man!

Unsure what to do, she turned in the other direction and strode off in a huff.

Who was that man? And why did he have the same eyes as Ransom? They obviously knew each other, but neither had acknowledged their connection. And Ransom…she'd never seen him so cold. There was that time in the library when she'd asked about his sisters, but that had been a light snowstorm compared to this blizzard.

Pain twisted in her chest, the agony so acute that she feared it would never go away. She had to find out who that man was and why he had Ransom's eyes.

Chapter Nine

Ransom walked briskly, but not too fast, as he enjoyed hearing the old bastard wheeze behind him. Maybe if he were lucky, Winford would keel over and die on the spot. He relished the thought of watching the life drain from his husk of a body.

Of course, Winford was here to ruin this perfect day. Ransom should have expected it. After all, what else was the old man's purpose in life but to destroy his? And to think, as he was hurtling towards the finish line, facing possible death, he had made the most terrifying and exhilarating decision of his life.

'Confound it, boy, stop!'

Ransom came to a halt by a line of trees that marked the edge of the village. 'I am not a boy.' He swung around to meet the old man's gaze, arms crossing over his chest, refusing to speak first.

'It's been four years and you haven't changed at all, Ransom.'

'Has it been that long? I can't recall.' It was a lie. Ransom remembered every second of the only time he had spoken with Winford.

'You should have stayed away. Stayed in whatever hole your mother whelped you. Bastard.'

'Aren't you going to ask what I'm doing here?'

Ransom remained impassive. 'If you think I care as to what you're doing at any given time, you are sorely mistaken.'

'Insolent boy,' Winford spat. 'Why do you want that land?'

'So you've heard about that. Why do you think?'

Winford raised a fist. 'Can you not let me have this *one* thing? Are you hell-bent on bankrupting yourself to spite me?'

'I could be starving on the street and I would still spend my last penny to spite you, *Grandfather.*'

'Don't call me that,' Winford raged. 'I have no grandson, no family!'

Ransom couldn't help but smile. 'And not a single heir. You know, I would give up my entire fortune right now if you expired on the spot, taking your title to hell with you.'

A fire burned in the old man's eyes. 'I had an heir. My wonderful Oliver, but he was taken from me. My son… killed in the prime of his life in that riding accident. His only sin was getting that tart pregnant. If it wasn't for her, I would still have an heir.'

Hurt filled Ransom, but he pushed it away, into that box of emotions where he could never feel it. He would not give Winford the satisfaction of a reaction. 'Did you come here to rehash the events of the past or did you have a purpose?'

Winford bared his teeth. 'Only to look you in the eye and let you know that you can snatch away every piece of property or art piece I want, but you will never win.' He sneered. 'You will never be more than the bastard son of a whore who tried to ensnare a lord, but ended up dead on the streets. It's a pity you didn't end up dead with her. Whatever scum took the lot of you in wasted their time clothing and feeding—'

'Shut your mouth!' Ransom flew at him, fuelled by wrath and years of resentment. He would not allow this bastard to speak ill of the woman who had taken him in and raised him. Grabbing the old man by the lapels, he shook him hard. 'Don't you speak of her—'

'Ransom!'

He stood stock-still at the sound of Persephone's sweet voice. Had his rage made him hallucinate?

'Ransom, let go.'

The soft burr and the dainty hand tugging at his arm told him she was not a figment of his imagination.

His grip on Winford slackened. 'You shouldn't be here, Persephone.'

'Aye, and neither should you.' Her hand encircled his wrist and gently pulled him away.

'You must be Lady Persephone MacGregor.' Winford straightened up and smoothed down his lapel. 'I've heard about you.'

'Y-you have?'

'Yes. I am neighbours with your sponsors, though I spend most of my time in London. I believe I've made acquaintance with your brother, the Earl of Balfour, at the Hayfield Ball.' He eyed her hand, which was still wrapped around Ransom's wrist, then *tsked*. 'My lady, do you know who this man is? His true character? His parentage?'

Persephone glanced at Ransom, her face filled with pity. Of course she knew; she had probably heard every word of his conversation with Winford.

'I imagine your brother would be interested to know

who his sister has been associating with,' Winford continued. 'As would the rest of the ton.'

A horrible dread filled Ransom. Though rumours had begun to circulate about their connection, neither of them had acknowledged the gossip. There was still plausible deniability, and there was no record of Ransom's birth. He'd done all he could to erase the traces of his impoverished background, learning how to speak, dress, and act properly, to appear only as a powerful businessman and owner of London's largest gentleman's club. If Winford were to confirm their connection, it wouldn't hurt either of them as their worlds didn't readily mix.

But Persephone—

'You vile man,' Persephone spat. 'Leave before I—I—'

'Before you what, my lady?' Winford barked. '*Hmmph.* Perhaps you do deserve each other.' He threw them one last viperous stare before he trudged away.

Persephone tugged at Ransom's wrist. 'Ransom—'

'What did you hear?'

'I—'

'What did you hear?' he repeated, this time more forcefully.

'Everything,' she confessed. 'I took a short cut around the other side of the meadow. I used it all the time while I was working on the brewery.' She turned to face him, threading her fingers through his. 'Please, talk to me. What happened?'

'What happened?' he scoffed. 'Where should I start, Persephone? From the beginning?' She was going to hear it all anyway, once Winford let out the truth about him. 'Winford is my grandfather. I'm the bastard son of his only son and heir, the late Oliver, Marquess of Havensworth. There were rumours that we were related swirling about once I became owner of The Underworld and then one day I saw it for myself when I ran into him on the street. I hired private investigators who dug up some clues; nothing concrete, but enough to piece my parentage together. Wanting to know the true story, I confronted Winford at his home.'

'Wh-what happened?'

'He told me everything. Even relished in it. His son had got a tenant's daughter pregnant, my birth mother, and when Winford found out, he had her kidnapped and taken to London. She died giving birth to me.'

'I'm so sorry. You father—'

'Fell off his horse. He'd been searching for her everywhere.' He shut his eyes tight. 'He's dead because of me. They both are.'

'Don't say that.' She stepped closer and laid her cheek on his chest. 'Don't say that.'

'It's true.'

'What…what happened to you after she died?'

'A couple from the rookeries adopted me. The kindest woman you ever met, and a bastard drunkard of a man.' His chest tightened. 'They had three daughters.'

'Your sisters,' she murmured against his shirt.

'They're dead too. All three of them, and Mum.' His throat burned, years' worth of unshed tears like hot knives. The tight, searing pain growing in his chest made it difficult to breathe. Taking hold of those emotions, he locked them up. He could not afford to break, not in front of her.

A sob escaped Persephone's lips. 'No…'

'There was a fever going 'round. Didn't even take my bastard adoptive father.' She flinched. 'Once they were gone, I left. Found a job at Hale's as a dishwasher. Worked my way up, eventually to the gaming floor as a croupier. Saved every penny I earned. I soaked up everything I could while dealing cards to fancy gentlemen. Stock tips, which businesses were about to boom and which were going bust. Invested everything until I had enough money to buy out Old Man Hale.' Since then he'd increased his personal fortune a hundred fold. He could buy anything and everything he wanted. Yet now there was one thing he could not acquire, not with all the money in the world.

As he faced his mortality during the race, he had come to the most profound truth in his life, and made a terrifying and exhilarating decision.

He would make Persephone his. Not for one tumble or some torrid affair, but his, for the rest of their lives.

He wanted her as his wife.

But all that would be lost, once Winford spread the truth about him. Persephone's brother would never approve of her marriage to a lord's by-blow who grew up in the slums.

Winford had finally taken away something Ransom wanted.

Persephone's hands slid up his chest and she lifted her head to look at him. 'Don't let that man make you think you are worth less than you are, Ransom.'

Tears streaked her cheeks, and he longed to brush them away. 'You should go, my lady. We should not be alone like this.'

Her fingers gripped his shirt. 'I don't care about that.'

'You should. Your brother will care. Everyone will care. Think of the scandal. Your mother's last wish.' Gently, he pried her hands away, then spun around to walk away from her. He quickened his strides, making his way down the hill, trying to put as much distance between himself and Persephone as possible. Spying a barn at the bottom, he made his way towards the structure, hoping to find some peace and quiet and respite from the heat.

It was cool inside, thankfully, and Ransom opened the

top two buttons of his shirt and wiped the perspiration from the back on his neck.

'Ransom?'

He spun around at the sound of the familiar voice. 'You followed me?'

Persephone stood by the entrance, the sunlight from the outside illuminating her like she was an angel sent from above. 'I had to.'

'Please, Lady Persephone, leave.'

'No.'

'No?'

She removed her spectacles, wiped her tears away with the back of her hand, then replaced them. Despite the clear glass barrier, her emerald gaze bore straight into him. 'What were you about to tell me?'

Ransom swallowed the lump in his throat. 'Tell you?

'Do not play games with me, Ransom. You said, "I thought I was going to die and I had this thought. What if I never got the chance to tell you something." Now tell me what that something is.'

Trust her to remember what he had said, almost word for word. 'Nothing.'

'It was not "nothing."'

'It was nothing important then!' he roared, frustrated. 'Just leave.'

'I am not moving from this spot, not one inch.'

'Then you'll be waiting all day.' He spun around to walk away from her, but she moved to block his path. 'Move, Persephone.'

'Are you going back to London?'

'Not that it's any of your business, but yes. My business here is concluded and I must return to The Underworld.'

'Will I ever see you again?'

'Perhaps.'

Her nostrils flared. 'That means no. You're just leaving me here then?'

'What would you have me do?' He raked his fingers through his hair. 'Persephone, we cannot…'

'Kiss me then, before you leave.'

All thought seeped out of his head. 'I beg your pardon?'

'You heard me.' Her arms crossed under her breasts. 'For God's sake—'

'Are you afraid?' she said, her tone challenging.

She then did something unexpected—she took a step towards him. Unsure how to react, he took a step back, which only made her advance further. He was taller and larger than her by far, and could easily knock her down, but he would never do that to her. More than that, he was afraid to touch her again, fearing he might lose control. That all those emotions he'd kept locked up would burst out.

'Let's not play this game. Stop this—Christ!' His back hit something solid. Persephone had trapped him against a wall.

'I will, but kiss me first.'

'Oh, for crying out—'

She lunged at him, arms wrapping around his neck. 'Kiss. Me.'

And because he was only human, he did just that.

Chapter Ten

As Ransom's head descended towards hers, only one thought remained in Persephone's mind.

Finally.

His lips melded onto hers, their mouths fusing together in the most curious, yet delightful way. His mouth was softer than she had imagined—and oh, did she imagine it then in just about every single way possible.

Concentrate, she told herself.

He shifted his head to the other side and to her surprise, his tongue licked at her lips. She gasped, which only allowed him to catch her bottom lip with his teeth and suck it deep into his mouth.

All right, so maybe she hadn't imagined his kiss in every way possible.

Heat gathered in that place between her legs, a tingling sensation pooling there with an intensity she'd never felt before. When he finally released her lower lip, she thought he was done, but no. He treated her upper lip to the same sweet torture. The pressure down there built up, and she sought relief by pressing her body against his.

'Persephone,' he murmured against her lips.

'Yes, oh, yes.' She didn't know what she was saying yes to, exactly, but she wanted whatever he had to offer.

Before she knew it, he had flipped her around so she was now the one trapped against the wall. 'Ransom...'

His mouth sought hers again, this time hungrier, more urgent. A hand cupped her jaw, fingers caressing her skin with soothing circles. His lower body pressed against her hips, and when she felt his strong thighs against hers, she gasped, allowing him to slip his tongue between her lips.

His tongue was gentle, probing her delicately, at the same time coaxing hers to respond. So she did, tentatively rubbing it against his lips. He moaned and pushed his hips into her, and something else hard brushed against her.

A thrill shot all the way through her. It was exciting, this feeling that she could make him pant and moan. She wanted more.

Her tongue became bolder, and this time she was the one urging him.

More, she pleaded silently with her hips. *And don't be gentle*, she encouraged, with her fingers gripping his shoulder. *Take as much as you can*, she ordered with her mouth.

It was like that wordless language of dance he had taught her.

Still he continued his gentle assault, so she decided to take the initiative. Her hands clutched at his shirt, and then pulled the hem out from the waistband of his trousers.

He muttered an oath against her mouth when her hands slid around his naked waist, the skin warm under her palms, his firm muscles going taut under her touch. With a feral growl, he thrust his tongue into her mouth once more, claiming her savagely. His hands found their way to her waist, then down to her buttocks, cupping them and pressing her closer to his hardness. He let out another moan as he rubbed rhythmically against her, obviously enjoying the feeling of her. The sensations were pleasant enough for Persephone, but there had to be more.

'Please, Ransom. I want to feel good.'

Slowing down, he said, 'I want to make you feel good.'

He pulled her towards him, hand running down her back. However, when she felt the fabric of her dress loosen, she realised that he had been unbuttoning the back of her dress. He caught the neckline with his teeth and dragged it down, exposing her neck and shoulders. His mouth trailed kisses down her neck to her collarbone, and down to the tops of her breasts. Deft fingers must have untied her stays somehow, as they too loosened and were pulled down, allowing him to cup a full breast with his hand through her chemise.

'Ransom!' She clutched at him as a thumb brushed her nipple, teasing it to hardness, while his mouth and teeth nibbled at the place where her neck and shoulders met. That pressure was building again, and she still wanted more.

Ransom was busy, so she raked her fingers across his scalp. 'Ransom, more.'

He let out a grunt, then ripped the front of her chemise, much to her shock and delight. When his mouth took in one bare nipple, she squealed in delight. 'Oh, yes.'

The cool air and Ransom's warm mouth made the most delicious contrast. She arched her body forward, pushing up towards his mouth. To her surprise, Ransom drew her entire nipple into his mouth. The sight of him hungrily devouring her bosom was shockingly erotic, sending more of those delicious sensations between her thighs.

'Need to—oh!' This time she didn't even have to demand anything. As if reading her mind, he lifted up the layers of her skirts, then hooked an arm under her knee before sliding her down to the ground, her back still pressed up against the wall.

Mother of mercy.

He knelt before her, propping one of her legs on his shoulder so that she was left exposed to him. A hand teased up her stockinged thigh, focusing on its target. Her hips jumped when his fingers touched her sex, probing gently at first. Then he began to tease her, caressing the outer folds, spreading the wetness around her nether lips.

More, more, more, she cried silently, thrusting her hips at him.

He answered by pushing one finger inside her.

It felt incredible. She pushed her hips towards him, and he slid the finger in deeper, then withdrew before thrusting it back in again. He repeated the motion a few times, her sex clenching at each thrust. When he pulled his hand away, she let out a protesting moan, but then his thumb found the crest of her sex, the bud swollen and throbbing.

'Oh!'

The sensations were indescribable, and the pressure building inside her seemed ready to burst. She rode his hand, chasing more and more of that sweet feeling. He spread her knees apart, then moved in to kiss her, all the while his hands never left her. His mouth plundered hers once more, and a finger thrust inside her core. The motions, his mouth, the air on her naked breasts—they all seemed to come together to give her that final push over the edge.

'That's it. Let go for me,' he growled against her mouth.

And she did, the waves of pleasure battering her body, making her shudder. It felt endless, yet at the same time, over too soon. She slumped against him, and he gathered her into the circle of his arms. Her limbs refused to move, and the feeling hadn't yet returned to her lower body. There was also the sense that she was sleepy, but not tired.

He kissed her temples as his hands rearranged her skirts over her knees.

'Ransom?'

His arms looped under hers, lifted her to her feet, and began to redress her. As she watched him put her clothes to rights, she could not help but notice the way his hands trembled as he pulled up the ripped chemise over her breasts.

'Ransom?' she repeated.

He gritted his teeth as he tugged her dress over her shoulders and pulled out bits of hay from her hair.

'Please—'

'We shouldn't have done this.' His voice was rough like sandpaper. 'Forgive me, I shouldn't have taken advantage of you.'

'I wanted it, Ransom. I wanted you from the beginning.' She balled her hands into his shirt. 'I ached so badly. The need for you burned hotter than fire inside me. I need you still.'

'I know,' he said. 'I wanted you too. But we cannot do this.'

'But I—'

'Don't make this any more difficult than it already is,' he said.

'But this isn't difficult. You want me.' She laid her palm against his cheek, looking at him pleadingly. 'And I want you.'

His eyes hardened like flint. 'For a quick tumble? Because that's what you ladies of the ton want with men like me, isn't that so? Why you propositioned me in the first place?'

'That's not what this is about and you know it.'

'Then what is this about? Aren't you heading back to Scotland at the end of the summer?'

'Yes, but I can change my mind. Ransom, you and I—'

'Can never happen.'

Her heart collapsed in on itself. Why was he acting this way? 'Don't go. Please. Don't leave me.'

'I'm done, my lady.' He raised his hands in the air. 'I'm done with the ton, done with Winford and   '

'Done with me,' she finished. Anger replaced her heartache. 'Go then and leave. Go back to your precious Underworld.' His expression faltered in a fleeting moment and she nearly begged him to stay a second time, but stopped herself.

His jaw hardened, but he didn't say a word as he turned on his heel and strode out of the barn.

Persephone bit her inner cheek so hard, it bled. But she would not cry. She refused to. From now on, no man would ever make her cry again.

Chapter Eleven

Ransom began his day on the main gaming floor as he had done every day for the past five years since taking ownership of The Underworld. Today, though, he woke up much earlier than usual, and he entered while the house-keeping crew was only just starting to clean up from the previous evening. The team of twelve was busy with their work as Hastings watched over them, directing them like a lieutenant-colonel commanding his soldiers.

'Come on, then, open the curtains and windows and make sure you tie them drapes up properly,' she ordered. 'Master Ransom wants to let the fresh air and light in.'

'Do we really have to do this every day?' one of the girls complained as she struggled to open the massive window. 'This thing is a pain in the arse.'

'Just do it, Lydia,' Hastings said. 'Light and air an' that helps keep the place clean.'

A little bit 'o light and some fresh air is just wot you need to feel clean,' Mum said as she pushed open the single window of their room, a luxury that no other family on their floor had. 'That's all we need.'

A pounding in Ransom's head hammered at his temples,

and razor-sharp pains cut at this throat as the tightness in his chest grew.

'M-Master Ransom!'

Hastings's surprised shout jolted him out of his memories. 'Hastings,' he greeted, then nodded at the other women. Half of them went pale and froze in fear, while the other half sent him lustful, inviting looks, which he promptly ignored.

'You're up early, Master,' Hastings noted. 'Can I do anything for ye? Did we miss anything yesterday? I told me girls not to be so sloppy with the dustin'.'

'Everything is fine, Hastings,' he said firmly. 'I have some matters to attend to. Carry on.'

Without another word, he strode away from them and made his way up to the open gallery. This morning, however, he only gave the gaming floor a quick glance before heading up to his office. He did not stop to admire the objects on the shelf or the paintings on the wall, but simply sat himself down on his chair. He also did not bother to fight the urge to reach for the object inside the right-hand drawer of his desk.

Gently, he picked up the spectacles inside by the delicate gold frames, raising them to the light, imagining emerald-green eyes behind them. This was a new ritual he'd adopted in the five days since he'd returned from Surrey. A ritual of torture, one that he deserved.

He did not want to forget Persephone nor lock his emotions in a box; he did not deserve that mercy after he'd left her the way he had. No, he would burn in the fires of his own hell, thinking of her every day, the image of her standing there in the barn after he'd all but ravished her, then left her while she begged him to stay.

Ransom allowed himself to continue his self-torment for another few minutes before he put the spectacles away. Though he could continue to torture himself for eternity, there was still work to be done. The Underworld employed nearly a hundred workers and they all were counting on him to keep the business running so they could put food on their tables.

The next few hours were spent mired in paperwork, correspondence, and meetings with employees and business contacts. He was knee-deep in reading a draft contract from his solicitor when Clyde knocked at the door.

'What is it?' he asked without looking up, as he had been reading schedule four, paragraph three of a new leasing contract for the past five minutes, yet still couldn't decipher what it meant.

'There's a man here to see you, Ransom. A solicitor.'

'From Chambers and Garland?' he said, mentioning the name of the firm he retained. 'Send them up.'

A few minutes later, he heard the door open again. 'Come in.' Picking up the contract, he rose from his seat to greet the man Clyde had brought up. 'Damned good timing.' He waved the pages around. 'I can't make head nor tail of this thing.'

'I—I beg your pardon?' the man sputtered.

Ransom frowned. The older man looked distinguished, dressed in a finely tailored suit, his hat still on his head, a heavy-looking valise in his right hand. 'Have we met before? I could have sworn I'd been introduced to all the senior partners at Chambers and Garland. Or perhaps you've recently joined?' He looked a bit too old to be a junior solicitor.

'No, we have not been introduced. My name is Robert Davis, sir. And I'm not from Chambers and Garland.'

'You're not?' He glared at Clyde. 'Why did you send him up here then?'

''Cause you said to,' Clyde replied with a shrug. 'Should I show him out?'

'Please, good sir, I must speak with you about a grave matter.' Davis's expression turned serious.

'I'm sure you must. But I do not meet anyone without an appointment, which you can obtain through my business secretary.'

The old man wasn't the least bit deterred. 'This is important, Mr Ransom. I must meet with you now.'

'It's just Ransom,' he corrected impatiently before nodding at Clyde. 'Escort this man out—'

'It's about the Duke of Winford.' Davis took his hat off. 'The late Leopold, Duke of Winford.'

The papers Ransom had been holding dropped to the floor with a soft *swoosh*. 'You can go, Clyde,' he said. Once the door had closed behind Clyde, Ransom turned to Davis. 'The only reason I haven't thrown you out is because I want to confirm that the old bastard's finally dead.'

Davis's face remained impassive. 'Yes.'

'Good riddance.' Ransom strode over to the glass cabinet in the corner to pour himself some brandy as he let the information sink in. After four years of waiting for this news, it now felt rather anticlimactic.

'Would you like one?' he offered Davis after he took a sip from his glass. 'It's the very best from France.'

'I'm sure it is, but no.'

'Suit yourself.' He took another gulp. 'You can go now.'

'I'm afraid I can't. I told you, I have a grave matter to discuss with you.' Davis cleared his throat. 'Regarding the title and the entailed property.'

'With no heirs, the title goes extinct and the property

reverts to the crown. You must be a terrible solicitor if you didn't know that.'

'But he did have a grandson via his only child, Oliver. You.'

Ransom burst out laughing, nearly spilling his brandy. 'That's a good one, Davis.' When the older man did not react, Ransom's instincts told him something was about to happen, something he might not like.

Davis opened up his valise and retrieved a large parcel. 'I think you should sit down.'

'No, I don't think so. I shall remain standing.'

'As you wish.' The solicitor strode over to him. 'I have served as the Duke of Winford's solicitor since the beginning of my career. It's true, His Grace did not have more sons or male relatives next in line to inherit. Some time ago, he asked me to prepare some documents should he pass on without any heirs.' He offered Ransom the parcel. 'Please have a look at this.'

Ransom glared at the parcel as if he'd been offered poison. 'You prepared these documents, did you not? Just tell me what they are so I don't waste any more of my time.'

Davis let out a long-suffering sigh, then broke the seal open, and retrieved a fragile, yellowed parchment from inside, and what appeared to be pages torn from a book. 'This is the register from the parish of the county of Holmstead. And this—' he opened the parchment '—is the marriage certificate of Oliver, Marquess of Havensworth, and Sophie Pryce, dated June the sixth, 1813. Your parents. This document makes you the new Duke of Winford.' He bowed his head. 'Your Grace.'

'You don't know that!' Ransom exploded. 'This Sophie Pryce could have been any woman. How do you know she was my birth mother?'

'Your grandfather confirmed it, Your Grace. This parcel also contains several corroborating written and signed oaths, such as the priest who married your parents and the witnesses, as well as a written confession from your grandfather, saying he had the registry record and the only existing marriage certificate stolen and concealed.'

A pulse pounded in Ransom's brain as he absorbed the information.

He was legitimate.

Winford knew it too.

And had hidden it.

'Does anyone else know aside from you and I?'

'No, Your Grace.'

'Stop calling me that,' Ransom barked. 'I'm not a duke.'

'Yes, you are.'

'No.' He shook his head vigorously. 'Why would he do this? The old coot hated me.'

'But he loved his legacy. Winford is one of the oldest and most prestigious titles in England, granted by—'

'Spare me the history lesson.' Ransom stalked over to his desk, finishing off the brandy in one gulp before slamming the glass down. 'Is there a way to stop this?'

'But, Your Grace—'

'I said. Stop. Calling. Me. That,' he said in his deadliest tone. 'Well?'

'In most cases, it's a matter of simply recognising your legitimacy, and then there's a legal process for you to take possession of all the entailed property and assets.' Davis paused. 'But this is an unusual case to say the least, as your grandfather committed a crime by stealing and concealing legal documents. There may be an investigation, but in my opinion, it should be a straightforward case since you are the victim of a crime and there is no one to challenge or obstruct your claim. So for all intents and purposes, the title is yours. You are Ransom, Duke of Winford.'

The sound of that name was like nails scraping on a chalkboard. 'If this was a crime, why didn't you go to the authorities?'

'I was bound by confidentiality to my client,' he answered.

'So…' Ransom clasped his hands together. 'If these documents did not exist, then there would be no other record of my parents' marriage?'

'As far as I know, none.'

'Am I obligated to submit these documents to the authorities?'

Davis paused. 'One could argue that as an upstanding citizen of England, you would report any crime you know of to the authorities.'

'All right then.' Ransom retrieved an envelope from the top left drawer of his desk, then threw it to Davis. 'Here.'

The older man caught it. 'What is it?'

'About five hundred pounds.' He walked over to Davis. 'More than enough for a retainer. You're my solicitor now, bound by confidentiality.'

'But—'

He ignored the man's protests and plucked the parcel from his hand. 'Thank you, Mr Davis, that will be all.'

'I implore you—'

'I said, that will be all.' He turned his back to him.

Davis huffed. 'If you change your mind, I'll leave my card with your man.'

Ransom didn't answer, but simply waited for the sound of the door slamming shut before exhaling. 'Damn you, Winford!'

The parcel in his hand crinkled as his grip on it tight-

ened. Marching to the desk, he threw it down, its contents spilling across the surface and onto the floor. With
another curse he began to gather the papers, shoving
them back into the parcel. As he reached for the papers
that had spilled on the floor, he spied a cream-coloured
envelope with an unbroken seal. Turning it over in his
hands, he read the name elegantly scrawled across the
fine linen paper: *Ransom, Duke of Winford.*

With a fierce growl, he tore at the envelope, took out
the letter within, then began to read.

Ransom,
By the time you read this, I will be dead and gone.
I trust you have read all the evidence and verified
the matter of your legitimacy and inheritance.

If you were hoping for a confession of remorse
from beyond the grave, then you will be sorely dis-
appointed. I do not regret anything I have done,
from banishing that trollop who whelped you to
stealing all evidence of my son's foolishness.

Then what is this, you ask? Why would I let my
family's most illustrious title pass on to a gutter-
snipe like you? The answer is not so simple, but
I'm writing it down in a way your uneducated mind
will understand.

When we first ran into each other on the street,
I had an inkling of who you were, but I ignored you
and the rumours swirling about. But there was no
denying who you were when you barged into my
home sometime later, showing me the proof from
your damned investigators, demanding answers. It
was one of the worst days of my life, second only
to the day my beloved Oliver died. I was living a
life of relative peace, not knowing of your exis-

tence, thinking you had perished along with your godforsaken mother. Then you come along, shattering this illusion.

And so I gathered all the evidence of your legitimacy, hoping to destroy the documents before your infernal investigators ferreted them out. Then you began to vex me, thwarting me at every turn, taking everything I wanted to acquire as your own. You would not let me have anything, not even the small things that were of no use to you but that would have given me pleasure. And so instead of burning all the evidence I had found, I thought I would leave you a gift instead.

That day you came to see me, I looked into your eyes and saw my Oliver's and my own eyes in your face. I knew who you were. But in your eyes I also saw something else—I saw hate reflected back at me, so intense that it scalded me. You didn't bother to conceal your contempt, and that was your biggest mistake.

So, as my parting gift to you, my grandson, you will be saddled with this title and a name you abhor. You will live with it and be known by it; you will be reminded of me for ever. The name will follow you around like a stench and it will be engraved on your tombstone so that even after your death it will be my legacy that will live on.
Yours, your grandfather,
Leopold, Duke of Winford
December 14th, 1841

Ransom crumpled the note into his fist, as if he could crush it into nothing. He'd wring the old man's neck if he weren't already dead.

If I didn't hate him so much, I'd admire his determination to have the last word.

Sinking back down into his chair, he unclenched his fist and stared at the letter.

There was one upside to inheriting the dukedom.

His head snapped to the right-hand drawer where Persephone's spectacles lay like a precious artefact in a museum.

If he were a duke, Persephone's brother wouldn't object to their marriage. Ransom would no longer be a bastard, but a true peer. There would be no scandal, and her family would not be shamed. She'd even fulfil her mother's dying wish.

Ransom felt the letter in his hand pressing down on his palm as if it weighed a ton. He had once thought that Persephone was the only thing in the world he could not acquire.

Now that was no longer true, but this was the one price he was not willing to pay.

Decision made, he picked up the parcel and hurled it into the fireplace, along with the letter, then plucked the box of matches sitting on top of the mantelpiece. He struck a match and tossed it in, the stick landing right at the edge of the parcel, the fire growing as it ate away at the paper.

'I ached so badly... The need for you burned hotter than fire inside me... Need you still...'

Persephone's confession rang in his head, sparking a flame inside him. Without another thought, he retrieved the parcel from the flames, dropped it on the floor, and stamped on it to extinguish the fire.

Ransom sent a barrage of oaths and curses to Winford—directing it above and below, just to be sure.

* * *

After Ransom's first formal consultation with Robert Davis, the solicitor had warned him that 'the wheels of justice turn slowly,' endeavouring to temper his expectations of the time it would take to conclude the investigation into Ransom's legitimacy. However, it was only a few days after Davis filed the necessary paperwork that the courts approved everything, and since the old duke was already dead, they didn't deem an investigation necessary. He was made Ransom, Duke of Winford, in the blink of an eye.

The ton, however, worked even quicker. The ink had barely dried on the papers filed at the courthouse, but the news of Ransom's legitimacy and new title were printed in the evening editions of the *London Tatler* later that same day.

Ransom rarely left the club, but when he did now, random men would come up to him, introducing themselves and giving him their cards. They were all especially eager to ingratiate themselves to him, even going as far as to imply that they had always known he'd been legitimate.

Since no one knew the precise location of his home, invitations poured in at The Underworld, and callers came at all hours of the day. Ransom had never seen Charon so flummoxed as when he had to tell the pugnacious Dowager Countess of Westix that no, he did not know what Ransom's receiving hours were, and no, she could not come in for a quick call.

'I'm happy to report that everything is settled with regards to your legitimacy and title,' Davis said. He had come this morning to deliver the news himself. 'There is now the matter of your grand—the previous duke's assets, the largest of which is Hollylane Manor and the entailed lands surrounding it.'

'I suppose burning it to the ground and salting the earth isn't an option?'

'You may do with it as you wish,' Davis replied. 'But there is the matter of the household staff and the tenants who rely on the ducal estate.'

Bugger. 'Do I have to make a decision now?'

'Not yet, but I wouldn't put it off for longer than six months.'

'So now I have to learn about crops and household accounting.' Ransom slapped his palms on the arms of his chair. 'Wonderful.'

'Might I suggest you enlist help from someone who knows about running an estate? From what I've heard, your closest neighbour, the Duke of Mabury, is an expert on such matters.'

'I'll keep that in mind,' Ransom said wryly.

'Is there anything else I can help you with, Your Grace?'

Ransom shuddered at the use of the title. 'Nothing I can think of.'

Davis bid his goodbyes and left, just as Clyde was coming in.

'Well now, Yer Grace,' Clyde said in a teasing tone. 'Would Yer Grace like some luncheon? Or perhaps some tea in a dainty cup? You can lift yer finger in the air while you sip it.'

Ransom scowled at Clyde. 'I'd like to show you a finger. Care to guess which one?'

Clyde let out a hoot. 'Some gentleman you are.' He leaned against the doorframe. 'Anyway, yer next appointment's with Gavin in the kitchens. Do you want me to send him up or are you comin' down?'

'Neither.' He rose to his feet. 'Cancel the rest of my meetings for the day. I'm going out. Tell Jones to come see me at home in five minutes and have Morton prepare my carriage.'

It was an impulse decision, but Ransom found he could not wait any longer. He had managed to stay away from Persephone for two torturous weeks, but he found that his patience had dried up. Now that he truly was a duke, he would proceed with the one thing he had wanted to do since the moment he fished those papers out of the fireplace.

He was going to see Persephone and propose.

I don't deserve her.

It didn't matter that he was now a duke. Ransom knew that he was still the same wicked, selfish, and soulless bastard he had been before he'd inherited the title. But every day without her was like being on that runaway wagon the day of the festival, wondering if he would die without ever knowing what her lips tasted like or how she would feel in his arms.

It was her damn fault, demanding that he kiss her as she had. And while he probably couldn't give her the love and tenderness she deserved, he was far too selfish to let anyone else have her. No, Persephone would be his, and much as he had vowed to rise up from poverty and exact revenge on Winford, he would not let anything or anyone stop him from getting what he wanted.

Ransom left his office and took the stairs two at a time until he reached the rooftop. He walked across the gravelled surface, all the way to the gigantic brick structure in the middle—his home.

Only a few people knew about his rooftop house, most of them his trusted employees. Ransom had lived in the building where The Underworld stood for most of his life, and even though he'd amassed a great fortune, he was reluctant to leave. Instead, he'd had this house built

on the rooftop. It wasn't very large, only a single storey
with six rooms, though he'd had it decorated lavishly with
Persian carpets, antiques from France, and the best furniture money could buy. The front door featured a beautiful stained glass window that was spectacular at sunset.

His housekeeper, Mrs Owens, looked surprised at
his arrival in the middle of the day, but welcomed him
warmly. He went straight to his rooms and awaited his
valet's arrival.

'Jones, I'm going out.' Ransom was in a hurry so he
skipped the preambles. 'I need to dress in whatever you
deem is my finest outfit. I trust your judgement.'

'Your Grace.' Jones bowed low. 'It would be my honour to assist you.' Ever since the news of Ransom inheriting the title broke, Jones had been walking around with
an expression on his face that looked like he was, as had
previously Clyde put it, 'creaming his britches.' 'Should
I take out your mahogany silk waistcoat? Or your silver
one? Or—'

'I don't care, Jones, as long as you're quick about it.'

'Of course, Your Grace.'

Jones moved as swiftly as the wind and soon Ransom was making his way out of The Underworld. His
reliable driver, Morton, already had the carriage waiting
outside and soon they were on the way to Mabury Hall,
the Duke's London townhouse. He'd sent one of his investigators to Surrey to keep a close watch on Persephone,
just in case she decided to leave for Scotland early—or
perhaps she'd changed her mind about leaving, in which
case he'd need to know about any potential suitors that
came sniffing about.

Much to his delight, his investigator reported back
that the entire Mabury household had returned to Lon-

don two days ago, including Persephone. It would save him the long coach ride to Surrey.

Ransom shifted in his seat. Now that he was drawing closer to the big moment, a nervous energy swirled in his stomach. Things had not ended well between them. Persephone was likely angry at him still, and why wouldn't she be? She had asked him to stay and he'd left her after using her so ill.

But Persephone was an intelligent and practical person. He would speak to her and make her see reason; he would make her understand that at that time, marriage between them hadn't been a possibility. But now that he was a duke, they could conduct a proper, scandal-free courtship.

The carriage slowed to a stop, and his footman, Orson, opened the door. As he stepped out, he instructed, 'I don't know how long I'll be, so tell Morton to wait.'

Ransom took a deep, cleansing breath as he alighted in front of the Georgian-style home in the fashionable district of Mayfair. He climbed the steps up to the front door and knocked.

A distinguished-looking butler answered the door. 'How may I help you, my lord?'

'I'm here to see Lady Persephone MacGregor.'

'My apologies, my lord. Lady Persephone is not accepting calls at the moment.'

Ransom clenched his teeth.

Calm yourself, this is merely a delay.

'During which hours is she accepting calls?'

'I'm afraid she is not accepting calls for the duration of her stay, my lord. Good day.'

Ransom braced his hand on the door, preventing the butler from shutting it in his face. 'What do you mean she's not receiving anyone?'

The butler's expression was impenetrable. 'Lady Persephone is not taking calls or seeing visitors while she is in London. Now please let go of the door, my lord.'

'It's Your Grace,' he corrected. 'I am the Duke of Winford. Is Mabury around? I want to speak with him.'

The butler let out a sigh. 'One moment, Your Grace.'

Ransom didn't release the door, but he remained outside, despite the temptation to sneak in and find Persephone. Why wasn't she receiving guests? Was she ill? Hurt?

Moments later, the butler came back. However, he did not bring the Duke with him, but someone else entirely.

'You have some gall coming here,' Kate, Duchess of Mabury, hissed at him. 'After what you did.'

'Good morning, Your Grace.' Ransom was not at all surprised that Persephone had told the Duchess what had transpired between them.

'Leave,' she spat. 'And never come back. She doesn't want to see you.'

'Well, that's unfortunate.' He stretched himself up to full height. 'Because I'm going to speak with her, one way or another.'

The Duchess didn't seem the least bit intimidated. 'Haven't you hurt her enough?'

'That's why I'm here. I want to explain everything and make her see reason.'

'See reason? That's all?'

'No, we have other things to discuss as well. Private matters,' he said firmly. 'Now, where is your husband? Perhaps he will be more level-headed.'

'Get out,' the Duchess bellowed. 'And don't darken my doorway ever again.'

'Your Grace, perhaps you aren't aware, but I now outrank you.' Saying the words aloud left the most unpleasant aftertaste in his mouth, but he wasn't going to let this tiny woman get between himself and Persephone.

'Yes, Your Grace.' Her tone was that of contempt, not deference. 'I'm fully aware of the changes in your circumstances, as is Persephone. However, that means nothing to her. She still doesn't want to see you.'

'Only because she hasn't spoken to me. I want to see her now. I promise not to upset her.'

'Oh? Not like you did at the festival?'

'I told you, the circumstances were different then.' He huffed out a breath. 'And now I require a private word with her.'

'You selfish ox. Listen to yourself.' The Duchess put her hands on her hips. 'You've had the coronet less than a fortnight and you're acting like an entitled peer already. Everything is "I want" and "I require." What about Persephone and her needs? Have you even thought to apologise to her?'

'I—' His mouth clamped shut. 'All right, I will apologise to her as well.'

'I'll extend your apologies, but you won't see her again. Not if she doesn't want you to. Now please—' She wrenched the door from his grasp. 'Leave.'

Ransom considered his options—or rather, his lack of them. He took a step back. 'Good day, Your Grace.'

The door slammed in his face.

Dejected, he returned to his carriage, tossing his hat onto the floor before plopping down on the seat. He had imagined that Persephone would be angry at him, but not so much that she would never want to see him again. If he could only speak with her, he was confident that he could convince her to marry him. No, not just marry him, but also forgive him.

But how was he to speak with her when she refused to see him?

Ransom now had money, as well as power and influence. All the peers of the realm would gladly open their doors to him. Yet he could not bypass one tiny woman who was worse than a three-headed guard dog.

There had to be a way in…a way to get past the gatekeepers and see Persephone.

Ransom was used to shady dealings and walking the line between what was legal and what was not. However, short of breaking into Mabury Hall and kidnapping her, he didn't know what to do.

'Uhm, pardon me, Your Grace?' It was Orson, rapping at the door. 'Mr Morton would like to know where you'd like to go next?'

'I don't know. Anywhere. Tell him to just drive.'

'Yes, Your Grace.'

Ransom sank back into the plush velvet sofa as the carriage began to move. They drove for about half an hour before he thought to look outside to check where they were.

Morton must have been driving around in circles because he saw they were still in Mayfair, but now inside Hyde Park. Fashionable ladies carrying parasols and gentlemen in shiny boots promenaded about, laughing and chatting without a care in the world. One man stopped in the middle of his stroll to tip his hat at a group of young, fresh-faced women, who all burst into a fit of giggles.

'Stop!' Ransom rapped on the roof. The carriage halted, and he lurched forward, grabbing the handle by the door just in time before he spilled over to the other seat.

'Your Grace!' Orson exclaimed as Ransom leapt out of the carriage.

'Stay here,' he ordered. 'I have to do something.'

Ransom stalked in the direction of the crowded footpath, his jaw set, a plan brewing in his mind.

This was the last thing in the world he wanted to do, and *he* was the last person he would ask for assistance in this matter. But what choice did he have? This was his new goal. Persephone would be his wife, and he would stop at nothing to have her for his own. He would do anything to have five minutes alone with Persephone, even make a deal with the devil himself.

Chapter Twelve

'Is he gone?' Persephone asked in a small voice.

'Yes.'

She let out a breath. Pressed up against the wall, her heart had been hammering so loudly the entire time that Ransom and Kate were speaking that she had nearly been deafened.

Kate pulled Persephone into a hug. 'I'm so sorry, Persephone, for what you had to endure at the hands of that beast.'

She gave Kate a grateful squeeze before stepping out of her embrace. 'It's all right. I told you, I'm fine.'

'No, you're not. Poor thing.' Kate *tsked*. 'I can't believe… What he did to you was unforgivable.'

Persephone hadn't given Kate all the details, but certainly enough to give her an idea of what had transpired between her and Ransom, as well as his connection with the Duke of Winford. Kate had been enraged on her behalf, of course, but Persephone made her promise not to tell anyone, especially not Mabury, as she didn't want any more trouble. She was certain that right after the wagon race, Ransom was going to propose, or at the very least confess his strong feelings for her. But then Winford had come along...

After learning about Ransom's parentage, she understood, of course, what his being a bastard meant for them if Winford admitted to being his grandfather. But they could have talked it out, found a way to solve the problem together. He had never met Cam and assumed he was just some snooty earl. She knew in her heart that Cam would have given them his blessing if she could have convinced him she would be with no other man.

But Ransom had lacked faith in her, in them. And he'd left her standing there in that barn, even while she begged for him to stay.

She wanted him, yes. She still did, perhaps, but she was not going to let him stamp on her confidence and pride. She knew she was worth more than that.

'Would it help if you went back to Surrey? Perhaps the distance will do you some good,' Kate suggested.

'No, I don't want to go back there.' Being at Highfield Park would only remind her of Ransom. Seeing all the places they had been together every day and remembering what they had shared had left her so downhearted that when Kate told her she was going back to London for a fortnight, Persephone had begged to come along.

But perhaps she should have stayed in Surrey, because as soon as they'd arrived in London, they'd heard the news about Ransom and his legitimacy. It was the talk of the town. The owner of London's most notorious gaming hell had been a long-lost duke all this time. It was better than fiction and the ton ate it up.

'You want to see him, don't you?' Kate ventured.

Persephone bit her lip. Despite everything that had happened, she'd been tempted to peek out the door just

for a glimpse of him. 'I can't help it. Kate, do you think…
I mean, should I hear him out?'

'That's up to you, Persephone,' Kate said. 'But only
if you're ready. Do you love him?'

Love? 'I don't know.' She was infatuated with him for
sure. 'How can I tell?'

'Only you can answer that.' The Duchess put an arm
around her shoulders. 'Now come. Let's have some luncheon and after that, we can go to visit the factory. Would
you like to see the plans for the engine I'm building? I
think we'll be ready to build a prototype next week.'

'That sounds wonderful.'

For the next two days, Persephone did as much as she
could to distract herself from thinking of Ransom: going
to the factory with Kate in the morning, shopping and
going out to tea. Today, however, the Duchess was expecting a visitor so they had to remain at Mabury Hall.
To pass the time, she sought out the comforting silence
of the library, and curled up in one of the comfortable
chairs with a novel she had chosen from the Duke's ex-
tensive selection of books.

'Persephone? Are you in here?'

'Kate?' Her head bobbed up from the book as she
heard the Duchess's call. 'Yes, I'm here.'

'There you are.' Kate breezed over and perched her
hip on the arm of the chair, her grin wide. 'I have something that might cheer you up.'

'Is it time for our tea with Dowager Viscountess Pearce?
If so, I'm sorry to inform you, your definition of "cheering up" is much different to mine.'

'No, no.' Kate shook her head. 'But thank you for the
reminder, the Viscountess is arriving anytime now.' Kate
had told her this morning about their visitor, an old friend
of Sebastian's grandmother, the Dowager Viscountess of

Pearce. She had apparently written to Kate and invited herself to tea.

'Anyway,' Kate said, pulling Persephone to her feet. 'Come with me.'

Kate was practically vibrating with excitement as she dragged Persephone out of the library. When they reached the foyer, Persephone realised why. The Duke was there, but he was not alone.

'Cam? Maddie?'

Her brother and his wife stood by the door, grinning ear to ear. 'Hello, Seph.'

The sight of her brother's warm smile, the sound of his deep familiar burr brought tears to her eyes. 'Cam!' She launched herself at him, wrapping her arms around his waist. 'Oh, Cam.'

'I'm glad to see you too, lassie,' he whispered, rubbing his hand down her back.

Cam's strong embrace soothed her, the tension and sadness seeping out of her body. 'I'm so glad you're here.'

When he let go, she turned to her sister-in-law. 'Maddie!' She was engulfed in another comforting, tight hug.

'Persephone, it's been too long.'

'Aye.' She sniffed, rubbing the tears from her cheeks.

'Don't cry, it's all right.'

'I'm just so happy to see you both.' She rubbed away the tears under her spectacles. 'But what are you doing here? We didn't expect you for at least another month.'

Kate embraced her friend. 'Yes, Maddie, you should have sent word—' A knock at the door interrupted her. 'Oh, dear.' She turned to Eames, who had been standing in the sidelines. 'That must be the Dowager Viscountess Pearce. Please do let her in.'

'Viscountess Pearce?' Mabury frowned. 'That old bat is still alive?'

'Sebastian!' Kate slapped him playfully on the arm. 'What a horrible thing to say.'

'It's just been a long time since I've seen her,' he explained. 'She's half deaf and mostly blind.'

'She can't be blind. She wrote me a letter—my lady.' Kate greeted the Viscountess as Eames opened the door. 'How do you do? Welcome to Mabury Hall.'

Persephone watched as an old woman with snowy white hair wrapped up in an enormous shawl toddled inside. But she was not alone. A tall male figure followed behind and the moment she saw his blond hair and handsome face she recognised him, as he'd been a guest at Cam and Maddie's wedding.

'Hello,' the Marquess of Ashbrooke greeted. 'My, you sure have a crowded foyer and—what a surprise. Balfour,' He slapped Cam on the back. He turned to Sebastian. 'And Mabury. Both of you, here in the same place. At the same time.'

'Ash? What are you doing here?' Kate asked.

'I'm here to accompany my wonderful Great-Aunt Agnes to tea. Please do take care with her, she's half deaf and mostly blind.' He placed a hand at her elbow. 'Aunt Agnes,' he said loudly in her ear. 'This is the Duchess of Mabury.'

'What?' the old woman shouted, her face straining. 'What did you say, dear?'

'I said I'd like to wear your bonnet while sailing down the Serpentine.'

'Ah, lovely dear.' She smiled and patted his hand. 'Such a sweet boy.'

'See?' Blue eyes sparkled with mirth.

'It's nice to see you, Ash,' Maddie interjected. 'And how fortuitous. Cam and I just arrived from Scotland.'

'Hmm.' He rubbed at his chin, as if he were thinking deeply. 'Yes, fortuitous indeed.'

'Shall we head to the parlour for tea then?' Kate said.

'About that.' Ash tugged at his collar. 'I'm not really here for tea. Er, this is embarrassing, but I had an ulterior motive.' He walked over to the door, nudging Eames out of the way. 'All right, the plot—er, surprise has been spoilt. Come on in.'

'Who— You!' Kate pointed a finger at the visitor. 'Didn't I tell you to never darken my doorway again?'

Persephone's knees turned to jelly and all the air rushed out of her body as those green and brown eyes pinned her to the spot.

'Hello, Persephone,' Ransom said.

'What's going on now?' Cam asked, lips peeling back. 'Who is this man?'

'Ash,' Mabury stated. 'Of course you're behind this.' He turned to Ransom. 'What did it cost you this time?'

'You don't want to know,' he said wryly. 'Ashbrooke, I thought you were going to sneak me in using this tea party ruse?'

'That was the plan, but how was I supposed to know everyone would be waiting here in the foyer? But you're in luck.' He gestured to Cam. 'Standing before you is my best friend, Cameron MacGregor, Earl of Balfour.'

'I thought Mabury was your best friend,' Ransom pointed out.

'I have two best friends, but I'm looking for a third if you're—'

'Ashbrooke!'

'Yes?'

'Shut up.' Ransom pivoted towards Cam. 'Lord Balfour, a pleasure to make your acquaintance. I am Ransom, Duke of Winford, and I'm here to ask for your sister's hand in marriage.'

Persephone gasped audibly.

Cam stretched up to his full height, which was a good half a foot taller than Ransom's. 'Seph, do you know this man?'

'I…' She tried to speak but nothing would come out of her mouth. She turned to Kate helplessly, but the Duchess could only flash her a tight smile. 'Yes.'

'And do you want to marry him?' Cam asked, his eyes never leaving Ransom's.

'No,' she said. 'I do not.'

'Persephone—' Ransom tried to move towards her but was blocked by Cam. 'Balfour, be reasonable. She's here for the Season, and I'm a peer of the realm. At least consider my offer.'

'Aye, it's true, you're a duke. But it's her choice who she marries.'

'I think it's time we give you privacy,' Mabury said. 'Why don't you continue this in the library?'

'Aye,' Cam growled and wrapped an arm around his wife. 'Come on, Maddie.'

Persephone's feet were like heavy lead weights as she made her way to the library with Ransom, Cam, and Maddie. She could feel Ransom's gaze burning a hole in her back, but she refused to look at him.

Oh, why couldn't he just have stayed away?

Why couldn't you let me be happy, Ransom?

Cam and Maddie were here, which meant that there was a possibility she could leave for Scotland sooner than expected. She'd be home, away from England and everything that reminded her of him.

When they finally reached the library, Cam spoke first. 'If she doesn't want to marry you I'll not force her.'

'Would it help if I told you I have compromised her?' Ransom offered nonchalantly.

Maddie gasped, while Cam's face turned red as a beet, but he didn't move.

'You did not!' Persephone denied. 'Stop lying, nothing happened. Cam, please, I didn't—'

'Of course you didn't,' Maddie assured her. 'We believe you.'

'We've met before.' Ransom pulled something out of his pocket.

The obol.

'Does this look familiar?'

Cam squinted at the card. 'Aye. Where did you get that? I thought I lost— Wait, you're Ransom? Of The Underworld?'

'Yes.'

'But how—' He inhaled a long breath. 'Seph, did you take my card?'

'I didn't… I mean, I saw it on the floor. Murray dropped it.' She chewed at her lip. 'I used it and sneaked into The Underworld.'

'Where she met me,' Ransom finished. 'She spent an entire night at my club. With me. Alone.'

'Nothing happened,' Persephone insisted.

'And nothing happened in the barn during the festival too, am I correct?' Ransom said.

Persephone's cheeks lit up as if someone had set them on fire. 'I—I—'

'I've taken advantage of your sister, Balfour. Perhaps not fully, but there are other ways a man can compromise a woman. Can't you see, I'm only trying to make things right here? And with my title, the match makes perfect sense.'

Cam looked about fit to be tied. 'That doesn't matter,

you stubborn goat. I told you, if she doesn't want to marry you, then she won't.'

'Persephone,' Maddie began in a gentle voice. 'Do you really not want to marry the Duke? Just say the word and we'll send him away.'

Persephone's eyes darted from Ransom to Cam, then back again. Still, she couldn't decide. She remembered the hurt she'd felt that day when he left her standing alone in the barn. What if he hurt her again? She thought she was starting to heal, and here he was, setting back her progress once again.

But her heart…oh, her heart…

'Five minutes,' Ransom pleaded. 'Just give me five minutes to talk to you, Persephone. If you don't want me after that, I promise I'll never bother you again.'

She must have stood there without speaking for the longest time because Maddie gave her hand a squeeze. 'Persephone?'

'Yes. I mean, all right.'

I hope I don't regret this.

'I'll speak with you.'

'Thank you.'

'I'll chaperone,' Maddie offered. 'Cam, you wait outside.'

Her brother gave Persephone's shoulder a squeeze. 'Remember, you don't have to marry him. I'll protect you. We all will.'

'I know. Thank you, Cam.'

Cam glared at Ransom before heading outside.

'I'll be in the far shelves,' Maddie informed them. 'You have five minutes, Your Grace.'

'Thank you, Lady Balfour.' Ransom turned to Persephone. 'I know I've hurt you, so allow me to say I'm sorry.'

'Fine. You're forgiven. Now please leave.'

'Persephone.' He advanced towards her. 'You're angry with me.'

'Of course I am, you daft man.' She raised her hands in frustration. 'I was willing to take a chance. To tell the world they can hang and just be with you. But you didn't believe in me, that I could weather any scandal. You didn't believe in us.'

'That's not—'

'You kissed me. Made me feel things I've never felt before. N-nearly made love to me and then left me there like a…a…' She didn't want to utter the word she truly wanted to use.

'No, don't say that. You're not *that*.' His fingers clenched, like he wanted to touch her. 'I would never think of you as anything less than you are.'

'And what am I?' she shot back. 'Some lady looking for a bit of rough? Isn't that what you called me?'

'No,' he said, his voice gravelly. 'You're the most beautiful and wonderful and brilliant woman I know.'

Persephone staggered back, his words hitting her like a bag of bricks.

'See? That's the problem,' he continued. 'It wasn't just that I didn't want to cause a scandal. No one would have believed I married you because of who you are. They would have all thought the same thing—that I was using you to elevate my status in order to spite Winford.'

'You mean, like you wanted to spite him with the land?'

A muscle in his jaw ticked. 'You know about that?'

'Y-yes.' Kate had told her about the Duke and Ransom's business at Highfield Park after the festival.

'It doesn't matter now anyway. But you're right. I should have had more faith in you. And I promise I will from now on.' He moved closer, leaning down so his mouth was right by her ear. 'I don't blame you if you don't want to marry me. I've told you time and time again, I'm much too wicked and selfish. I can't be redeemed either, as I'm afraid I have no soul.'

Did he truly believe that? Why did he think he was so irredeemable? Did he think himself unworthy?

And why?

'But, because I'm wicked and selfish, I don't want you to go. I want you to be mine, to stay here with me. Don't go back to Scotland. Marry me.'

'Wh-why should I?'

'Because I can give you what you want.'

She scoffed. 'I don't need your money or your title.'

'I know that. You wanted a dalliance, an affair before you settled into life as a spinster. But I know the real reason you asked me for an affair.'

'Y-you do?' Her heart thudded in her chest. She was thrilled—yet scared at the same time.

'Yes. You wanted to know what it was like to be with a man without compromising your freedom, with the limited choices you have. Most women could only choose a life with a husband or as a spinster, and you thought an affair with me was the only way you could experience passion without losing yourself.'

She'd never felt as exposed as she did now, not even when she was nearly naked in front of him. This man knew who she was, even better than she did herself.

'Marry me and you can have both. I'll not interfere with your work. You can build a hundred breweries and distilleries at inns all over England. I'll even help you. But I'll also give you the passion and excitement you crave.' He was so close to her now, she could feel the warmth of his breath. 'Marry me and I promise to give you a lifetime of adventure.'

Persephone had anticipated that he would try to bribe her with jewels, clothes, or other material things, like he always did when he wanted to get his way. But this…this wasn't at all what she expected.

'Please, Persephone. Say yes.'

How could she possibly say no?

And so she did say yes—by turning her head to press her mouth to his.

He groaned her name, and his hands cupped her cheeks. She wrapped her arms around his neck, pulling him closer, wanting more, parting her lips so she could once again taste the mouth she'd been dreaming of.

'Ahem,' came Maddie's delicate cough. 'Is everything settled then?'

Ransom tried to pull away, but Persephone refused to release him, her arms tightening. 'Surely that wasn't five minutes?'

Maddie smiled wryly. 'You have two minutes and thirty-five seconds before I call Cam,' she said, before turning away and marching back towards the shelves.

Persephone waggled her eyebrows at Ransom. 'Now, where were we?'

'Minx,' he teased, before seizing her mouth once again.

'A toast to the happy couple!' Maddie cried as she raised her champagne flute.

'To the happy couple!' Everyone cheered and clinked their glasses together.

'Now,' Kate began after everyone had taken a sip. 'While I'm not one to talk to speedy weddings—' she beamed at her husband '—I think it's important we keep this engagement a secret for at least two weeks. Just to keep tongues from wagging.'

'I think it's far too late for that,' the Duke said. 'Besides, the gossip over Ransom's true parentage is still the talk of all the balls and drawing rooms of London. This engagement is but a drop in the ocean.'

'For him, perhaps,' Ash said. 'Because he's a man. Everyone will be gossiping about Persephone and the newspapers will go wild because it means selling more of their tawdry papers.'

'They wouldn't dare,' Ransom said in a deadly serious tone. 'I won't let them.'

Ashbrooke rubbed his hands together. 'What will you do to them, Ransom? Will you send some of your men to burn down the presses?'

'No, I'll buy them.' He smiled at Persephone. 'And then I'll make sure they never print a single bad word about you.'

'Pfft.' Ashbrooke finished the rest of his champagne. 'I'm afraid I must leave you all. I was hoping for a fist-fight or a duel at dawn, but alas, nothing more exciting than another engagement.' He put an arm around his aunt. 'Come along, Auntie Agnes,' he hollered into her ear and steered her towards the door. 'Let's get you home.'

'What did you say?' the Viscountess shouted back.

'I said we're going to stop at some bawdy houses in St James's.'

'That's lovely, dear. You are such a sweet boy.'

Cam rolled his eyes as Ashbrooke and the Dowager Viscountess left, turned to Ransom. 'He'll still want an invitation to the wedding.'

'And he'll insist on being your best man,' Mabury added.

Ransom's mouth pulled back into a tight line. 'The man does have a point, though. As much I want to marry you right away, I won't have even a hint of scandal touching you.'

A tenderness warmed Persephone's heart. 'Do you think that's possible?'

'We will find a way, I promise. I will do anything.'

'You could wait six months and marry in the winter,' Cam suggested.

'Except that,' Ransom replied quickly.

'A speedy wedding would be ideal for us, Cam.' A smile touched Maddie's lips. 'Then we could leave for Scotland before… Oh, never mind.' Her cheeks turned pink.

'What is it?' Persephone asked. 'Is there anything wrong?'

'No, no.' Maddie shook her head. 'I don't want to overshadow your engagement.'

'No, please go ahead,' Persephone urged.

Cam and Maddie looked at each other before Maddie spoke. 'We decided to come to London early before it became too uncomfortable for me to make the journey.' She pulled back her travelling cloak, which she had been wearing the entire time, to reveal a small but noticeable bump.

Persephone gasped. 'Are you—?'

'Yes,' Maddie burst out. Cam beamed with pride and wrapped an arm around his wife.

'That's wonderful news!' Persephone hugged Maddie.

Everyone came forward to give their congratulations and best wishes except for Kate, who burst into tears.

'Kate?' Maddie rushed to her side. 'Kate, what's the matter?'

'There, there.' Mabury tucked her into his side. 'Kate, darling, it's all right.'

'Is she ill?' Maddie cried. 'Kate, what's wrong? Please tell us.'

'It's all right,' Mabury soothed. 'You can tell them.'

The Duchess took a deep breath, then smiled. 'Sebastian and I are expecting as well.'

'What? Oh—' Maddie embraced her friend. 'How far along are you?'

'Not as far as you,' Kate replied with a hiccup and a laugh. 'Sorry, I just… I can't seem to control my emotions these days.'

'I understand,' Maddie said. 'Oh, how wonderful. Our children will be the same age.'

'More champagne,' Mabury said.

'A speedy wedding it is then,' Cam said begrudgingly. 'We were planning to leave at the end of August, if that suits you.'

'We can wait two months,' Ransom said. 'Can't we?'

Persephone bit her lip. 'I suppose so.'

Ransom grinned and then leaned down to whisper in her ear, 'Don't worry, it will be worth it.'

Persephone shivered with delight, but cleared her throat when Cam sent her a warning look. 'Yes, we can have the wedding in August.'

'That settles it then,' Kate said. 'Ransom, you'll have to make a few public appearances as the new Duke of Winford. We shall attend one of them—a ball of course— and you'll be "introduced" to Balfour, Maddie, and of course, Persephone. You'll dance with her and after that, you'll pay her a few calls, go on a few outings, and then announce your engagement. If anyone asks why the wedding is so soon, Lord Balfour will give the excuse that he'd like to see you settled before he leaves for Scotland with Maddie.'

'My, my, you've certainly become a proper society matron, love,' Mabury teased.

'You know I'm a quick learner.' Kate's blue eyes sparkled. 'Now I think it's time for Ransom to leave, before anyone sees him here and casts a shadow on our plan.'

'As you wish.' Turning to Persephone, Ransom took her hand and kissed it. 'Until I see you again.'

Persephone's mouth went dry at the contact of his lips on her skin. 'Until then.'

'Balfour and I will see you out,' Mabury said.

Once the men left, Kate took Persephone's hands in hers. 'Is this really what you want, Persephone?'

'Yes,' she assured her friend. 'I want Ransom.'

'But do you love him?' Maddie asked.

She blinked. Kate had asked that as well. 'I… Does it matter?'

'Only if you would be happy if he doesn't love you either,' Maddie said. 'It's obvious he's mad for you, and you for him. But I hope you don't confuse infatuation with love.'

Persephone knew, of course, what infatuation was. But how did it differ from love? 'I don't know…all I know is that I can't be without him.'

Maddie put an arm around her. 'I'm sure he loves you. He might not say it, but he'll show it.'

Persephone had never even thought about that, whether Ransom loved her. He wanted her, surely. They wouldn't be engaged otherwise. But love? Did he even have room in his heart for her?

'You'll have enough time to discover the answer yourself,' Kate said. 'And— Oh, I must write to Mama. She'll be so thrilled, and she can help us with our plan.'

'There will be so much to do, I hope you're ready,' Maddie said. 'You'll have to stop disappearing behind topiaries and start dancing.'

Persephone couldn't help but smile. 'I know. And don't worry, I've started learning to dance.'

'Truly? Did the Dowager hire a new dance master?' Maddie asked.

She shook her head. 'No, Ransom taught me.'

'Ransom?' Kate's jaw nearly dropped to the floor. 'He taught you?'

'Yes.' And she couldn't wait to have her very first dance with him.

Chapter Thirteen

'I don't think this is going to work.' Ransom gritted his teeth. 'They'll see through it. Through me.'

His eyes scanned the room, at all of the elegant people gathered in Lord Dalworth's ballroom. They were London's finest, dressed in their best gowns and coattails, their eyes hawk-like as they watched and waited, hoping perhaps for someone to commit a faux pas so they could gossip about it amongst themselves.

Ashbrooke picked up two flutes of champagne from a passing footman and handed one to Ransom. 'Here, this should help.'

Ransom drank it down in one gulp. Sadly, it did not ease his nerves.

Damn these people.

When he was just Ransom, owner of The Underworld, he could feel superior and lord his power over them, watching them from his private gallery above the gaming floor as he laughed at their foolishness while they gambled their fortunes away.

Now he was on the opposite end, receiving judgement instead of passing it. They were the ones watching him now.

Probably waiting for me to make a mistake.

He wouldn't usually give a whit, except this wasn't just about him. He had to do things right, for Persephone.

As the Duchess of Mabury had advised, Ransom went out into society with his new title. The Dowager Duchess and Miss Merton had been most helpful, advising him on how to best handle his debut. He accepted a few invitations to balls and events, sat through more opera and ballet performances than he'd ever seen in his life, and more importantly, acted like the proper duke that he was, mostly by imitating the other lords he'd encountered in his line of work. Stock tips and business deals weren't the only thing he'd learned during his time serving drinks and dealing cards to the gentlemen of the ton.

'Why are you so worked up anyway, Winford?' Ashbrooke asked. Somehow the Marquess had heard of their plan and accepted all the same invitations as Ransom, as well as attending all the same events. He was grateful for the Marquess's presence, though he would only admit that on pain of death.

'Ransom,' he corrected. The very sound of the name *Winford* had never failed to rankle him, but now it was even worse. 'I need another drink.' He craned his neck. 'Where is that blasted footman?'

'Look, Ransom.' Ash gripped his shoulders. 'Everything will be fine. You've done everything the ton expects of you and it's obvious they've welcomed you like a long-lost son instead of a pariah.'

'Do you think so?'

'I've lived my whole life with these people. I know it. The title you carry has more weight than you think and no one cares who has the coronet, only that they get as close to it as possible. Now that your legitimacy has been proved, no one would dare question your right to be here, nor your right to choose your bride.' He glanced around slyly. 'In fact, in case you haven't noticed, the vultures have begun to circle.'

'Vultures? What vultures?'

'For a man as intelligent and observant as you are, I find it quite hilarious you haven't noticed all the mamas of the ton eyeing you like a piece of meat.'

'If they're vultures, then shouldn't I be a carcass?'

'Exactly. Dead meat. They all want you as a son-in-law, and why not? You're the most eligible bachelor here. The most eligible bachelor in all of London.' Ashbrooke *tsked* and shook his head. 'You could probably commit several crimes in the middle of the ballroom and all the mamas would still want you to marry their daughters.'

'Well, I only want to marry one.'

'Monogamy is such a mystery to me,' Ashbrooke sighed. 'Why shackle yourself to one, when there is a myriad of choices all around you? Unless you and Lady Persephone have some sort of understanding?'

'No. Never.'

'Of course not,' Ash said drolly. 'But, really, stop acting like a nervous fool. You need to start getting your head on straight.' He nodded towards the doorway. 'They're here. The butler just announced Mabury and Kate.'

Ransom's heart thudded against his ribcage. He swore to himself that he would not look at Persephone when she arrived, so as not to betray their previous acquaintance. Everything had to be right and proper.

'The Earl and Countess of Balfour! Lady Persephone MacGregor!' the butler announced.

Ransom allowed himself one glance their way. However, it was difficult to tear his eyes away, not when Persephone looked so lovely in her blue satin ball gown, her luxurious red curls piled on top of her head.

'Close your mouth, Ransom,' Ashbrooke said cheekily.

'And you shut yours,' Ransom retorted. 'Come, introduce me to more of these damned lords and ladies.'

'As you wish, Your Grace.'

They had all agreed that the Dalworth Ball would be where Ransom and Persephone would be introduced, though it had to be played out perfectly. Ash and Ransom would not approach Balfour for an introduction until at least an hour after they arrived. That hour seemed to crawl by as the Marquess introduced him to several gentlemen and ladies; Ransom didn't bother to remember their names as he kept his eye on the grandfather clock. It was a minute past the appointed time before Mabury and his group eventually made their way across the room. Ransom had never been more relieved to see Mabury or Balfour.

'Ah, look who it is, one of my best friends, the Duke of Mabury himself, and the lovely Duchess of Mabury,' Ashbrooke announced rather loudly. 'And my other best friend, back from Scotland, Cameron, Earl of Balfour, with his enchanting wife.'

'Good evening, Ash,' Mabury greeted, and the Duchess did the same.

Cam merely nodded, his jaw clenched.

'Ash…' The Countess of Balfour offered her hand, which the Marquess kissed. 'How nice to see you again.'

'My lady, you look beautiful tonight. Have you or Balfour made the acquaintance of my companion? No? Allow me to make the introductions. This is Ransom, Duke of Winford.'

Ransom stepped forward. 'How do you do?'

Everyone except Mabury bowed or curtseyed, then Ashbrooke introduced everyone in order, one by one.

'And finally, this is Balfour's sister, Lady Persephone MacGregor.'

'Your Grace.' Her gaze lowered.

Ransom's very breath stole away at how lovely she was tonight. Her fiery red curls shone under the chandelier, the light shooting gold through the strands of scarlet. Her skin was smooth as silk, bared by the low neckline of her satin gown. And the sound of her voice after two long weeks away from her made him ache with longing.

When the butler announced the waltz as the next dance, he could not stop himself from saying, 'Lady Persephone, will you do me the honour of this next dance?'

The Duchess and Countess looked at each other while Balfour sent him a death glare. He was supposed to write his name on Persephone's card and wait for one of the group dances, like the quadrille or cotillion, and not ask outright.

'Yes, Your Grace.' The excitement in Persephone's voice pleased him very much. 'I would love to.'

He took her offered hand and brought her over to the middle of the floor.

'I—I'm afraid I haven't practised much.' Lifting her head, she added, 'But my dance teacher said anyone can learn to dance.'

The glimmer of humour in her emerald eyes spread warmth in his chest. 'He must be a clever man.' When he placed her hand on his shoulder, he felt her tremble. 'You will be fine,' he said. 'Don't look at anyone, just look at me.' He leaned closer to her ear and whispered. 'And remember what I taught you. We are equals, working towards one goal.'

'Not to look foolish.'

He bit his lip to stop himself from laughing. 'The music's about to start. One, two, three...'

Ransom guided her through the dance, silently communicating to her which way they should turn and move. Persephone performed beautifully—in his eyes, at least. She was responsive and graceful, and this close to her, he wondered if she would be as pliant in the bedroom as she was on the ballroom floor. The thought had him taking a misstep.

'Ransom?'

Thankfully he recovered. 'Loose floorboard,' he said with a cough. 'Sorry. But keep going, you're doing marvellously.'

The waltz eventually drew to a close, but the floor underneath him continued to spin. He was breathless and dizzy, but it wasn't the dance. It was all her.

'You did well,' he whispered to her when it was done.

'Thank you for being my first dance.'

'You're welcome.' Taking her hand gently, he led her back to her companions. 'Thank you for the lovely dance, Lady Persephone.' He turned to the others. 'It was a pleasure to make your acquaintance. If you don't mind, our wonderful hostess has promised me the next dance and I should make my way to her.'

Ransom did not want to dance with Lady Dalworth or any of the matrons and misses at the ball. No, he would dance every dance with Persephone if he could, but the Dowager and Miss Merton advised that they only dance once during their first meeting, and he must also dance with other women of marriageable age. No doubt he'd already set tongues wagging by not waiting to write his name on her card or for a more appropriate first dance than a waltz, but he didn't care. For now, though, he would play his part and do things their way. Once he secured Persephone, they'd be doing their own dancing, behind closed doors.

* * *

The next two weeks passed in a whirlwind for Persephone, with all the various balls and dinners and events she'd attended. When she first arrived in London, every outing seemed like a dreary task, one she loathed. Balls, especially, took up a lot of her energy as she spent most of them hiding from the gentlemen who wanted to dance with her.

However, now she looked forward to every single time she was required to dress up and leave Mabury Hall. Because that meant she would be seeing Ransom. There hadn't been a day in the last two weeks they hadn't seen each other.

The day after their first dance, he had paid her a call. It was all proper, of course. He arrived two minutes before the start of her calling hour, and gave her a gift which she promptly declined. They sat down in the parlour, with Maddie and Kate in the room, talking about the weather. Once his fifteen minutes were over, he left.

The next day, they had attended a dinner party at the home of one of the Marquess of Ashbrooke's mutual friends. They did not converse because she sat far away from Ransom, but they exchanged a few glances. It wasn't until the day after that, when they were both at the Hathaway Ball, that they danced again, but only once, though that allowed him to pay her another call, and he invited her for an open carriage ride in Hyde Park the following day with Miss Merton as their chaperone, though it was not necessary.

After that, Ransom had been invited along to all their social events—more dinners, garden parties, and the opera, where he sat behind her in Mabury's private box. As soon as the lights were turned down, he leaned over to whisper in her ear how lovely she looked. Persephone thought she would expire right there, beside Miss Merton as the overture for Mozart's *The Magic Flute* played.

And now it had been a whole month since she'd accepted his proposal in the library, so if they wanted to be married in four weeks, they had to announce the official engagement soon. For their final appearance out in London society, they'd gone sailing on the Serpentine with Cam and Maddie yesterday, a very public outing that had no doubt shown the ton that Ransom had her family's approval.

Tongues were wagging for sure, but if the Marquess of Ashbrooke was right, it was in a good way. At this point it would be a bigger scandal if they didn't announce an engagement.

'How are you feeling?' Maddie asked. Her sister-in-law was already dressed up, but she stopped by Persephone's room in Mabury Hall to check in on her.

Tonight, Kate and Mabury were hosting a ball at Mabury Hall. It would be the perfect place to announce their engagement and they had it all planned. Despite every lord and lady in England clamouring for an invitation, only the elite would be in attendance. They were the ones whose opinion mattered. Their seal of approval would ensure that the engagement would push through without a whisper of doubt or scandal.

'You look beautiful. Green is your colour,' Maddie continued.

Mrs Ellesmore had outdone herself with her newest creation—a frothy concoction of tulle and silk in various shades of green. It made Persephone feel like a fairy princess.

'So do you, Maddie.' She took one of Maddie's hands in hers and squeezed it. 'Pregnancy suits you.'

'Do you think so?' Colour crept into Maddie's cheeks

and she placed a hand over her visible bump. 'I was worried I look fat in this dress.'

'Nonsense. Cam tells you you're beautiful, does he not?'

'Every chance he gets. He's so happy—and so am I.' She chuckled. 'I'm so glad you cooked up that pretend courting scheme. Otherwise, we wouldn't have fallen in love.'

'And I'm glad for you both.'

'But I came here to talk about you.' Maddie sat her down on the bed. 'This is what you want, isn't it?'

'Of course,' Persephone said with a laugh. 'We've worked so hard to get here.'

'I just want you to be happy. We—Cam and I—both do.' Maddie cleared her throat. 'And I know you were telling the truth that nothing has happened between you and Ransom. But if you have any questions about the, uh, wedding night, you can ask me.'

'Oh, I—' A rap on the door interrupted her. 'Uhm, I suppose that means we should go. The ball's about to begin.'

'Are you ready?' Maddie asked.

'I am,' Persephone replied resolutely.

The two of them made their way downstairs and towards the ballroom. The room was beginning to fill up, as Eames announced name after name of the arriving guests. Anticipation squeezed the very air out of Persephone's lungs as she waited for the one name she wanted to hear.

'Ransom, Duke of Winford!'

She could not take her eyes off him as he entered the ballroom. Despite the frown on his face, he looked so handsome in his dark formal clothes. A few people approached him, greeting him and trying to draw him into conversation, but he quickly brushed them away. As he drew near, their eyes met. His frown instantly dissipated, and he moved towards her with purposeful strides.

'My lady, you're looking lovely,' he greeted as he took her offered hand and kissed it. 'Would you care for a dance?'

'I would love to.'

Persephone let him sweep her onto the dance floor. By this time, they had danced so many times that her body was in tune with his hands, fluent in that silent communication that passed between leader and follower.

'God, I can't wait for this night to be over,' he confessed.

'Me too. Courting is exhausting.'

'Exhausting?' He smirked at her. 'Once we are married, you will know the true meaning of exhaustion.'

She inhaled a sharp breath, feeling the heat creep up her neck and to…other places. Lower places. He had never spoken so intimately in the last month; in fact, he was the perfect gentleman. His words were shocking. And thrilling.

The dance was over much too soon. Before she knew it, he was bringing her back to Maddie and Cam's side. He didn't leave, however, and stayed to chat with Cam. Despite the friction between them during their initial meeting, both men seemed to have put the past behind them and now had a cordial relationship. Persephone flashed Cam a grateful smile as she caught his eye while he and Ransom talked about Glenbaire's current grain harvest.

She danced with Ransom once more—a reel this time, much to her disappointment. However, her second dance with him brought her so much closer to the third and final dance they would have for the evening. It would be her last as an unmarried debutante, as on the stroke of midnight, Cam would announce their betrothal and they would dance a waltz.

Persephone's stomach churned. The moment she'd been waiting for would soon be here. 'Air,' she gasped. 'I need air.'

'Seph?' Cam looked at her with concern. 'Are you all right? Do you want me to get you some water?'

She waved him away. 'I'm...fine. I just need some air.'

Quickly, she ran towards the balcony doors. She heaved in a big breath the moment she was outside. Her corset suddenly felt like it was being laced tighter, and she braced herself against the balustrade as she took in heaps of air.

What was going on? This was what she wanted, wasn't it? What she and Ransom had worked so hard for? Why was she suddenly wracked with nerves, now that they were so close to being officially engaged?

'Oh, Lord.' She took another deep breath. Ransom was going to be her husband. But did she even really know him? They would be bound together for the rest of their lives. Yet doubt crept through her mind, nestling, burrowing in there so deeply, she feared she would never be rid of it.

'Persephone?'

She whirled around. 'Ransom?'

He stepped out onto the balcony and closed the door behind him. 'I saw you run out. What's the matter?'

'Nothing.' She shooed him away. 'You shouldn't be here. The guests might see—'

'Hang the guests. They all know what's coming anyway.' Crossing the distance between them in giant strides, he was beside her in an instant. 'What's wrong?'

'N-nothing,' she said, half laughing. 'I'm just...after all this time... I'm just nervous.'

The corner of his mouth turned up. 'I'm not. This is

what I've been waiting for. What I've wanted for so long. But if it makes you feel any better, I was a wreck that first night we danced.'

'You were?'

'Yes. Ask Ash,' he said with a smirk. 'But we're nearly there. You can do this. Just like you learned how to dance.'

'You taught me how to dance,' she reminded him. 'I'm just… All those people…looking at us…'

'Don't think about them.' Taking her gloved hand in his, he pressed her palm to his cheek and kissed it. 'I'm glad we have this time alone.'

'You are?'

He nodded. 'I just realised I haven't done a proper proposal.'

'Yes, you have. In the library. I mean, that was a real proposal, wasn't it?'

'I mean, a proper one. I proposed for real that time, but I didn't do it properly.'

She pursed her lips. 'What was your plan that time anyway?'

'Ash was supposed to distract everyone while I sneaked in. I just wanted five minutes alone with you, to convince you to marry me.'

'And if I said no?'

A devilish smiled touched his full mouth. 'I would have carried you away to The Underworld.'

She gasped. 'You would not!'

'I suppose we'll never find out.' Still grinning, he reached into his pocket. 'Lady Persephone,' he began, then got down on one knee. 'Will you marry me?'

'Ransom…' In between his thumb and forefinger was the largest diamond she had ever seen. It was five carats at least, surrounded by smaller emeralds. 'It's beautiful.'

'Well?'

'Well, what? Oh!' She nodded. 'Yes, of course. Yes, I will marry you.'

He slipped the ring onto her finger. 'Thank you.' As he stood up, he ran his hand up her wrist, elbow, all the way up to her shoulder. 'I wish I could kiss you.'

'Then do it,' she found herself saying.

His eyes darkened with passion as he slipped an arm around her waist. Slowly, he lowered his head. He was so close now she could feel the warmth from his body as he—

The sound of the balcony door opening had them pulling apart.

'Persephone? Your Grace?' Maddie asked as she stood in the doorway. 'Uhm…it's almost midnight.'

Ransom blew out a breath. 'You should go. I'll follow right behind.'

Without another word, Persephone hurried towards Maddie, who was smirking. 'Come along,' she said. 'Looks like I found you at the right moment. We don't even have to fix your hair this time.'

Her blush deepened. 'I'm just glad you were the one who found us and not Cam.'

The two of them made for the middle of the ballroom dance floor, which was now empty of people, except for Cam. Once they joined him, he turned to the guests. 'Good evening, everyone, thank you for coming. First, I'd like to thank my good friend the Duke of Mabury for hosting this ball in honour of our return.' Everyone applauded. 'England is very important to me, as this was my dear mother's homeland and where I met Maddie, which is why we plan to come here as often as we can manage. But, as some of you may have guessed, my lovely countess and I must return to Scotland by the end of August.' He briefly glanced down at Maddie's obvious bump, and her hand immediately rested on top of her belly. 'Which is why I wanted to make this announcement sooner rather than later.'

A hush fell over the room as he gestured for Persephone to come forward. Scanning the room, she found Ransom just at the edge of the ballroom. They locked eyes, not caring that everyone was staring at them.

'My dear sister, Persephone, has accepted the proposal of His Grace, the Duke of Winford.'

Cam had barely finished when the guests' cheers rang in the air. However, Persephone did not miss the way Ransom flinched when Cam called his name. He also remained rooted to the spot, until Ashbrooke poked him in the ribs and urged him to come forward. He blinked, then nodded and strode towards the dance floor.

'My lady.' He took her hand and kissed it after she curtseyed. As the orchestra began to warm up for the waltz, he guided her to the middle of the dance floor.

She bit her lip. 'Ransom, is everything… I mean, are you all right?'

'Me? I'm fine.' He pulled her close—much closer than he'd ever done before in public, their bodies nearly touching. 'It's over. This part anyway. We are now officially engaged.'

Her worries melted away as he smiled down at her. 'Indeed we are.'

'And now we just have to wait for our wedding.' He leaned down closer to her ear. 'And our wedding night.' He whirled her around and at the same time brushed his lips against her neck. It was over quickly, but it had made her head spin.

'Afterwards, where would you like to go on a honeymoon?'

'Oh.' Persephone paused. 'I hadn't thought about it. Must we decide now?'

'No, we don't have to decide now.'

'But won't we have to make arrangements soon? If we are to leave in a month?'

'We don't have to leave right away. This is our honeymoon and our marriage. We can leave for our honeymoon anytime. In fact, we can have several honeymoons, if you want.'

'Truly?'

'Whatever you want. Anything and everything you want, you shall have.'

Persephone had no doubt he could provide her with what she wanted. And while the nerves surrounding the engagement had ebbed away now that it was over, there was still some doubt left in her.

She shook her head inwardly. No, the time for doubts was long past. She had accepted his proposal, and his offer of an adventure. And now she had to stand by her decision.

Chapter Fourteen

Eight weeks.

Eight torturous weeks.

Ransom didn't think he would survive their long, drawn-out courtship and engagement. By society's standards, of course, it was scandalously short. But to Ransom every single day Persephone was not his was like a lifetime.

Yet he did not dare stray away from what was proper, not a single inch. There were a few whispers here and there, but they were able to quash any rumour the moment it reared its ugly head. And of course, the ton being as predictable as they were, everyone wanted to be at the wedding. The women had been especially insistent—Lady this, Countess that, and the Honourable whatshername, all of them pressing for an invite. Ransom had never seen such fierce competition, and he'd spent most of his life watching degenerates gambling away their fortunes at *vingt-un*.

There were more events after the engagement of course, but Ransom didn't remember any of them. All he could remember was Persephone, there by his side each time, smiling at him.

Ransom counted every day, every hour, every second until the day of his wedding to Persephone, and it had been perfect. The ceremony at St George's was followed by the wedding breakfast at Mabury Hall. There had been scrumptious food, cheers and jeers—mostly from Ashbrooke, who did not have to beg for an invite or worm his way into becoming his best man because that, unfortunately, was the second favour he had asked for in exchange for that tea party ruse that hadn't quite worked out.

But once the festivities were over and they said their goodbyes to their guests, Ransom tucked Persephone away in his coach and they drove away from Mayfair.

And now it was finally his wedding night.

'Where are we going?' Persephone asked as she looked out the window of his carriage. She looked absolutely ravishing in her white gown and veil, like a cake, in the sense that he wanted to eat her up.

'To my home, of course.'

'I know that,' she said with a laugh. 'I mean, where is it?'

He frowned. 'I never told you?'

She shook her head. 'Never. We were too busy and you never hosted any event at your home.' Even their engagement ball had been held at Ashbrooke's home.

'I suppose not. We're heading to The Underworld.'

'Your club?'

'Yes.'

'That's where you live?'

'Of course.'

Her face faltered. 'Oh.'

A feeling of dread wrapped itself around his chest like a fist. In that moment, he felt like he was once again Ransom, bastard son of a marquess, staring up at the moon where Persephone lived, unreachable. 'I hadn't thought…

It's inappropriate, of course. We could go to a hotel, if you like. Something glamorous. Or back to Mabury Hall. Maybe I could find a terrace for the evening?' He knew of at least two men in his membership file he could press to give up their luxurious homes for a few days.

'I beg your pardon?'

'Tomorrow we'll start looking for a house. In Mayfair, Upper Brook Street. Or I'll build one for you, something glamorous and fit for a duchess. One bigger than—'

'Oh, no, no.' She gripped his hands in hers. 'You don't have to.'

'But I must,' he insisted, that fist around his chest squeezing tighter. 'You deserve more than living in a sordid gaming hell.'

'What—? Oh, Ransom, it's not that. I love The Underworld. It's so mysterious and exciting…but, I was wondering, if you ever had a real home?'

He rubbed his jaw with his thumb. 'As far as I can remember, I've always had four walls and a roof over me. After I left that filthy room in the rookery, the cook at the club let me sleep on the kitchen floor. Then when I became a runner, Old Man Hale gave me an old broom cupboard to use as a room. Would you like to know the rest?'

'I've upset you,' she said, her voice shaky. 'I just meant… I'm sorry, please forgive me for bringing that up.'

Her remorse, in turn, upset him too. 'Come here,' he urged, opening his arms to her. She sidled closer to him and he placed an arm around her. 'There is no need to apologise. Please, do not distress yourself over my past. That's dead and gone and we never have to speak of it.' He pressed his lips to her temple, breathing in her familiar floral scent with a tinge of citrus and spice. 'I've missed this.'

She turned her head up to his, her eyes inviting. Had

he forgotten she was his wife now? That they could do whatever they wanted?

And so he kissed her, capturing that sweet mouth of hers. It had been too long for both of them, as they never dared anything more than a few stolen kisses during their engagement. She responded right away, opening up to him, her tongue tangling with his.

The carriage stopped abruptly. 'We're here, Your Grace,' Orson called with a sharp rap on the door.

Ransom released Persephone reluctantly. 'Come, my bride.'

He helped her down from the carriage, and up the black marble steps of The Underworld. The door opened and Charon and Clyde waited for them on the other side.

'Yer Grace,' Clyde said. This time his tone was completely respectful. 'Welcome.' Charon said nothing but only bowed low.

'It's so quiet,' Persephone remarked.

'We've shut down for the evening,' Ransom informed her.

'You have?'

'I didn't want to be disturbed.' Placing a hand on her back, Ransom led her through the secret passage and up the winding stairs and hallways until they reached the rooftop.

'Where are we—Ransom!' Persephone covered her mouth with her hand. 'Is that—'

'My house.' He swept his hand towards his brick structure in the middle of the rooftop. 'Would you like to go inside?'

'Yes, please.'

He guided her across the gravelled path, all the way to the front door where Mrs Owens was already waiting for them.

Persephone gasped as they entered. As the sun was sinking behind them, the light hit the stained glass on the front door, painting the room in a rainbow of colours. 'This is beautiful… Ransom, I'm sorry to have implied that your house wasn't—'

'Shh, I told you, we'll have none of that talk.' He kissed her when she tried to speak again. 'Come, let's go on a little tour.' He had waited eight weeks to have her; he supposed that he could wait a little longer.

Ransom showed her around himself, starting with the parlour, dining room, his private study, and a large terrace that had a magnificent view of London. He took great pride in showing her all the expensive antiques he had acquired, the lavish furnishings and carpets, and the extravagant décor all over the house.

'This is extraordinary, Ransom,' she said. 'And you had this built to your specifications?'

'Yes,' he replied. 'It's not as big as Mabury Hall and definitely nowhere near your Kinlaly Castle.'

'But it's still so grand. Is there more?'

'Just one more room.' Holding her by the elbow, he guided her down the hallway to the last room at the end. 'My bedroom.' Her obvious shiver made his anticipation rise. 'Do you mind that we have to share one room?' He had honestly thought he would never take a wife, so he didn't have an adjoining bedroom built.

'Share? Why—? Oh.'

Once again disappointment marred her face, and he felt as if he'd been doused by a bucket of cold water. 'It's just for the night,' he muttered. 'I'll find us a house in Mayfair tomorrow. Even if I have to throw out whoever's living there. We—'

'Ransom.' Her grip on his wrist was gentle, but firm. 'I don't care about having my own bedroom. What I am concerned about is that…' Her teeth bit into her lower lip. 'You've probably had a lot of women before me, I assume.'

The question set him off balance. 'I don't want to lie to you, Persephone. Yes, I've had lovers before you.'

'And they were experienced?'

'Yes.' She flinched. 'What is this about, Persephone?'

'They've all shared your bed, all these beautiful, experienced women.' Her voice shook. 'How could I possibly compare?'

'Wait…you're upset about other women I've bedded?' He cupped her cheek, tilting her face up and staring deep into her emerald eyes. 'Persephone, first of all, I've never brought a woman up here.'

'Never?'

'Never.' He kissed the tip of her nose. 'And second, you cannot compare to any of those women.'

Her expression fell. 'Oh— *Mmph!*'

He pressed his lips to hers firmly, kissing her thoroughly until she was clawing at him. 'I misspoke. What I meant was they cannot compare to *you*. Your beauty, your mind, and your sweet, responsive body. May I show you?'

She nodded.

He took her hand and slid it down to the front of his trousers where he was already half hard. 'See what you've done to me? Just by kissing me?'

She gasped when he pressed her palm to his erection.

'You know what to do,' he whispered. 'Go on.'

His hand never left hers, but he let her take the lead. She rubbed gingerly at first, as if she were handling some delicate porcelain figurine. He moaned aloud, thrusting into her hand. Though she let out a shocked sound, her fingers gripped the stiffening erection tighter.

'That's it,' he encouraged. 'Hold it, feel it. That's all

you, Persephone. You make me ache. This need for you…
if there's anything hotter than fire, then that's how I feel.
How much I need you.'

Her eyes grew wide as his cock continued to strain
against her hand. She stroked him through his clothes, in-
creasing the pressure. The sensations were driving Ransom wild, and soon he was grunting like a savage beast,
rubbing against her hand. He held on as long as he could,
still enjoying the way she pushed him to the limit, but
then he had no choice but to take a step back.

'Ransom?'

He let out a guttural moan, then inhaled. 'Bloody hell,
Persephone… I…'

'Was it…good?'

She looked at him so sweetly and hopefully that he almost laughed. 'It was good. More than that. But I fear if
we had continued, this night may have been over before
it's begun.' And he planned for this evening to go on a
very long time. 'You drive me mad with desire. Never
doubt that.' He kissed her again, roughly until she was
gasping for air. 'Now, wife, would you like to come into
our bedroom?'

She reached for the doorknob. 'Yes, husband, I would.'

He allowed her to enter first, to explore the room with
her eyes. He wasn't lying—she was the only woman to
have ever entered this room.

When he had an architect draw up the plans for his
rooftop home, the only thing he'd asked was that the bed-
chamber be the largest room in the house and for there
to be windows that would let in plenty of morning sun.
And so one entire wall was made of glass doors, which
opened up onto a small balcony. Every morning, he would
stand out there, basking in the cleansing light. Tonight,
though, he'd had the curtains drawn for privacy.

Persephone stopped in the middle of the room, just beside his enormous four-poster bed. He'd had the finest mattress maker in London custom make it to his exact specifications, with extra cushioning so it would feel soft as a cloud. And while most households used lower-quality linens for normal use and higher ones for guests, he had instructed Mrs Owens to use only the best linens for his bed, which were changed at least every other day.

She turned her head towards him and smiled shyly. 'Will you help me, please?'

So polite and proper, his wife. He remembered the night she had sneaked into his office and given him that outrageous proposition.

'I would like to have an affair with you, please.'

'Of course.' Brushing her veil aside, he reached for the tiny pearl buttons on the back of her dress, unbuttoning them one by one. There was a time when he'd have ripped them off—which surprisingly most women enjoyed—but tonight, he relished the moment. She was like a present, one that he'd been waiting for eagerly, and he didn't want to rush.

With the buttons undone, he let the dress fall to the ground, then undid her corset and tossed it aside. He expected one last layer—a cotton chemise—but was pleasantly surprised by the silk-and-lace concoction underneath that clung to her curves.

His eyes traced the silk fabric skimming down her back, clinging to her small waist and flaring out at her hips, his cock throbbing at the sight of the outline of her buttocks.

'Do you want to see the front?'

Bloody hell, if he was nearly spent at the sight of the back, the front would surely kill him. 'Yes,' he said roughly. He would not die in vain, anyway.

She turned to face him, her arms covering her breasts at first, but then she lowered them. He muttered an oath, but couldn't tear his gaze from her. The silk chemise was held together tightly in front by small ribbons, which pushed her breasts high.

She really did look like a present.

'D-do you like it?' she asked. 'Mrs Ellesmore said it's all the rage in Paris.'

Thank the good Lord for the French.

'It's beautiful.' He planted a kiss on her mouth. 'You're beautiful.' With that, he untied the ribbons one by one, letting the garment fall away and exposing her breasts. They were quite generously sized and firm, but their crowning glory were the nipples—large areolas with puffy pink tips. They were begging to be put in his mouth, and so he did.

She let out a squeal when he captured the left nipple with his lips. Her drew it deep into his mouth, bringing her to just the edge of pain. She let out a disappointed mewl when he slowed down and released the bud, but he quickly put the other one in his mouth and gave it the same treatment.

He could feast on her nipples the whole night, but there would be time enough for that. So, he pulled away and removed the rest of her clothing until she was standing there naked, except for the sheer veil on her head. He took that off too, then released her coppery curls from their prison by pulling out the pins and throwing them aside, allowing her hair to tumble in soft waves down her shoulders.

Stepping back, he looked at her. She was magnificent, her creamy skin glowing in the light, her breasts high, nipples puckered, belly flat, leading down to a nest of fiery curls covering her sex.

'Persephone...' He cupped her chin, and kissed her deeply, their tongues clashing. She had obviously never kissed before, but she was a quick learner and so eager to please.

'Wait,' she said, pulling away.

'Yes?'

'This isn't fair.'

'What's not fair?'

The deepest blush he'd ever seen coloured her face. 'I want to see you too. It's your turn to be naked.'

'It's your turn to be naked.'

Saying the words caused perhaps the deepest and most profound mortification Persephone had ever felt, but she could not help it. The desire for him was burning, and she was not afraid of it. Not with Ransom, who made her feel safe.

The corner of his lips turned up into the slightest smile. 'Of course. But you know, it's only fair that you undress me.'

'Me? Undress you?' It was shocking to think about. She wanted to do it.

'Yes.' He unbuttoned his frock coat. 'Go on.'

She took a shaky step towards him, reaching for the lapels of his coat. She pushed it off his shoulders and allowed it to drop onto the carpeted floor. Then she untied his silk ascot, and pulled his suspenders down.

She unbuttoned his shirt, letting it part, revealing a thick mat of black hair on his chest, which she tentatively touched. She'd never seen a naked chest before, so she was surprised by its springiness and the flat nipples hiding underneath.

'They're sensitive too, just like yours.' He had obviously noticed her observing his nipples. 'Would you like to touch them?'

She nodded wordlessly and pressed a forefinger to one. 'Interesting.'

'Can we continue?' he asked, amused.

'Yes, of course.' She finished unbuttoning his shirt and pulled it out from his waistband. He shrugged it off.

Next, the trousers.

There were buttons on the sides, so she assumed that's how they were fastened. Her heart raced at the sight of the large bulge under the fabric, so instead she focused on undoing the buttons until the panel fell forward. She tugged at the trousers so they joined the rest of his clothing on the floor, leaving on his cotton drawers. Her eyes grew wide as the bulge seemed even larger now, the outline thick and ample.

'Wait,' he said in a low tone. 'I can't… If you touch me, I might not be able to hold on.' With a sharp inhale he stepped back and out of his trousers. 'Get on the bed.'

She shivered at the order, and did as she was told, scrambling up naked to the top of his mattress. Her hands caressed the fine linens, perhaps the smoothest she'd ever felt in her life. It was rather vulgar to think about her naked skin against them, but she found she liked it.

'Persephone.'

Slowly, she turned to him, stifling the gasp threatening to escape from her mouth at the sight of him fully naked—the long, sinewy muscles of his arms and legs, the broad shoulders, his furred chest, leading down his hips and—

Mother of mercy.

His erection jutted out from the springy curls between his legs, long and thick, bobbing up and down as he walked towards her. 'You know what's going to happen, don't you?'

She licked her lips. 'Aye.' She was innocent, but she'd spent a lifetime around men, many of whom didn't realise she'd been listening to what they said when they thought they were alone.

'I must make you ready first,' he said.

'Ready? How?'

'You must be slick so I fit inside you.'

'A-and how will I become...slick?'

'There are many ways.' He climbed up on the bed, slowly advancing towards her. 'Do you recall, after we kissed, if you ever felt dampness between your legs?'

'Aye.'

'And when I put my fingers between your legs and made you climax that day in the barn?'

She swallowed, remembering. 'A-aye.'

'I will make you climax again,' he said. 'Perhaps you'll climax more than once, at least until I'm satisfied you are sufficiently wet. But not solely with my fingers.'

'How?'

He didn't answer, but tilted his head.

Oh.

'I know you are a bold little thing, Persephone. And you follow your instincts and desires so well, but I want to prepare you so you are not shocked, which is why I'm telling you all this.' He crawled towards her, over her. 'So, will you let me make you ready for me?'

'Aye.' *A hundred times aye.*

He smiled before planting a soft kiss on her lips, trailing them down her neck, pausing so he could suck on her collarbone. Then, he kissed each nipple, and proceeded lower.

Persephone closed her eyes tight. She couldn't breathe,

anticipation keeping the air inside her from escaping. When she felt the first touch of his lips on her sex, she exhaled. It was just like a kiss, but still...the sensation of his mouth there was a shock to her senses, so new and strange. Slowly, he kissed her there, mouth moving, tongue lapping at her. The entire time, she'd had her eyes closed, but the sounds of him made her curious, so she opened them a crack and peeked down.

Oh, Lord.

His head was there, bobbing up and down as he continued to pleasure her. The very tips of her ears burned as she watched him, but she couldn't turn away. A hand grabbed her thigh and pushed it up, and his tongue licked at the edges of her entrance. She moaned aloud when it probed at her, teasing her. Then, a finger replaced it, slipping inside her, and his mouth moved higher, right to the bud above her sex.

She dug her fingers into the soft mattress. His finger thrust in and out of her, while his mouth teased, lapped, and sucked at her. She cried out his name, but he didn't stop as he pushed her further and further. Her hips lifted off the mattress as an explosion sent her body shaking wildly.

When the last vestiges of the pleasure ebbed away, she expected him to stop. But no, she had barely recovered when he started his efforts once again.

After the second time he had her twisting in pleasure, she pushed him away. 'Please... I cannot... I must breathe.' Her body was weak, her muscles sore.

'You were magnificent.' He kissed all the way up her belly, her breasts, before kissing her open mouth. 'Before we continue, it might be best if we take these off?' He gestured to her spectacles.

'Why?'

'The next part will be…vigorous. I don't want to damage them and hurt you.'

'I suppose so.'

She let him remove them and place them on the night-stand.

'Can you see me?'

'Mostly,' she said. 'When you're over me like that, you're mostly a blur. I cannot see your features.' Or his beautiful eyes.

He moved closer, between her legs, and then covered her body with his. 'And like this?' His face was now right in front of her.

'Now I can.'

He nipped at her lips. 'You are slick and ready, Persephone. Your body is ready. Will you let me make love to you?'

'I can't wait any longer, Ransom. Please.'

'You know it may hurt?'

She nodded, then pulled his head down for a kiss. 'I trust you.'

His eyes burned with a different kind of fire, one that sent sizzling heat down to her core. She couldn't look away—she focused on them as she felt something blunt at her entrance. A gasp tore from her mouth as she felt the invasion, the pushing. When she flinched, he stopped.

'I'm sorry, Persephone.'

'It's all right.' She continued to look at him, every-thing else outside his handsome face blurred. 'Please.'

He continued to move in, the burning pain building. 'Just— Oh!' He pushed all the way inside, the agony un-bearable, but surprisingly brief. They lay there together, unmoving, for what felt like the longest time.

'I think…the pain has lessened.'

'I'm sorry, I had to do it.'

'I know.' She kissed the side of his face. 'Please.' She wiggled her hips, a shock of pleasure making her shiver. Repeating the motion, she found the next one even more intense than the last. 'So…good.'

'Is it? What if I do this?' He lifted his hips away from her, then pushed back in again.

Her eyes nearly rolled to the back of her head. 'Aye…' When he rolled his hips forward, she let out a soft squeal. 'Oh, Ransom…more, please.'

He gave her a tight smile. 'So polite, my Persephone.' He adjusted his position, looming over her as he planted his hands on either side of her head. His face was a blur, but she did not tear her gaze away.

His hips moved, slow and deep first, angling upwards. Nudging, seeking. Persephone found herself pushing up to meet him, as if her hips had a mind of their own, wanting so badly to be close to him.

'You're beautiful…so beautiful…'

And when he said it as his body worshipped hers, she believed it to be true.

The speed of his hips increased, once again that pressure built up inside of her. The pain was long forgotten—only ecstasy and Ransom were on her mind. He shifted positions again, pressing down to her torso, forcing her hips upwards so she had no choice but pull her knees up. When he withdrew and thrust into her, it hit a different part of her, and she let out a gasp as a jolt of pleasure tore at her. Hands slipped under her, cupping her buttocks, and he rode her harder, faster, bringing her to new heights with each stroke as she reached her climax.

She hadn't even reached the ground yet when he changed position once more, this time moving his head lower so once again he could devour her mouth. His tongue matched the rhythm of his hips, pushing deeper, further.

'One more, Persephone,' he coaxed. 'For me. Don't fight it. Let go.'

She cried out against his mouth as he wrung another climax from her. A hand thrust into her hair, twisting the locks and giving them a sharp pull, which to her surprise doubled her pleasure. His movement turned erratic, his body jerking forward as he let out a series of grunts and pumped furiously, grinding into her until he let out one final growl before slumping on top of her, his mouth breathing heavily against her neck.

Her body relaxed, her fingers unclenching from where they had dug into his back—when had she even done that?

'Persephone,' he murmured against her neck. 'Are you all right?'

'Wonderful.' She kissed his temple. 'I— Ah!' The burning pain returned as he withdrew from her, now that her mind was no longer preoccupied with pleasure.

He tensed. 'I need to make this—' He pulled all the way out.

She flinched at the motion, but the pain quickly subsided. There was, however, a soreness that remained.

'Stay here.'

The bed shifted as he left, and without her spectacles all she could see was a big blur moving to the other side of the room. He returned quickly. 'Here, open your legs.'

She did, and felt a warm, wet cloth pressing between her thighs. 'Oh…that's good.' When she sighed with relief, he let out a breath.

'I was a brute, forgive me,' he said. 'I shouldn't have been so rough.'

'No, no…' She placed her hands over his, where he held the cloth against her. 'It was wonderful. The pain couldn't be helped.' A few days before her wedding, Maddie had sat her down, just to ensure she knew what to expect on her wedding night. They'd spoken honestly and openly about it, including the pain. Maddie had promised her that after the first time, the pain would go away.

He kept the cloth there for a few more minutes, until the warmth was gone. 'Thank you,' she said with a great big yawn.

'You should get some rest. We both should.' He put the cloth on the nightstand next to her, then climbed into bed. Drawing away the covers, he helped her slip under them, then joined her. Strong arms slipped around her, pulling her closer, so her head lay on his shoulder.

A few minutes passed, and even though she was tired, sleep escaped her.

'Ransom?' she whispered.

He didn't answer, but continued to slumber. Reaching up, she brushed a lock of mahogany hair off his forehead. He looked so peaceful like this, his face relaxed. Earlier in the evening, when they were in the carriage and she asked if he had a home, his expression had turned sombre and humourless. She had felt awful, upsetting him like that, and so she had quickly changed the subject.

She hadn't meant to insult him. No, she wanted to know if he had ever had a home—not just four walls and a roof—but a place where he felt safe.

'Home is where you're loved and you feel secure,' Da always said. *'You could live in a hovel or a palace, but if that's the one place you want to be at the end of the day, then that's your home.'*

Did he feel that way about his home in the rookery? Or here in The Underworld?

Ransom frowned in his sleep, a small line appearing between his eyebrows. Wiggling from his arms, she moved up to kiss it.

Perhaps, one day, she could be that for him. A home. The one place he would always be safe.

Chapter Fifteen

No one could call Persephone's childhood conventional, at least not after her mother died. She'd been raised by four older brothers in a whisky distillery after all, and it was a miracle she hadn't grown up feral. But she never imagined that she'd be living atop a gaming hall in London married to the lord of The Underworld—Mama was probably laughing up in heaven right now.

But she rather liked her new home, liked its cosiness and that she didn't wear out her slippers walking from room to room. The interiors were comfortable and certainly the furnishings and décor luxurious, but her favourite place was the terrace, where she sat every morning, sipping her hot chocolate and nibbling on her toast, marvelling at the rooftops. From here, she could practically see the entirety of London.

If she did have a complaint about the house, it was its proximity to her husband's place of work. Ransom didn't keep regular hours as The Underworld operated from late afternoon 'til dawn, so several times now he'd had to go downstairs in the middle of the night to personally deal with a few issues. And during the day he had to attend to other business, like his investments, a variety of business interests, and other paperwork that pertained to the club itself, such as membership requests and supplier contracts. Persephone did not enjoy having to share her new husband with the club.

Of course, there was one advantage to living so close to his office, and which she was enjoying right this moment, splayed on top of Ransom's desk, her skirts around her waist, and her husband making furious, urgent love to her in the middle of the day.

'Persephone,' he groaned as his body shuddered in pleasure.

She dug her fingers into his hair and raked her nails across his scalp, a gesture which she'd discovered drove him wild. He bucked into her a few more times, then his entire body relaxed. She found his weight pleasurable, especially after they'd made love. How she enjoyed the feel of his naked skin against hers, the smell of his aftershave mixed with sweat, and the warmth of his body. She lay under him, basking in the moment as the pleasure eddied away from her like waves created from throwing a rock in a pond.

'The tea's gone cold,' he murmured.

'Hmm?'

Ransom lifted his head. 'The tea.' He nodded at the tea tray she'd brought in, balanced on his chair. She had initially brought him the tea tray for, well, tea. However, he'd had other plans for her that had nothing to do with the fine brew or the cakes and sandwiches that Mrs Owens had prepared.

'And whose fault is that?' she asked with a lift of her eyebrow.

He laughed, then reached up to right her spectacles. 'Mine. Totally mine. I confess, constable. Lock me up.'

'Should I take you off in cuffs?'

'I'm afraid the ones I had made for us haven't arrived—
Oy!' he protested when she gave him a playful slap on
the shoulder.

'Beast,' she said. 'Are you certain no one will come
in and discover us?' She'd been reluctant to accept his
advances in his office, for fear that Clyde or one of the
other employees might come in at any moment.

'They know to knock, and if anyone even got within
five feet of the office door, they'd surely know we were
busy from your screams of pleasure.'

'I do not scream,' she protested, feeling her entire face
turn hot, all the way to the tips of her ears. 'You are in-
corrigible, husband.'

His eyes lit up whenever she said that word. 'You
enjoy it, wife.'

She flashed him a coy smile. 'I do…but you really should
let me up before my leg cramps up and I fall down again.'

'All right.' He gave her one last kiss and slid off the
table, pulling her along. 'But now that we are married, I
plan to be around to catch you when you fall.'

Her heart thumped madly. 'I shall hold you to that.'

Ransom assisted her in redressing, and she was thankful that he didn't bother with her chemise and stays because although he was proficient in removing said items
of clothing, he was helpless at putting them back on. The
other day, he'd come up to the house for luncheon and
she'd ended up in a similar situation as today's teatime,
except on the dining room table. Unfortunately, she was
running off to go shopping with Maddie right after, and
when he attempted to help her dress, he ended up with
her stays knotted and her chemise bunched up around
her hips. Red-faced, she'd had no choice but to ask her
maid to help her dress again.

'Now, where are my stockings?' She glanced around.

'I thought you— Oh, how did that get there?' She spied the tube of silk on one of the shelves behind Ransom's desk, hanging from an enormous gold mask. 'That must be very old.' The mask was that of a man's face, wearing some type of striped headdress with a cobra in the middle. 'And… Egyptian? I think I've read about this in a book.'

'Hmm?' Ransom was fixing his waistcoat in front of the mirror by his desk.

'The mask. A funeral mask, if I remember correctly. A king, perhaps?' She plucked her stocking from it and offered a silent apology to His Majesty. 'Well? Who is it?'

'I don't know,' he said nonchalantly.

'You don't?' She whirled around to face him.

'Should I?'

As she put her stocking back on, Persephone examined the other items on the shelf. When she first came here, she'd been curious about the objects, and now she finally had the chance to ask him about them. 'How about that one?' She pointed to the long, curved object displayed on a wooden stand. 'The carvings remind me of the writings from the Far East.'

'It's a sword.'

'Oh!' She clapped her hands together. 'Tell me more. It is from Japan? Or China? Was it owned by a famous warrior?'

'I suppose so. It's a sword.' Ransom shrugged his coat back on. 'Ah!' He picked up something from the floor, then strode over to her. 'Your other stocking, *madame*.'

'Thank you. And the sword?'

'What about the sword?'

'What else do you know about it? Did the auction house not give you any pamphlets regarding its origin or maker?'

'They must have, I probably stuck them somewhere here. Or I likely tossed them in the rubbish when I was clearing away a few things.'

'Is there anything you can tell me about these objects?' There had to be a dozen other things on the shelves—a fancy lace fan, a wooden clock, a porcelain plate. 'Ransom, all of this must have cost a lot of money.'

'It did. A great deal of money, in fact.'

'Do you know anything about any of them?'

His expression turned grim. 'I do. The only thing important about them. That Winford wanted them, and therefore I had to have them.'

The frosty Ransom she'd seen that day at the festival had returned. A chill went through her. 'So this is a shelf of spite.'

'You could call it that.' He gestured to the paintings on the wall. 'And these are spite paintings, all of them depicting property I bought from right under his nose.' He looked especially proud when he told her that.

Persephone felt the warmth drain from her body. Where was her tender, caring husband? While she had initially been fascinated by the objects, she now could not stand the sight of them. 'Put them away,' she said, rubbing at her arms to ward off the chill.

'I beg your pardon? Put them away? Why would I do that?'

'Why in the world would you keep them up, Ransom?' She balled her hands into fists. 'Why do you want to be reminded of that horrible man?'

'I'm already reminded of him, every day.' The cold was gone, but instead, a fire raged in his eyes. 'I will be reminded of him when people bow and call me by that despicable man's title. A title, if you recall, I took to—' He snapped his mouth shut.

'You took to what?'

'Nothing.'

'You took so you could marry me,' she finished, her voice cracking. 'Ransom, please. Take these down. Take them all down. He's gone, you've won. You're here.'

I'm here, she wanted to say.

'They're my things now. Why should I take them down?'

A knot of fear tightened in her belly. 'Because I fear for your soul and what could happen to it if you stay mired in the past.'

His nostrils flared and his shoulders stiffened, but he said nothing. They stared at each other, neither one speaking.

A knock on the door broke the tension stretching between them.

'Come in,' Ransom called.

''Scuse me, Yer Graces,' Clyde said. 'Sorry to interrupt. We have a situation in the sporting club.'

'I was just on my way out.' Brushing past Clyde, she left the office and went back upstairs, her heart heavy. Not even the sight of the beautiful stained glass window could bring her cheer.

'Beggin' your pardon, Your Grace,' her maid Clara said as she approached Persephone. 'But did you decide on the green or the gold dress for tonight?'

She slapped a palm on her forehead. 'That's right. The dinner party.' Kate and Mabury were hosting a farewell dinner party at Mabury Hall for Maddie and Cam, and she and Ransom were supposed to go.

Would she and Ransom still attend, now that they were in the middle of a row?

I can't not go.

She would not see Cam for at least another year, as

they would not be able to travel once Maddie had the baby. But to show up alone would be humiliating, not to mention they would all ask questions, and Persephone could not even think of making up some excuse to cover up for the fact that her husband was a stubborn goat.

'The green,' she said to Clara, her mind made up. She could not miss out on seeing her brother and sister-in-law before they left. Perhaps Ransom would come up soon, and they would make up before the party.

It was early yet, and there was still time for Ransom to come to his senses.

When Ransom didn't show up at home by the time she was dressed, Persephone's heart sank.

'Maybe His Grace is attending to some business,' Mrs Owens said as they stood in the foyer. The sun was nearly gone from the sky and the dazzling hues from the stained glass were fading fast.

'Did he or Clyde send word if he's indisposed?'

'I'm afraid not, Your Grace.'

She glanced up at the window, watching as the final shafts of light disappeared, changing it back into ordinary coloured glass. 'I should leave or else I will be late.'

'Your carriage is waiting, Your Grace.'

Persephone made her way down to the ground floor, but before she could head towards the secret passageway, a familiar face greeted her at the bottom of the stairs.

'Your Grace,' the boy greeted. 'Good evening.'

'Hello—Thomas, right?'

'Yes, Your Grace. Come with me, please.'

'I'm sorry, Thomas, I cannot. I must leave as I'm already running late.'

'That's why you need to come with me. Master Ransom—er…His Grace, said you'll not be using the front entrance.'

'What?' Persephone fumed. 'So, I'm to sneak off where no one will see me, like some...some—'

'Please, Your Grace, just come or His Grace will be cross at me.'

'Oh, all right.' Not that she had much choice, unless she wanted to walk or hire a hackney cab.

She followed Thomas in the opposite direction, then through another secret hallway.

How many nooks and crannies did this place have?

Thankfully, they didn't have to walk too far, and at the end of the hall, they arrived at a foyer where a footman she did not recognise held the door open.

'There, Your Grace.' Thomas pointed to the coach waiting outside.

'What is that?'

'Your coach, Your Grace,' Thomas offered.

She shook her head. 'No, Ransom's coach is dark brown.' This one was all white, not to mention extremely extravagant, with gold leaf flourishes, mother of pearl inlay, and even a team of sleek white horses.

'The Duke took his coach when he left this afternoon,' Thomas explained.

'And where did he go?'

'I don't know, Your Grace. But he said to tell you that you were to take this one tonight.'

Persephone pursed her lips. Ransom was not only abandoning her during their first event as a married couple, but he was going off somewhere without her? If it weren't for Cam and Maddie, she would have turned around and gone back upstairs.

'Your Grace?' Thomas asked.

'Er...yes. I mean, all right, I should go. Thank you, Thomas.'

'You're welcome, Your Grace.' He bowed.

The footman helped her up into the coach, and soon, she arrived at Mabury Hall.

'*Crivvens*, I'm so terribly late.' She rushed up to the front door and nodded her thanks to Eames, who directed her to the parlour. 'Good evening, everyone, I'm so sorry for being— *Oh!*' In her haste, she tripped on the carpet on the way inside. She braced herself for the fall, but a pair of arms caught her just in time.

'Now, aren't you glad I'm here to catch you all the time?'

The voice made her pause. 'Ransom? What are you doing here?'

He set her down on her feet. 'What am I doing here? I was invited. We both were.'

'I know that, but how—'

'Thank goodness you're here, Persephone,' the Dowager greeted. 'We were about to sit down to dinner without you.'

'Apologies for being late,' she said.

'It's all right, dear.' The Dowager nodded to Eames to indicate they could start. 'I'm just glad you made it. Ransom was worried you were caught up with something at home.'

Ransom had been worried *she'd* be late?

He was the one who left me alone.

However, she didn't have the chance to protest as Eames announced that dinner was about to be served and everyone moved to the dining room.

It was a pleasant dinner for the most part, and Persephone enjoyed spending time with her family and friends. Ransom too acted as though he were having a good time, and was the perfect, charming, and attentive husband, as if they had not just had the most terrible fight less than five hours ago. Throughout the entire dinner, she observed him, tried to pick apart every word he said, interpret every gesture he made, but he was acting in a completely ordinary way. Try as she might, she could not figure out what was going on with him.

When they finished the meal, Mabury announced that the men would have cigars and port in his study while the ladies had sherry and tea in the library, though they would all meet up in the parlour once again for some wine later. As everyone rose to leave, Persephone waited for Ransom to say something—anything—about what happened in the afternoon or where he'd been, but he merely nodded at her as he left with the men. Flummoxed, she followed the ladies.

'Your Grace?'

She halted in her steps and turned around. 'Yes?'

The man who had spoken bowed deeply and handed her a slip of paper. As she stared at it, the most curious feeling came over her, as if this had happened before. She squinted at the footman—he was the same one from Highfield Park, the one who handed her the note from Ransom asking her to meet him in the library for their dance lesson.

Taking it, she read the message in the same handwriting.

Meet me in the garden pavilion.

'Who is this fr—? Oh, never mind.' Of course she knew who it was from. 'Which way?'

The footman pointed at a set of double doors to her right.

'Thank you.'

Pushing the doors open, she stepped outside. The scent of primrose was heavy in the air as she made her way down the path to the pavilion in the middle. Sure enough, waiting by the steps was Ransom. Under the blazing lights surrounding them, he looked especially dangerous—and wildly attractive. Persephone cursed her knees for weakening at the sight of him.

'Hello, Persephone.'

'Hello, Ransom,' she greeted back, because she didn't know what else to say. 'What is this about? Are you here to explain yourself?'

'What am I to explain?' He looked thoroughly confused.

'About wherever you took your coach this afternoon.' Her stomach clenched as a maddening thought entered her head—had he gone to see someone else? Another woman? A woman who didn't vex him and act like a shrew over a pile of priceless objects?

'Persephone, what are you talking about? And why do you care about my coach? Aren't you happy with yours? If you don't like it, I can buy you a new one.'

'B-buy me a new one?' Now it was her turn to be confused.

'Yes.' He clucked his tongue. 'I should have consulted you and let you choose your own colours and horses, but the carriage maker said white was all the rage these days for women. He promised me it would be fit for a duchess.'

'You bought that carriage? For me?'

'Of course,' he said matter-of-factly.

'Today?'

'No, I had it ordered weeks ago. It was to be a wedding gift, but there was a delay in production. Fortunately it arrived today, so you had your own ride here when I had to run off to buy something else.' He retrieved a large package that was sitting on the steps of the pavilion. 'For you.'

She stared at the wrapped parcel. 'What is it?'

He grinned. 'Open it.'

She tore the paper away, revealing a black velvet box. Prying the lid open, she gasped when she saw what was inside—a diamond tiara with a large emerald in the centre. 'It's beautiful. Is it for me?'

'No, I bought it for Charon.'

She laughed out loud. 'It will look stunning on him, though it might make your members less intimidated. But Ransom, it must have cost a fortune. This is too much.'

He brushed her protests away with a wave of hand. 'No such thing when it comes to you. Would you like to know more about it?'

She couldn't help but smile. 'There's a story behind it?'

'Yes. It belonged to a baroness who was said to have been one of the most beautiful women of her time. In fact, her beauty was so renowned that men came from far and wide wanting to be her lover, offering her gifts. Apparently, this was one such gift, from the King of Prussia himself. He begged her to be his queen.'

'Did she go with him?'

'Sadly, she did not. She loved her long-dead husband too much and she vowed never to take another lover or husband after him.'

'That's sad,' she said.

'Because she didn't become a queen?'

'No, silly.' She nudged his side with her shoulder playfully. 'Because she loved him so much that she spent the rest of her life waiting to be reunited with him.'

'She probably spent it receiving gifts like this,' he said. 'Anyway, would you like to try it on?'

'Don't you think it's too much for a dinner party?'

'Nothing is too much for you.' He took the tiara and placed it on her head. 'There. You really are my queen.'

'Queen Persephone of The Underworld,' she said, smiling wryly.

'The name fits you like this crown does.' He lay a hand on her cheek. 'May I kiss you?'

The way he sounded so hesitant made her heart melt. 'I'm your wife, of course you can kiss me. In fact—' She took his hands and planted them around her waist. 'I'd be disappointed if you didn't.'

Ransom's mouth was on hers, devouring her, drinking her in as if he were dying of thirst. As his tongue tangled with hers, a hand moved up to the low neckline of her dress, delving inside to pull out one breast.

'Ransom,' she cried. 'We can't. Not here. The other guests—'

'Won't suspect a thing.' He lowered his head and sucked at her nipple.

'Oh, that feels heavenly—what do you mean they won't suspect a thing?'

He released the bud with an audible pop. 'I told Mabury and the Duchess that I needed to speak to you alone, that we had quarrelled and I was going to go down on my knees to beg for your forgiveness. Mabury said he'd take care of everything and the Duchess would make up an excuse to bring you upstairs for half an hour. Why do you think the torches out here are lit?'

'You planned this? And the Duke knows and—'

'No more talking.' His expression turned dark, his eyes reflecting the torchlight, making them look as if they were aflame. 'I'm about to go down on my knees.'

Mother of mercy.

As he promised—or more like threatened, from the tone of his voice—Ransom sank down in front of her, lifting her skirts up to her waist. She held them in place as he parted her thighs and the slit of her drawers, his fingers teasing her until she moaned his name over and over. Then, his mouth replaced his fingers, and Persephone held on to his shoulders, clutching at them as he tortured her with his talented tongue. By now he knew all the right places to touch her, where to swirl his tongue, and which crevices drove her wild. Her body quaked with pleasure, her legs barely able to keep her standing.

'Now, my queen.' He took her hand, as he sat on the steps and she stood above him. 'Do with me as you please.'

The most delicious thrill seized her. They had made love so many times in the last week that she'd lost count, but never like this. 'H-how—'

'You know how,' he encouraged. 'Like you knew the first night.' He unbuttoned his trousers and slipped his hand underneath the fabric, stroking himself.

Just as she had done on their wedding night, she let her feelings and desire guide her. She moved forward until she stood over him, then sank down. She reached under her, searching for his hand as it moved rhythmically over his shaft, covering it with her own fingers. Together, they guided him into her.

She descended onto him, letting him fill her up. 'Oh…' It felt good, as it always did, but different. She moved her hips, first side to side, then forward and backwards. It was when she leaned over him, however, that felt the best as the friction of his hips against her sex sent little shocks of pleasure up and down her body.

'My queen,' he groaned. 'What do you want? I am yours to command.'

'Hold me. Grab me.' Hands cupped her breasts, his thumb teasing one exposed nipple to hardness. 'Oh, yes.' She leaned forward, pressing down even harder. 'I… Oh…oh…take it in your mouth.'

'As you wish, my queen.' He drew the nipple in deeply, the pain and pleasure melding together.

She planted her hands on his chest and continued to ride him, his hips thrusting up to meet hers. The pressure building inside her was immense as she raced to the peak, biting her lip to keep from screaming. Looking down, she saw that he too, was struggling to remain quiet. As his face twisted in silent ecstasy, she could help but feel a sense of power. She was doing this to him, giving him mindless pleasure. It was an intoxicating sensation.

Just as she was reaching her climax, she felt him begin to pulse. She rode harder, knees squeezing his hips as her body was wracked with shivers. He bit the back of his hand, his hips bucking wildly, then after one last thrust, she felt him flood her. Her body spent, she collapsed on top of him and remained there until she felt his nudge.

'We should go,' he whispered in her ear. 'Mabury said he'd do what he could, but eventually, we'll be missed. And your brother and the Countess are leaving early tomorrow.'

She sighed against his chest. 'All right.'

They scrambled to put themselves to rights, and Ransom put the tiara back in the box, then winked at her. 'We can use that again later, my queen. Maybe with those cuffs.'

She smirked at him. 'Come, let's go back inside.'

They followed the path back into the house, hand in hand. She leaned her head against his arm, taking in the scent of primrose as she declared that all was right in the world again. She looked up at her husband, her warm, gentle, and sensuous husband, all traces of the cold, hard king of The Underworld gone.

For now, a small voice inside her said. *You know things aren't settled.*

No, everything is fine, she argued.

Really? Did he even apologise? Promise to remove all the objects from his shelf of spite and take down the artwork?

She quickly quashed that voice. Yet, if she were truly honest, a tiny seed of doubt had planted itself in her heart.

Chapter Sixteen

'Oh, bother.'

Persephone shook the pen in her hand, willing the ink to flow out. It was just after luncheon and she was writing letters to her family, as well as responding to all the invitations that had arrived since the wedding. That was nearly three weeks ago now, so the pile was considerable. When she had finally finished, she opened up her notebook to sketch out a few ideas.

She'd been inspired when she visited Kate's locomotive factory, the ideas coming to her easily as she toured the facility. There were some new methods and materials that she might be able to use and modify to improve production at the distillery. However, she hadn't had time to sketch and write them down because she'd been too busy with the wedding and married life.

And now that I finally have the time, my pen runs out.

She tutted to herself, then went in search of Mrs Owens for some ink.

'Apologies, Your Grace,' the housekeeper said. 'I just ran out myself. Why don't I send for some from downstairs?'

'All right, thank you, Mrs Owens, I'll be in the parlour.'

Persephone sat at her desk, sealing her letters, when the knock came. 'Come in, Mrs Owens.'

It wasn't Mrs Owens, however, but rather Thomas. 'I have your ink, Your Grace.'

'Wonderful, bring it over here, please.'

As Thomas walked inside, his eyes grew wide at his surroundings. 'If you don't mind me saying, Your Grace, your house is beautiful.' He attempted to touch the porcelain knobs on her desk drawers, but quickly drew his hand away.

'Thank you,' she said when he placed the bottle of ink on her desk.

'Is that real gold?' He pointed to the elaborate clock on the mantel.

'Perhaps, I shall have to ask Ransom.' Knowing him, though, it probably was.

'We all knew that His Grace lives on the roof, but I ain't never imagined it'd be a grand house like this.'

'Have you never been here?'

'No, Your Grace, I ain't never been up here.' Thomas swallowed a gulp and peered at her notebook.

Sensing his interest, she picked it up. 'Would you like to see it?'

'N-n-no, Your Grace.' He shook his head vigorously.

'It's all right, it's just my notebook.' She spread the pages towards him. 'See? I'm making sketches about this new idea I had for a brew kettle.'

Leaning forward, he squinted. 'That's what them scribbles are?'

'Yes.' She flipped the page. 'And I write down my notes here.'

'Oh.' He frowned. 'What do you do with all these then, Your Grace?'

'Eventually, I shall build it. Or my brothers will,' she laughed. 'I'm not very good with a hammer and saw, I'm afraid.'

'But you think of it, then you build it?' Thomas's eyes nearly popped out of his head.

'Yes.'

'But you're—'

'A woman?' she supplied when he clamped his mouth shut. 'It's all right, I'm not cross with you for saying that. I grew up with only brothers, you see, and they took me to work with them in our family's distillery. I started to learn how to make whisky at a young age. Eventually, I became really good at it and I helped my brothers make a few modifications to increase our production.'

'It's grand that you can think of things and build 'em. I wish I could do that too.'

'Really?' She leaned forward. 'You can learn it too, if you want.'

His expression turned stricken. 'I… I couldn't, Y-Your Grace.'

'Of course you could,' she assured him. 'I did and I was only, oh, about a year or two older than you when I began.'

'N-no, Your Grace, it's not that.' He glanced at her notes once more. 'I really can't. I ain't never going to learn nothin'. Not if I need to make scribbles.'

'What—? Oh.' Realisation dawned on her. 'You've never learned to write? Or read?'

His face turned red as a beet. 'N-no, Your Grace.'

'Why not?'

'I was too busy workin'.'

'Working? How long have you been working here?'

'Six years, Your Grace.'

'Six?' she exclaimed. 'And how old are you now?'

'Turning thirteen, Your Grace.'

'You've been working here since you were seven years old?' Persephone could not believe it, but Thomas nodded. 'What about your parents? Did they not send you to a parish or ragged school?' She'd heard about these free schools for the disadvantaged children and orphans around London while attending a charity event with Cam and Maddie a few weeks ago. According to the organisers, the schools were started by one man, Thomas Cranfield, who established nearly two dozen schools before his death.

'No, Your Grace,' Thomas said in a soft tone. 'No time for school, not when Da expects me to bring home me earnings.'

'And what about your mother?'

'Gone.'

'I'm sorry. My mother's gone too. She was sick and Da followed right after. What did yours die of?'

Thomas's face turned pale, and his lower lip began to tremble. 'Beggin' your pardon, Your Grace, but I needs to go back to the kitchen.' He turned and quickly scampered off.

Persephone fought the urge to run after him. She wanted to pull him into a hug and tell him everything was going to be all right.

That poor boy...

While she knew of the plight of poor children in London, it had never truly been as real to her as it was now. Tears sprung to her eyes. She had thought perhaps that at his age, Thomas was an apprentice of some sort and had just started at The Underworld the first night she saw him here, not that he'd been working here half his life.

'Persephone, are you in here?'

Ransom's voice startled her and she sat up straight and wiped the tears from her eyes. 'Yes, I'm here.'

Her husband walked in, his expression lightening as he saw her. 'There you are. I was coming home for—' He paused, watching her. 'You're upset.'

She pursed her lips, not knowing what to say.

He marched to her side. 'Tell me.'

'It's silly.'

'No, it's not.' He knelt down. 'What has upset you?'

'Thomas.'

'Thomas? The errand boy?' He shot up to his feet. 'What did he do? Did he say something bad to you?'

'No!' she cried, grabbing his arm. 'He didn't upset me.' Taking a deep breath, she told him what she had learned about the boy's circumstances, but to her surprise, he didn't seem at all perturbed.

'And so?'

She cocked her head to the side. 'What do you mean "and so"?'

'The lad makes a good living, certainly more than boys his age who are just starting their trade. And he's treated well here. Clyde and Cook watch over him and make sure the other employees don't bother him.'

'That's all you have to say? Ransom, I told you the boy cannot even read.' The look on Thomas's face when he had said there was no way he could learn to build things had just about broken her heart. 'The only thing he's known is this gambling hall.'

'So have I,' he replied in a curt tone.

'That's different and you know it. How could you employ him at seven years old? That's not right.'

'I didn't employ him, Old Man Hale did. His mother was a cleaner here and brought him with her while she worked during the day, so she wouldn't have to come home to him black and blue after his useless father knocked the snot out of him.' Persephone gasped, but he continued. 'Then one day, in a fit of rage, the man stabbed her dead and the boy ran away to the only other place he knew in London. Hale let him stay, gave him a few errands in exchange for some coins. His father was furious but once he saw what the old man was paying the boy, he allowed it. Then I took over five years ago and what was I supposed to do, Persephone? Fire him because "it's not right" to employ someone so young? What do you think his old man would do if Thomas couldn't provide him with gin money?'

She flinched. 'I didn't know. I'm sorry.' She straightened her spine. 'But it's not too late. We can still do something. In fact, we should do something about it.'

'And what's that? Take in every street urchin in London? Thomas is one of many.'

'So were you. Think of all the good we can do in the world for children like Thomas. We can give them a home, where they'll be safe. You were in his position once. You and your sisters. Think of what could have happened if someone had come along and helped you.'

The air in the room went still, and that frosty mask once again slipped over his face. Without a word, he turned on his heel.

'Wait, Ransom,' she pleaded. When he didn't stop but instead kept on walking, a pit began to form in her stomach. 'Don't go, please. I'm sorry to have—'

Slam.

Persephone dropped down to her chair. She had thought that everything was settled between them, after that night at the pavilion. But then she'd once again said something to upset him. This time, though, he didn't even stay to fight with her. Instead, it was like all his emotions evaporated.

She slumped back in her chair, the strength draining out of her. Would she have to live like this for the rest of her life, walking on eggshells around Ransom, afraid to say something that would make him explode, or worse—lock himself away?

Putting those thoughts away, she turned back to her notebook. There was nothing she could do about it now, so she refilled her pen and pressed it against a fresh new page, filling it up with her ideas and sketches.

She wasn't sure how long she'd sat there, but it must have been hours as she had nearly finished half the pages with her sketches. Mrs Owens had left her some tea and scones at some point, and by the time she rose from her chair to stretch her aching back, the sun was nearly sinking in the distance.

'Would you like to dine in your room tonight, Your Grace?' Mrs Owens asked as she entered the parlour.

'Why would I want to dine in my room?'

'Because His Grace said not to expect him for dinner. I could still set up the dining room if you wish.'

Ransom was not coming home.

Since their wedding day, no matter how busy he was with the club or with his other businesses, Ransom never failed to show up for dinner. He even told all his employees to disturb their meal only if something or someone was on fire, but other than that, they were to stay away.

Persephone attempted to hide the disappointment on her face, but from the housekeeper's pitiful expression, she knew she had failed. 'A tray would be fine, but have Clara draw a bath first.'

She soaked in a long, warm bath and later took a few nibbles of the ham and potatoes Mrs Owens had brought, but it all tasted like ash in her mouth. So she crept under the covers and closed her eyes. She drifted off to sleep at some point, but was awakened by the sound of the door creaking.

'Ransom?' She sat up.

'We should get that oiled,' he said sheepishly. 'Did I wake you?'

'It—it's fine. I wasn't sleeping deeply.' Her fingers gripped at the edge of the covers. 'You didn't come home for dinner.'

'I know.' He padded over to her, sat at the edge of the bed, and placed a long velvet box on top. 'Here. This is for you.'

Curious, she took the box and opened it. Inside was a diamond-and-ruby bracelet. 'Ransom—'

'Do you like it?'

'It's beautiful.' She supposed she liked it well enough. 'Thank you.' Reaching for him, she touched his cheek. He turned his head and kissed her palm, then trailed his mouth up her arm, all the way to her neck.

'Ransom…'

Persephone found herself on her back as Ransom captured her mouth, while his hand gripped the hem of her nightrail and lifted it up to her waist. Neither of them spoke for the rest of the evening, and Ransom made love to her until they were both exhausted.

The light was turning pink outside their window, but Persephone still hadn't slept a wink, despite being worn out. Ransom's head lay on her breast, and she ran her fingers through his hair in a soothing manner, the diamond-and-ruby bracelet a heavy weight around her wrist.

Her thoughts turned to that conversation with Kate and Maddie the day Ransom proposed, when she told them she didn't know if she loved him. However, the answer had never been clearer to her than in this moment. And despite what had happened yesterday, she could no longer deny it.

I love him.

But did Ransom love her back? And could she continue to be with him if he didn't?

Chapter Seventeen

'Thank you, Cook, all the accounts seem to be in order.' Ransom closed the kitchen's ledger, satisfied with what he saw. 'And if that new fishmonger gives you any trouble, send him directly to me.'

'You don' have to worry 'bout me, Ransom. You know I can hold me own,' the plump, white-haired woman said with a wide grin. 'That young man thinks he can pull the wool over me eyes, just 'cause I'm an old crone now.'

Ransom smiled. 'You have not changed a bit, not since the first day I saw you.'

'Yeah, she's been old all her life,' Clyde interjected.

Cook raised a wooden spoon at him. 'And you, Clyde, have had no brains all of yers.'

'Maybe it's you who's lost yer mind. Don't you remember, he's a duke now. Can't be goin' around callin' him Ransom no more.'

'I've known him since he was in short pants, and he'll always be Ransom to me. And he says he don't mind, ain't that right, Ransom?'

'All right, children.' He gave them a stern look. 'No more fighting.' He rubbed a hand over his eyes. 'And yes, you can still call me Ransom, as you'll always be

Cook to me. And Clyde, you know you only call me Your Grace as a joke.'

Clyde placed a mocking hand over his heart. 'Yer Grace, I'm offended you think of me that way.'

'You're doing it right now,' he pointed out, which only earned him a laugh.

Still, he couldn't help but be amused by their antics. Cook and Clyde had been his constants in the last twenty years. When Ransom began working here, Cook had taken him in, patiently showing him the ropes around the kitchen. Clyde, who had been working as a hall boy, kept watch over him, ensuring none of the other employees picked on him and more importantly, that he was never alone with any of the patrons. Ransom still shuddered to think of what could have happened to him growing up here and while it had not been an ideal childhood, he'd always been fed, had a roof over his head, and been safe.

Why couldn't Persephone see that Thomas was in the same lucky position?

A dark cloud crossed over his head at the thought of his wife. It had been a few days since their fight over the boy and while they had not rowed since then, the truce between them was silent and tenuous. He avoided her during the day and had dinner alone in his office or with a few patrons at the club, but each night he would come home and make love to her until dawn. She didn't turn him away, and was eager as ever. He thought that after a night of passion she would soften towards him, but when morning came she turned away and pretended to sleep as he awoke.

He would have to do something about this. She would not see reason, but short of sending the boy away so that the topic would never come up, he did not know what to do.

'If there's nothing else, I'll see you later,' he said to Cook. 'I'll be up in my office if you need me, Clyde.'

It was the middle of the afternoon and they were just about to open. The heavy drapes on the main gaming floor were drawn closed and the chandeliers were newly lit, bathing the room in a rich, sensuous glow. The employees were taking their places at the table, acknowledging him with a 'Your Grace' as he walked by. He stopped by the hazard table, looked up at the mirrored ceiling, and nodded to his eyes in the sky before he headed up the stairs to his office. To his surprise, it was not empty as he had left it.

'Persephone?'

She stood in the middle, a tray of food in her hand, staring at his shelves.

'Persephone?' he repeated.

Her face turned towards him, her emerald eyes glittering like diamonds, and just as hard. 'They're still here.'

'What's still here?'

The tray clattered loudly as she dropped it on his desk. 'All of them.' She gestured to his shelf. 'And the paintings.'

'As long as they're mine, they will stay.'

'It's been two weeks since our fight. You've had all this time to take them down and yet you haven't.'

'I didn't say I would take them down. Whatever gave you that idea?'

'B-but the pavilion at Mabury Hall…you said you would ask for my forgiveness—'

'By getting down on my knees. And I bought you that tiara, remember?' Not only had he paid a fortune for it, but he'd had to sit down to an hour-long history lesson about some fancy baroness and a prince. 'I just want things to be right between us.' He didn't care how much money it cost him, as long as they could go back to the way things were before their stupid argument over this shelf. Why could she not be content with her gift and forget about the fight?

'You think that's all you need to do? Buy me some trinkets and make love to me and everything will be all right?'

'Isn't it?' He had thought so. 'What is this about, Persephone? Do you really care about all these things on my shelf and the paintings?'

'No, you dimwit!' She threw her hands up in the air. 'I don't care about these stupid things.' Her shoulders slumped. 'And neither should you. Please, just put them away.'

'Still worried about my soul?' he scoffed. 'While the Underworld of Hades might have collected souls, I myself have none. Whatever soul I had is long gone, and was even before I crossed paths with Winford.'

'You mean, when you lost your sisters and Mum?'

Faces flickered at the edge of his mind. It had been so long ago, he wasn't even sure if the faces were truly theirs or just something his mind had conjured up.

Amelia.

Carrie.

Dorothy.

Mum.

That same searing hot pain began to build in his chest, but before the emotions could take over, he seized them and threw them into the box. This time, he not only locked it, but also threw away the key. 'What do you want from me, Persephone?'

'Why don't you ever talk about them, Ransom? Each time I try to bring them up, you shut yourself off. It's like…it's like you're a completely different person. Not the man I—'

'The man you what?'

'Nothing. Ransom, please talk to me. I don't want to live like this, always tiptoeing around you, waiting for you to get upset at me for saying something wrong.'

'Then stop bringing up the past. It's done. Why would we even need to talk about this?' He raked a hand through his hair. 'Aren't you the one telling me not to get mired in the past? Why should I get rid of my things? You cannot have it both ways, Persephone.'

'That's not the same thing.' Her hand curled into a fist. 'It is one thing to let the past hinder you and another to honour it and let go. Can't you see that in both these instances, you're still holding on by keeping these objects and locking your emotions away?'

Locking his emotions…

How did she…?

'This is a ridiculous conversation.' His chest tightened, like a giant fist had wrapped around his torso and squeezed. 'I'm going to find something more productive to do, and I suggest you do the same.'

Ransom stomped out of the office, slamming the door behind him. He made his way down to the main gaming floor, which was already beginning to fill with members.

'Your Grace!' someone called from the roulette table. 'It really is you,' he slurred.

Ransom stared at the man, who was obviously already in his cups, without returning his greeting.

'Pritchard, look! It's the Duke of Winford himself.'

Ransom stifled the urge to strangle the man. While he tolerated the 'Your Graces' from his employees, he forbade them from calling him by that title.

'Winford?' The man called Pritchard looked up, squinting. 'But Ransom hardly ever comes down here. I've been a member two years and I've only seen him once.' He blinked several times. 'By Jove, it is him. Join us, Your Grace.'

'No, thank you,' Ransom replied curtly. Though he had learned how every game in the club was played, he never participated or placed any bets himself. It was one of the most important lessons he had learned from working here, as he saw the most desperate, degenerate gamblers lose entire fortunes while clinging on to the hope of 'one more win.'

He continued to roam around the gaming floor, whispers following him as he moved from table to table, never speaking or acknowledging anyone else. Having made a full round of the floor, he decided to go to the basement where the sporting club was located. Aside from gaming tables, The Underworld also held prize fights there every night. He was about to descend the stairs when he heard footsteps quickly approaching from behind.

'Your Grace!' It was Thomas. 'Your Grace!' The boy nearly collided with him.

Ransom caught him by the shoulders. 'What is it?'

'Your… Grace…' He took a deep breath and bowed. 'Your wife, Your Grace.'

A sense of dread washed over him. 'Persephone? What about her? Is she hurt?'

He shook his head. 'No, Your Grace. But…' He took another gasp of air. 'She's outside in her carriage, wantin' to leave.'

'Where?' he thundered.

'She called for me an' said she was takin' me home.'

'What in blazes—did she say why?'

'Yes. She wants to talk to me Pa. I told her I had to get me hat first.' His eyes grew to the size of saucers.

'You can't let her, Your Grace. That's why I came and got you quick.'

'Good boy.' He ruffled his hair. 'Go and stay with Cook. I'll handle this.'

Ransom had never run so fast in his life. What was she thinking, attempting to go into the slums in her fancy carriage, with nothing but a boy for protection? The thieves would have divested her of all her belongings before she even put one slipper down on the filthy street.

'Stop!' he called as he sprinted outside. The door to Persephone's carriage had just slammed shut and the driver was ready to snap the reins. 'Stop this instant!' The driver recognised him and immediately lowered his hands.

Yanking the door open, he hurled himself inside. 'Are you mad?' he shouted at Persephone, who started at the sound of his voice. 'Do you have some kind of sick wish to put yourself in harm's way?'

'What are you doing here? Where is Thomas?' she demanded.

'He called me as soon as you told him your plan,' he growled. 'I'm glad one of you had some sense in their brain.'

'I just wanted to talk to the boy's father,' she reasoned. 'I want Thomas to go to school.'

'He'd never agree to it, not when he depends on the boy for his gin habit. What was your plan? Sit him down for some tea? Tell him about the benefits of schooling? Do you think you have any chance to make a man who only cares about when he's getting his next drink see reason?'

Persephone's lips tightened. 'Someone had to do something.'

'Are you still angry at me? Is that why you're doing

this, to drive me crazy because I won't do as you say? Because I won't speak about the past?'

'Ransom, please.' She scooted closer to him. 'I just want you to be at peace. To feel safe and secure.'

'You want to know all about my past? Then I'd be happy to oblige.' He stuck his head out of the window and called up to the driver. 'Bring us to St Giles.'

'Your Grace? Are you sure—'

'Now!'

Persephone clutched at the seat cushion as the carriage lurched forward violently. 'Wh-where are we going, Ransom?'

All he said was, 'It's a surprise.'

After a long, silent ride, the carriage finally stopped. Ransom pushed the door open, hopping out first, his boots making a squelching sound as they hit the muck pooling on the ground.

'What is this place, Ransom?' Persephone asked as she peeked out from the carriage.

'The place where you wanted to go. St Giles, one of the biggest rookeries in London. My former home.' He made a sweeping gesture behind him, where the tall buildings were squashed together, shoulder to shoulder like the crowds at Vauxhall Gardens, and casting their shadow over the street so that no light could touch it. 'Come, let me give you a tour.'

Persephone alighted and she winced when her slippered foot hit a puddle.

'Watch where you're stepping. I don't know what that liquid was, but I believe it's *mostly* water. But do not worry, after tonight, you'll probably want to burn your slippers and that gown anyway.' Catching her hand, he dragged her down the street, and into one of the dark alleyways.

'St Giles is one of several rookeries in London. Do you know why they're called such?'

She shook her head.

'Have you ever seen how rooks nest? No? Well, rooks like to build their nest in big groups. One tree might have dozens, perhaps hundreds of nests. These buildings you see here house hundreds of families, each one squeezed together in one room, just like mine was. Shady landlords do this to maximise profits.' He continued down the street, ignoring the curious eyes from the residents peeping out from their windows.

'Can you guess what type of people roam these alleyways?' He nodded to the old woman dressed in rags, hobbling down the street with a rickety cane. 'Keep looking forward, don't look anyone in the eye,' he said when they passed by a group of suspicious-looking men coming out of an alley. 'That's the number one rule here in the rookeries. One wrong look, and you might find yourself with a knife in the gut. Keep up.'

He picked up his pace and turned into another dark alley. 'It's been a while since I've been here, so I'm afraid I can't remember where it is I lived.'

A tight, hot knot formed in his chest, like a piece of coal roasting in the hearth—cold and black, turning red-hot once exposed long enough over fire. A voice in his head screamed that he should stop. Persephone's entire body had gone stiff as a board as he dragged her along and the fear in her face was evident.

Good.

She should fear him and everything he stood for. She was getting much too close to him, worming her way under his skin and he could not let that happen. He was being harsh, but it was like someone else had taken over him, controlling his actions. As if he was once again a passenger in that wagon, holding on for dear life while someone else drove them towards death.

And so he let that driver take over.

'I wouldn't be surprised if that building's collapsed, seeing as it was already falling down when I lived there,' he sneered. 'I remember Amelia's foot once punched a hole right through one of the rotting planks of the stairs.'

They turned another corner, down a narrow street, then walked up some steps. 'Oh, but this place, I still remember.' He stopped right at the corner, where the spire of St George's loomed in the distance. 'Every other shop on this street sells gin. This was my adoptive father's favourite place. When he failed to come home, my mother had to leave my sisters in my care so she could come down here and look for him. She often did find him, as well as a box to the ears. When she got sick, I went down here myself to tell him and got beaten black and blue for the—'

'Ransom, stop!'

He dropped her hand. 'Have you had enough? Is this little jaunt into my past too much for you? I promise you, the stench in your nose isn't burned in there for ever. It goes away. Eventually.'

She was breathing hard. 'Let's go back to the carriage. Please.'

'How can I deny you when you say please?'

As quick as he could, he led them back to the waiting carriage. Once they began to move, the knot in his chest loosened.

'Well, Persephone? Do you have anything to say?' He stared at her, waiting for an apology or some sort of remorseful confession.

Persephone glanced outside, her mouth pulling back into a tight line. 'I see it now, so clearly.'

'I doubt that, with all the smog.'

'No, not that.' She bit at her lip. 'It upsets you to talk about them, I understand that.' She took a deep breath. 'Do you know what the most dangerous thing is at a distillery? Some might think it's fire or the boiling of the fermented mash. But it's not.' She shook her head. 'It's the vapours, you see, produced during the distillation process and while the whisky is in storage. You can't see this vapour or smell it but it's highly flammable. One spark could cause an explosion, which would be bad enough in itself but when it's in a place with dry grain and alcohol, it could be—'

'Catastrophic,' he finished. 'Is there any point to this story?'

'That's why all the rooms have proper ventilation. By airing out the rooms, the vapours disperse into the outside air and prevent any disasters. Ransom,' she said, her tone shifting. 'You cannot keep your emotions inside. Otherwise, you'll explode. Maybe not now, but one day you will. Something will set you off, like a spark inside a room full of vapours.'

She reached over to touch him, but he flinched away. 'It's okay, I understand. You loved them so much. Your sisters, your mum. You lock away your feelings so you don't feel the hurt. And you feel guilt because you survived. You made it out of the slums. And then Winford came along, and he became the target of your hate because you still can't let go. But you must. You have to let go of the guilt. Remember your family. Honour them, but not by ignoring how you feel. You can't keep your heart locked up. At least, I hope you won't.'

He kept his stare focused ahead, refusing to look at her even as she gave her impassioned speech. 'And why not?'

'Because… Because I'd like to have it, please. And I can't have it if you keep it locked away in a box.'

His head snapped towards her. Even behind that barrier of the glass of her spectacles, he could see her eyes shining bright with tears. 'You do not want my heart.'

'I do. And, well… I don't have much choice, really, because I've already lost mine. You have it, Ransom. I love you.'

He stared at her for the longest time, his entire body frozen. 'You do not. You *should* not.'

'But I do. Why do you think I married you?'

'You love a man that shouldn't exist. We should not have married. I should have just stayed as I was, a man without a name or title.' He should have burned that letter the moment he read it. 'We wouldn't have married if I wasn't a duke.'

'If you think your title makes a difference to me, you're wrong. I was ready to marry you during the festival, hang all and whatever society would have thought of it. I—I loved you then, back when you had no title. I love *you*, Ransom with no last name. All of you—the parts that are tender and caring, the determined and hardworking parts that built an empire, and yes, even the broken boy who thinks that by locking his feelings away, he won't feel pain. That's all of you and I love you. You just have to decide if you want to stay in the past or join me in our future together.'

'I do not know this person you're describing, but it's certainly not me. I'm the wicked, selfish, and soulless man I have always been.'

The air in the carriage was suddenly suffocating. He had to get out of there. Knocking on the roof, he yelled,

'Stop.' The carriage had barely halted when he flung the door open. 'Go home, Persephone. And don't even think about attempting to see Thomas's father or I'll lock you up and throw away the key.'

She smiled sadly at him. 'I think you love me too. You just don't know how to say it aloud. That's all right. Once you've thought about what I said, I have faith you'll make the right decision.'

Ransom slammed the door. 'Send her home,' he barked at the driver, then stood there, watching it roll away until it disappeared in the distance. Once the carriage was gone, one thought rang in his mind.

Marrying Persephone was a mistake.

He'd been blinded—no, confused—by all these emotions he was supposed to keep locked up in that box. Caring for others only meant you could get hurt once they were gone. All these years, he had put all his energy towards building his fortune and plotting ways to make Winford miserable so he wouldn't have time to think about sentiments like love and guilt and pain. Somehow, Persephone had opened that box and he hadn't even seen it coming. He'd left himself open and vulnerable, two things he swore he would never allow himself to be. But then, he only had himself to blame, as he'd let it happen.

A stiff breeze blew by, making him shiver. There was a crispness in the air he had only just noticed.

It was nearly October.

How had time passed so quickly? One day it was summer, and now it was autumn.

Pulling the collar of his coat up his neck, Ransom stuck his hands deep into his pockets and walked.

He wasn't sure where he was going, only that he couldn't be anywhere near The Underworld. Not tonight, while she was there.

Chapter Eighteen

'Is there anything else I can do for you, Your Grace?' Mrs Owens asked as she placed the tea tray down on the desk.

Persephone looked up from her notebook. 'Perhaps something to help remove these stains?' She wiggled her ink-blotched fingers at the housekeeper. 'I've scrubbed my skin raw every night but I can't get them to wash off completely. Then I start writing again in the morning and the ink just builds up.'

'I'll see what I can do, Your Grace. Perhaps one of the cleaning women downstairs knows a trick or two.'

'Thank you, Mrs Owens,' she said, then nodded at the older women to dismiss her. The moment she was alone, Persephone slumped back in her chair, took her spectacles off and closed her eyes.

Three days.

That's how long she'd been working on her sketches. She'd written down enough ideas to fill a whole notebook and perhaps build two more distilleries. From morning until evening, just scribbling away.

Three days was also the amount of time Ransom had

been away. After he'd stepped out of the carriage, she hadn't seen him again.

She was mad with worry when she woke the next day and he wasn't by her side. However, Clyde was already waiting for her in the foyer by the time she quickly dressed, to inform her Ransom had travelled to Swindon on business. When she asked when he'd be back, he couldn't give her a concrete answer.

That was three days ago. And there was still no sign that he was returning.

Persephone suspected that he had shown her the rookeries so that she would cease to bring up the past. Instead, it had only opened her eyes more. He needed to let go of the past and everything that was weighing him down, to stop drowning in guilt because he had survived.

She feared that the guilt, along with the anger and resentment, building up inside him would find its way out, one way or another. As long as he clung to that guilt and kept everything else locked up, he would never be happy, never feel safe and secure. Never accept her love and return it.

But he does love me.

She had to believe it, even if with each day he was away, the hope slowly trickled away.

Opening her eyes, she retrieved her spectacles, put them on, then stood up and stretched her arms over her head. She drew the curtains back and opened the windows, allowing the fresh air to come in.

While she did manage to accomplish so much in the last three days, staying inside was slowly driving her mad. She supposed she could go out for a promenade in the park or shopping, as the other ladies of the ton did, but she had never really enjoyed those activities, not even while she was an unmarried debutante.

An idea popped into her head. *Kate!* It had been so long since she'd seen the other Duchess. Perhaps she could press on her for an unscheduled visit today. Maybe even to the locomotives factory.

Decision made, she scrawled a note and asked Mrs Owens to call Thomas so he could deliver it to Mabury Hall. She thought he might rather like a ride in her carriage, and if nothing else, it would get him out of the club for some fresh air.

'I'm sorry, Your Grace,' Mrs Owens said when she returned some time later. 'I'm afraid Thomas is unable to deliver your letter, but if you give me your note, I'll have someone else run it over to Mabury Hall.'

'Is he running another errand? When will he be back?'

Mrs Owens fiddled with the hem of her apron, her eyes cast downward. 'I don't know…that is, I'm not certain…'

'What do you mean? Mrs Owens, please tell me. I shan't be angry.'

'It just…according to Mr Clyde, Thomas is no longer working at the club.'

'I beg your pardon?' Persephone shot to her feet, gripping the side of her desk.

'Mr Clyde said that His Grace sent his instructions from Swindon that Thomas is not to work here any longer.'

That…that monster!

Ransom had actually sent him away? Because he didn't want to speak about him any more?

He really was selfish and wicked.

She let out a huff. 'And where is Mr Clyde?'

'I believe he's in the kitchens. Your Grace, perhaps you should stay here and I'll call for—'

Persephone ignored Mrs Owens's protests and stalked out of the room. Though she'd never been to The Underworld's kitchen, she eventually found her way there. One of the maids directed her to the pantry where Clyde and Cook were talking.

'It's not right, Clyde, I tell you, the way he's treatin' his wife.'

Persephone halted just before she crossed the threshold into the pantry. She didn't even need two guesses to figure out who the 'he' and 'his wife' Cook was referring to were.

'What would you have me do? Drag him back here? You know Ransom—stubborn as an ox.'

'And just as stupid.' Cook clucked her tongue. 'He shouldn't be lying to her. Or rather, have you lie to her by tellin' her he's in Swindon when he's just staying at The Greenbriar Hotel.'

A dull ache throbbed in Persephone's chest as she heard those words.

Ransom hadn't gone away on business. No, he was right here in London, just around the corner. Apparently, he was still overseeing The Underworld, just not from within its walls.

He just didn't want to come home.

He didn't want to come home to her.

Disappointment, grief and rage all swirled within her. Without thought, she marched inside. 'So, my dear husband has been in London all this time.'

Clyde and Cook halted their conversation, their expressions turning to horror and embarrassment as they turned to her. 'Your Grace,' Cook cried.

'Well? What have you two got to say for yourselves?'

'I… Yer Grace… I couldn't…' Clyde stammered. 'It was Ransom's orders. Said he would fire me if I told anyone else the truth.'

'I had to pry it out of him,' Cook added. 'I swear, I won't tell no one else.'

'At least he had the decency to spare me the humiliation from everyone finding out,' she said sarcastically. 'Do give His Grace my thanks for his kind consideration next time you run off to see him.'

'Yer Grace, I'm sorry,' Clyde murmured. 'I had to.'

'Aside from my thanks, could you kindly give him another message, please? Tell him that he's a heartless swine and a coward for firing Thomas.'

'F-firing Thomas?' Clyde cocked his head to the side. 'What do you mean, Yer Grace?'

'That's what you told Mrs Owens, did you not? That on Ransom's instructions, he "is not to work here." That's why he was unable to deliver my letter.'

Clyde slapped a palm on his forehead. 'I told her that he's unable to deliver your letter *right now*. Yer Grace, Ransom didn't fire Thomas.'

'He didn't?'

'Of course not. Ransom gave instructions that the boy was to have reading and writing lessons every day in one of the private card rooms, from noon until we open. He still has to do some work at the club in the mornings, sweepin' and whatnot, so he can earn his food and lodging at the rooming house next door with the other employees.'

Persephone's jaw nearly dropped to floor. 'He—he—Ransom—really asked you to do that?'

'Yes, Yer Grace. I found the tutor meself. They're upstairs now, if you'd like to see them.'

Still in shock, she simply nodded her head and followed Clyde out of the pantry and upstairs to the third floor. He led her to one of the many card rooms, and sure enough, Thomas was there, sitting in a plush velvet chair, while a stern-looking older man with powder-white hair stood in front of him, holding a chalkboard with letters on it.

'Your Grace,' Thomas exclaimed as he jumped to his feet and bowed.

'Thomas,' she greeted as she approached him. 'How are you? How are the lessons?'

'Good, Your Grace.' His grin spread from ear to ear. 'Mr Walker's been teaching me all the letters, so I can recognise them.'

'That's wonderful, Thomas. What about the rooming house? Are the other employees treating you well?' She swallowed. 'And your father?'

'Yeah, they're all right. They don't beat me up or nothin' and the beds are nice and clean. And Pa, well he don't know about the lessons, but His Grace said he'll continue to pay me the same. He says I'll have to earn my keep by learning to read and write. And that he'll give me a raise if I can write him a letter.'

She chuckled and ruffled his head. 'That's wonderful, Thomas.'

Persephone listened to Mr Walker report on Thomas's progress. The tutor said the boy was bright and eager and had already memorised half the alphabet in just two days. Then, she stayed to watch for half an hour before she bid them goodbye.

'Is everything to your satisfaction, Yer Grace?' Clyde asked.

'Yes, Clyde. Thank you.'

Hope sparked in her—tiny, but it was there. Perhaps Ransom was finally starting to open his eyes.

Clyde crossed his arms and leaned against the wall. 'Reminds me so much of Ransom, that one. Scrappy little thing when he first got here, but he survived.'

Yes, that was her husband. A survivor.

And perhaps, not so selfish or wicked, nor soulless.

'How is he, Clyde?' she asked, unable to hold on to her emotions.

'He's…breathin'.' Clyde clucked his tongue. 'Stubborn fool. I don't know what's passed between you, but you don't deserve this at all.'

She smiled. 'Thank you, Clyde.'

'Will that be all, Yer Grace?'

'Yes, thank you.'

He bid her goodbye, and turned to leave.

Persephone clutched a hand to her chest. A flicker of hope sparked there. It was tiny, but it was there.

If only he would come back…

Unsure of what else to do, she decided she needed to clear her head.

Perhaps a walk outside.

She retraced her steps and found her way back to the staircase. As she made her way down, she halted, recognising her surroundings. This was the same set of stairs Ransom had first taken her to, the one that would lead to the room with his eyes in the sky.

Where it all began.

Mind made up, she stopped at the second floor. The guard looked surprised to see her, but made no attempt to stop her from entering. Inside, a few of the men were already in position, while the others who were still getting ready looked taken aback by her presence.

'I'm not here,' she declared, pressing a finger to her lips.

That was enough for them; they shrugged and continued with their business. Once everyone was in place, she saw one empty pallet.

Why not?

She lay down on her stomach, put her spectacles away,

and looked through the spy hole. The main gaming floor was already filling up with patrons, scattering about as they took their positions at the tables of their choice. The last time she was here, she didn't get a chance to observe the games as she didn't stay too long, not to mention, she was distracted by the woman on that gentleman's lap.

A furious blush rose in her, remembering what she had seen, as well as all the things she'd done with Ransom. An ache built in her core, the need for him like a burning ember ready to burst into flames.

Please, Ransom, she pleaded silently. *Come home.*

Pushing those thoughts aside, she continued to watch downstairs. More men arrived and the gaming tables were all full. The movements, the lights, the noise—it all looked dizzying from up here and she wondered what it was like in the thick of it. Fascinated, she continued her observation, watching the roulette wheel do spin after spin, the dice roll across the hazard table, and the cards flipping on the green felt.

Time lost all meaning as she watched. It wasn't until she felt the sharp pain in her leg that she realised she must have been here a good hour at least.

Blasted cramps.

Sighing, she pushed herself up, and flipped over, then put her spectacles back on. She bit her lip to stop herself from moaning in pain. Just as she reached down to massage her leg, a loud *boom* echoed through the room, making the floorboards shake.

What was that?

All the men lifted their heads and looked at each other. When nothing else happened, they resumed their work.

Shrugging, she lifted her skirt and pressed her fingers to her calf. After a few minutes, the pain subsided. She was about to resume her position when a loud bell began to ring. This time, all the men scrambled to their feet.

'Wh-what's happening?' she cried. 'What's going on?' And what was that loud explosion?

'Danger, Yer Grace,' one of the men said as he helped her up. 'That's the bell to warn us to leave the building.'

'Danger? What kind of danger? Inside here? Does it have anything to do with that boom earlier?'

'I don't know, but it's safer to just leave. Master—His Grace had the alarm bells installed to give us early warning should anything happen. Said that if we were ever to hear those bells, we should flee. Come, Yer Grace.'

'B-but the house… Mrs Owens… Clara!'

'The bells go up to the roof. Mrs Owens'll know what to do.'

Oh, please, let that be the case, Persephone prayed silently as she allowed the man to drag her out of the room.

As they made their way down, the telltale smell of burning assaulted her nostrils and when they turned a corner, dark bursts of smoke blew their way.

'Out to the main floor!' someone called.

The hand on her arm gripped her harder, hauling her along until they reached the gaming floor. The crowds were making their way to the front door as Charon held it open, screaming for everyone to get out. Thankfully by the time they reached the golden doors, the mob had thinned and Persephone and the rest of the eyes in the sky were the tail-end. A hand—probably Charon's—pushed her forward, propelling her down the black marble steps. Spectacles askew from the narrow escape, she pushed them back up her nose and blinked until her vision focused.

Mother of mercy!

The scene before her was chaos. It was evening now and

St James's Street was already packed enough at the best of times, but the deluge of patrons and employees flooding the street caused further pandemonium. Persephone craned her neck, searching through crowds. An exclamation of relief burst forth when she saw Mrs Owens and Clara, as well as Clyde and Cook, across the street.

'Your Grace!' Mrs Owens's face paled when she saw Persephone. 'You made it out.'

'I did. And so did you.' She hugged the old woman, as well as Clara. 'Thank goodness.' She looked to Clyde and Cook. 'Any idea what happened?'

'Musta been the boiler in the basement that exploded,' Cook bawled. 'We started havin' some trouble a few days ago. Hadn't been able to bring it up to Ransom, seein' as he's away.'

'Is everyone out?' she asked Clyde. 'No one else is inside, are they?'

'Everyone should know to leave when they hear the bells,' he answered. 'But I'm going to go 'round, make sure we didn't miss anyone.'

The women huddled together, watching as thick plumes of smoke curled out. Another blast erupted and they screamed in fright. Soon, flames followed, and the orange and red tongues began licking at the windows.

Oh, no.

The Underworld was Ransom's most precious possession. It was the only home he knew that was still remaining. Perhaps it was the one place left he did feel safe and secure, even if he didn't know it.

'The fire engines are on their way,' Clyde reported as he returned to them.

'And the employees?' Persephone asked. 'Everyone's accounted for?'

He did not answer right away, but the crestfallen look

on Clyde's face told her something was very wrong. 'Clyde?'

'I heard… I mean… I'm not sure.' He swiped his hat off his head and clutched it with both hands. 'One of the dishwashers said they saw Thomas walking into the broom cupboard next to the pantry with a book just before we opened. Was supposed to be going home, the idiot.'

Persephone's heart sank as she watched the flames blazing across the street helplessly. 'No…'

'He wasn't certain it was him, but who else could it be?'

'Couldn't he be at the rooming house?' she said. 'Did anyone else see him?'

Clyde shook his head. 'Everyone there heard the alarm bells and went out too.'

'Thomas,' she sobbed.

They couldn't just leave him in there. Taking a deep breath, she gathered her thoughts. From what she remembered when she went in there this afternoon, The Underworld's kitchens had a big door in the back where their suppliers brought crates of produce and meat and whatnot. There should be some kind of alleyway there, and it would have to be big enough for a horse and cart.

Hmm.

It was the other day, as she took a stroll with Clara outside The Underworld, that she spied a wagon filled with vegetables entering a huge gate on the west side of the building.

Persephone broke away from the others, their protests swallowed by the growing crowds around them. She weaved through the throng of people, and darted down the west side of the street and found the gateway, which thankfully was left open.

No fire.

That was a good sign, as that meant the blaze hadn't yet reached the kitchens. Smoke was blowing out of the rear door, but only in thin, irregular gusts.

'Thomas!' she screamed as she entered. 'Thomas!'

The smoke was choking her throat and making her eyes water, so she covered her nose with the inside of her elbow and rushed to the broom cupboard, flinging it open. 'Thomas!'

'Your Grace!' The boy was huddled in the corner, a book clutched to his chest.

Relief washed over her and she rushed inside, the door slamming behind her. 'Thomas, we have to go.' She pulled him up. 'Before the fire reaches us.'

A loud crash made her jump, and the entire cupboard shook, raining dust on them. She pushed the door—but it would not open. She jiggled the knob and then gave another push. 'I think there's something blocking the door.'

'Maybe something fell in front of it,' Thomas cried. 'Your Grace, what should we do?'

'We have to push it out of the way.'

Both of them braced themselves against the door and pushed.

And pushed again.

It did not budge an inch.

'I'm sorry, Your Grace.' Big fat tears rolled down Thomas's cheeks. 'I just… I didn't wanna go back to the roomin' house yet. I just needed a quiet place to study my letters.' He glanced at the discarded book on the floor. 'I'm sorry.'

'Shh…it's all right.' Not sure what to do, Persephone took his hand and dragged him to the corner where she sat him down. 'Clyde said the fire engines are on the way.' She pulled him close to her and rubbed his back as he sobbed. 'They'll find us,' she promised. 'It'll be fine.'

The calming words were meant to soothe the boy, but they were empty to her ears as she saw the curls of smoke seeping under the crack between the door and the floor.

Oh, Lord, someone please help us.

Chapter Nineteen

'Blast it!'

Ransom put his pen down, rose from his desk and marched over to the windows to draw the drapes shut. He was already having a difficult enough time concentrating on his correspondence, and now the growing din from outside was driving him mad. He supposed he should be used to noise by now—this was St James's, after all—but the racket was completely out of control.

Probably a fight between some drunk lords over cards or women.

He marched back to the desk and sat down, then picked up the pen.

There was a reason he had his office at The Underworld far in the back, away from the main commercial area, and high up on the fourth floor of the building. When he checked into The Greenbriar Hotel, the manager had been so delighted to welcome him, declaring he would give Ransom 'the finest suite' they had. The three-room suite was lavish enough, he supposed, but the large window faced the street, which made it impossible to get any sleep, especially at night as garrulous groups of men, screeching women, and all sorts of noisy, drunken revellers seemingly converged right under his room.

But that was not the only reason he couldn't sleep.

Putting the pen back down, he gripped the side of the desk and pushed himself away, the chair legs scraping loudly on the hard wooden floor. When he didn't allow the noise or his work distract him, his mind drifted to only one person.

His wife.

'Persephone,' he whispered, as if saying her name aloud would conjure her up.

He wanted to go back to The Underworld.

Back to his home.

To his bed.

To her.

He walked over to the cabinet stocked with a variety of liquors, then poured himself a glass of cognac.

I could go home anytime, he told himself as he took a sip.

No, he could not.

Because it might be too late.

Because surely, after three days of silence, there was nothing to go home to. By now Persephone surely would have realised what a truly wicked and selfish man he was and had decided she no longer loved him.

The very thought had him finishing the cognac in one gulp.

It had been a foolish mistake, coming here. Not the biggest mistake he'd made in the last few days—no, that was leaving Persephone in the first place. But he should not have stayed away for so long. The decision to leave had been made in anger. Staying away was just because of his damned, foolish pride.

He slammed the glass down on top of the cabinet.

The faces of his sisters and mum came back to him. He'd felt so much guilt over their deaths. Losing them had destroyed him. The only thing that had kept him alive was the drive to pull himself out of poverty. But then he achieved that after he bought Hale's and transformed it into his own kingdom, amassing a fortune that rivalled the Queen's.

Still, his guilt festered, and when he found out about Winford, a new goal appeared before him, something to distract him from the pain and guilt of his past.

Persephone was right. The emotions he locked up inside were going to explode soon. And—

'Damn!' he cursed as the ringing alarm bells pierced the heavy drapes. 'What the blazes is going on?'

Dashing over to the windows, he yanked the curtains back. Three horse-drawn wagons rushed by. People scattered about, making way for them as they thundered down the street. Why did they look familiar? He searched his memories until it dawned on him.

The London Fire Engine Establishment.

Like any good businessman, Ransom took out insurance on all his properties. It cost him a fortune, but knowing that life could throw anything at him, it was worth it. One of the services he bought was fire insurance, which included paying into the private London Fire Engine Establishment, which dispatched firefighting engines to their clients.

His stomach churned. The engines were moving up the street. Towards The Underworld.

It couldn't be…surely someone would have sent for him by now…

Well, they would have if they knew where he was.

Ransom shot to his feet, bolted out of his room. By the time he rounded the corner and spied The Underworld in the distance his lungs were burning, but he ignored the pain. Thick smoke rose from the all-black building as the fire blazed bright.

Dear God, no.

He fought his way through the crowd, pushing and shoving until he reached the corner. The street was teeming with his employees, along with well-dressed gentlemen of the ton. When they saw him, they clamoured for his attention, grabbing at him, all talking at once.

'Let me go!' he roared.

'Ransom!'

The familiar voice caught his attention, and his head snapped in the direction of where it came from. Sure enough, Cook was on the other side of the street, along with Mrs Owens and Clara.

But where was his wife?

'Ransom!' Cook exclaimed as he rushed to them. 'Thank God you're here! The Duchess—'

'Where is she?' He gripped her shoulders. 'Did she make it out?'

Oh, Lord, please...

'She did.' It was Mrs Owens who answered. 'B-but we think she went back in.'

Blood roared in his ears. 'Are you certain?'

Mrs Owens blubbered through her explanation about Thomas and the cupboard, but Ransom understood enough.

That fool!

'She disappeared not too long ago. Clyde went after her,' Cook added. 'Lost her in the crowd, but I know he'll find her.'

'I have to go in after her.' Ignoring the women's protests, Ransom ran across the street. The fire engines were now in position and ready to pump out water to douse the flames, but they might still be too late.

Think, Ransom.

Persephone was a clever woman—she wouldn't just run off without a plan. She wouldn't go in through the front door. It would take too long to go to the kitchens. His brilliant but foolish wife would have known that there was another way to get in.

The delivery entrance.

He turned westward down the street and spied a familiar figure ahead of him. 'Clyde!' He must have had the same thought.

The man stopped and turned. 'Ransom!'

He quickly caught up to him.

'Yer wife, she—'

'I know. No time, let's go!'

The two men sprinted down the street, through the gates, and in through the rear door. The entire kitchen was filled with smoke and the heat of the fire was nearly unbearable.

'Persephone!' he shouted into the black void.

'The broom cupboard,' Clyde reminded him.

The broom cupboard. *His* broom cupboard, the one he had slept in when he was younger. 'Follow me.'

Ransom could find that broom cupboard in the dark, so he quickly guided them to where it was. Thankfully the fires had only consumed the other half of the kitchen, though it was growing by the second, the flames licking at the ceiling.

'Something's blocking it, Ransom.'

He saw the thick beam that had fallen across the door through the thick smoke. Without another word, the two men braced their shoulders against one side and lifted it out of the way.

Ransom kicked the door open with his boot. 'Persephone!' He spied her in the corner, huddled up along with a smaller figure. Both were distressingly still. 'Clyde!'

They wasted no time; Ransom picked up Persephone as Clyde slung the boy's body over his shoulder, then they raced outside.

Ransom took a gasp of the cold autumn air, allowing it to clear his lungs of the smoke.

'Where should we go?' Clyde asked.

Ransom glanced around. The streets were still in utter chaos. 'My hotel.'

They carried Persephone and Thomas back to The Greenbriar. Ransom barked at the staff to call for a doctor as they hurried back to his room. Clyde put the boy on the settee and Ransom took Persephone to his room. She let out a cough as soon as he put her on the mattress, then fainted.

Fear gripped him like never before. He tore at her clothes, tearing her dress down the middle, then he untied her stays. He opened her mouth, clearing the way for air to come in, but she remained unconscious, so he pressed his mouth to hers, hoping to flush the smoke from her lungs.

After four breaths, her eyes opened, then she let out a cough. Ransom jumped back, giving her room. She gasped, taking in a deep breath before another fit of coughs overtook her.

Not knowing what to do, he dropped to his knees beside her. 'Persephone,' he cried. Her coughing slowed and their eyes locked.

After one more deep inhale, she whispered in a rough voice, 'Ransom.'

All the tension, worry, and panic drained out of him. 'You're alive.'

She smiled weakly, then closed her eyes and fell back against the pillows.

'No!'

'Your Grace, the doctor is here,' the manager bellowed as he burst into the room. Behind him, a distinguished-looking man in a tweed coat entered, carrying a large leather bag.

'Dr Talbot, Your Grace,' he introduced himself. 'Please move out of the way so I may examine her.'

'Will she be all right?' Ransom asked, his voice shaky. 'She was just awake—'

The doctor raised a hand to silence him as he turned to Persephone. He checked her eyes, her mouth, and her nostrils, then took out a variety of instruments from his bag and began to prod and examine her.

With each passing second, his anxiety, panic, and worry returned. As soon as the doctor stood up, he asked again, 'Will she be all right?'

Dr Talbot nodded. 'She just needs rest and some medication. I'll explain in greater detail later, but now I must attend to the boy.'

'Thomas.' He'd been so concerned about Persephone that he'd forgot about the boy. 'Thank you,' he called as the doctor left the room.

Ransom collapsed on the floor by Persephone's side. She looked so frail, lying in bed like that, her hair fanned out around her. He cupped her jaw and brushed his thumb along a soot-streaked cheek. She was alive—that was all that mattered.

He buried his face in the covers and wept in relief.

When Persephone was younger, she had taken to her bed with a fever which had lasted several days. She recalled having several hallucinations and strange dreams, including one of a giant bird that flew her around the world.

At first she thought she was reliving that experience now, but then she remembered she was not a child any more, nor was she back in her room at Kinlaly Castle. She didn't know where she was but nothing around her felt familiar.

She opened her eyes.

The fire.

Thomas.

The broom cupboard.

'Hel—!' Her throat burned as she tried to shout.

'Persephone, you're awake.'

She froze. Ransom? 'What—' The ache in her throat was like swallowing hot nails.

'Shh, don't talk.' A big, Ransom-shaped blur knelt down beside her. 'It hurts. I know.'

Bed...she was in a bed. The fire... How had she got out? She opened her mouth to talk, but even breathing sharply made her chest hurt. She grasped at her throat.

'Water?'

She nodded.

The Ransom blur moved, then she felt a glass press against her lips. 'Sip slowly,' he instructed. 'Swallowing will hurt too.'

When he tipped the glass, she followed his instructions. Once she finished with half the glass, she pushed it away.

'That's it. Can I get you anything else? More blankets? Some broth?'

She shook her head with each suggestion. *My spectacles*, she wanted to say. She made two circles with her thumb and forefinger then put them up to her eyes.

'Ah, yes.' The Ransom blur moved again, then she felt something familiar land on her nose. 'There you go.'

She blinked several times until her vision came into focus and Ransom was a blur no more. She smiled at the sight of him. However, she couldn't help but notice how unkempt he looked—hair tousled, jaw unshaven, dark circles under his eyes. Then she remembered.

Fire, she mouthed at him. *Thomas.*

'He's fine. Resting back at the rooming house. In better condition than you are, apparently, according to Dr Talbot.' With a deep sigh, he embraced her. 'I can't believe you went inside after him. You could have been killed,' he said in an anguished tone, barely able to finish the last word.

Oh, Ransom.

She wrapped her arms around his middle, squeezing tight. They stayed there for a while, but then she let go and mouthed, *What happened?*

Ransom explained everything to her, from the boiler explosion, all the way up to when he and Clyde found the two of them in the broom cupboard.

Ransom had gone in after her?

'You don't know how lucky you are,' he continued. 'The fire could have trapped you there or…' He cleared his throat. 'You will never put yourself in danger like that ever again, do you hear me?' He didn't bother to wait for her reaction as he pulled her into another embrace. 'Persephone…'

She was glad to hear Thomas and everyone else was all right, but what about club? She pushed him away.

The Underworld?

He smiled. 'It doesn't matter. That doesn't matter.' Fluffing the pillow behind her, he said, 'Dr Talbot doesn't think the smoke did you any lasting damage. You only need time and rest to heal your throat, though he did leave some medicine. We'll stay here for a few days until you've recovered, and we can decide what to do.'

What to do? What did he mean? And where were they?

She attempted to hold on to him and make him listen, but he gently pried her hands away. 'Rest, please. Your body needs it to heal.'

Seeing as she had no choice, she fell back against the pillow. Despite her protests, her lids became heavy. He kissed her on the temple. 'Have a good rest.'

For the next few days, Persephone stayed in bed. She felt weak at first and slept most of the time, and Dr Talbot—who visited at least once a day—said that was normal and she should regain her strength soon. At first she could not eat much—just cold broth, pudding, and puréed vegetables—but after a day or two she could tolerate some soft foods, like bread soaked in milk and mashed fruit and potatoes.

Though she was bored most of the time, she passed the hours by reading, though she could hardly get through the single book Ransom brought her because she kept falling asleep. She wondered if her notebooks and sketches had survived the fire, but Ransom still refused to tell her what had happened to the house or The Underworld.

By the third day she was allowed visitors and of course, Kate and the Dowager were the first ones to arrive. Both women were deliriously happy to see her, and told her that they had already written to Cam and Maddie. She felt relieved, as she knew her brother and sister-in-law would be glad to know she was safe. Kate also relayed to her the progress on her locomotive engine prototype, which was nearly finished, while the Dowager informed her that she had taken a new protégée under her wing.

'I missed having all that young energy around me,'

the Dowager explained. 'So I decided to sponsor another debutante.'

Persephone scribbled on a notebook.

What is she like?

It was not the most efficient way to communicate, but talking still hurt and exhausted her.

The corner of Kate's mouth quirked up. 'Interesting.'

Aside from the Duchess and the Dowager, Mrs Owens, Clara, Cook, and Clyde came to see her. On the fourth day, Thomas was well enough and came to visit as well. Just as Dr Talbot said, he was in a better condition than her, as he was able to rasp a few sentences without wincing. She was glad to see him, though with their limited means of communication he left after a few minutes, promising to come by every day.

And then there was Ransom.

Her husband came in and out of the room at all hours. She suspected he was busy because of the implications of the fire, so she did not mind that he was not by her side all the time.

However, what did annoy her was that although he spoke to her about trivial matters, held her, even gave her a few kisses, he didn't say or do more than that. Whenever he came in, there was always a deep line of worry between his eyebrows, but it disappeared the moment their eyes met. Though she tried to ask him about The Underworld, he would brush away her questions.

By the seventh day, Persephone felt well enough to speak, the burning in her throat limited to a few spots. As soon as Ransom walked into the room, she rose from the bed.

'Get back to bed,' Ransom ordered as he rushed to her side.

She folded her arms and shook her head. 'Talk,' she rasped. 'Now.'

'Persephone—'

'Now.'

His shoulders slumped in defeat. 'Fine. But you must sit.'

She plopped back down on the bed. 'Talk. Underworld.' She cocked her head to the side. 'Gone?'

'Not all of it.' He sat down beside her. 'The entire basement and sporting club were completely obliterated. However, the foundation is still solid, as is the structure itself. But the rooms closest to the boiler were burned in the fire. The gaming room, the second floor, the kitchens, the storage rooms, anything and everything inside them. Only the fourth floor and rooftop were spared.'

'I'm sorry, Ransom.' She took his hand. 'I'm so sorry.'

'Don't be. It's all right.'

She swallowed to moisten her throat. 'It was your home,' she declared. 'The most important thing in the world to you.'

'No, no, Persephone. It's not the most important thing in the world to me.' His large hands covered hers. 'That's not my home. You are my home.' Lifting her hands up to his mouth, he kissed each of her fingers. 'Persephone, forgive me. Forgive me for being so blinded by guilt and rage. Forgive me for leaving you alone. I promise, if you do forgive me, I will always be by your side. I want to leave the past behind and build a future, a new home, with you. I give you my heart—miserable, cold thing that it is. I love you.'

Tears sprang to her eyes and she feared her heart would burst right out of her chest. 'I love you too, Ransom.'

'And you're right.'

'I am?'

'Yes. About everything. My sisters and mum. Winford. The guilt.' He swallowed hard. 'I couldn't let go. After Mum and my sisters died, I thought that if I got out of the slums, made enough money, I would be happy. But then I bought the club and became richer than Midas, but the guilt was still there. So I found a new obsession.'

'Winford.'

'Yes.'

He tipped up her chin to meet his eyes, one green and the other brown, both looking at her with all the love in the world. He would be the most beautiful man in the world to her for ever.

The corner of his mouth lifted slightly. 'But then one day, I found this slip of a girl who had sneaked into my office.'

'And then?' she asked, grinning at him.

'And then she changed my entire world by asking me for an adventure.'

Epilogue

'*Achoo!*'

Persephone had felt the tickle in her nose, but the sneeze came so fast, she had no time to retrieve her handkerchief. 'Pardon me.'

Ransom retrieved a square of cloth from his pocket and handed it to her. 'There you go, love. It's all the dust from in here.'

She accepted the cloth, delicately wiping her nose with it. 'Thank you.' Glancing around what was the former main gaming floor of The Underworld, she let out a gasp. 'It's hard to believe this was the same room after the fire.'

As Ransom had told her, the main gaming floor had completely burned down. After she had recovered from her injuries, they paid a visit to what was left of The Underworld to survey the damage. The sight of the charred remains of the gaming tables, chandeliers, décor, and the mirrored glass ceiling had so broken her heart that she nearly wept.

That, however, was months ago. After the debris had been cleared and the plans drawn up, the rebuilding of The Underworld began. The gaming floor was empty for now, but the scorched walls had been repaired and repainted.

A few workers were unravelling rolls of beautiful dark blue-and-gold damask paper for the walls, while two men perched on high ladders were carefully placing mirror shards on the ceiling, piecing them together like a puzzle.

It was easier and quicker to rebuild the rooms the same way as they were before the fire. But even though Ransom didn't plan to change much, it still felt like a new beginning. Just in time too, as spring was already in full bloom. The curtainless windows allowed the bright sunshine to fill the space, bathing it in warmth, and the entire room was like a promise of better things to come.

'Do you really think it'll be ready by summer?'

'I hired three separate companies to ensure we finish on time,' he said. 'Each one is assigned their own section of rooms, and of course, there's the fourth company we selected for the basement. Shall we go and check on the progress there?'

A frisson of excitement ran through her. 'Oh, can we?'

'Of course, love.'

While Ransom was keeping things the same for most of the rebuild, he did ask the architects to make one major improvement.

'The fermenting casks have arrived!' Persephone dashed to the row of enormous oak barrels, each one the size of a carriage. 'Think of it. In a few months we'll be brewing our own ale.'

Since the boiler had levelled the entire sporting club, Ransom decided to rebuild part of it as a brewery, which of course would be Persephone's domain. She'd been thrilled when he offered her the opportunity and immediately said yes. Using her notes and sketches, she planned everything, including making a few improvements from her original design at The White Horse Inn that she was certain would produce a high-quality product that even the most discerning members of the club would enjoy.

Ransom had given her free rein on the design and build of the brewery, and agreed to all of her requests and changes, though there was one matter they could not come to an agreement on—naming the brewery.

Persephone reached up to trace her hand along the name stamped on the side of the barrel. 'What do you think?'

Her husband walked over to her and leaned casually against the oaken cask. 'I think it's perfect. Winford Brewery will be a smashing success, and it will be all thanks to you.'

Initially, Ransom had forbidden her to use that name.

'I'll not have another reminder of him anywhere near me. It's bad enough I have to keep hearing it when we're out and about, but to have to see it in my club is absolutely unacceptable. Why would you even suggest that, knowing how much I despise that name and what it stands for?'

She'd known he would object of course, as she had noticed his reaction whenever they were at a ball or at the opera or some other event. He would flinch ever so slightly whenever his title was announced or introduced to someone new.

But she had a reason for wanting the name for the brewery, and so she'd calmly told him, *'You cannot let this name hold power over you for ever, Ransom. I won't allow it. That is why I want this name on our ale—so that we may reclaim it and make it our own. So that it will no longer hold that meaning for you and in the end, we will have won.'*

Ransom had not reacted to her speech, but neither had he refused her the use of the name. However, Persephone was certain he took much pleasure in knowing that the ton was scandalised by the use of the illustrious name in a commercial venture, and thus he never brought up any objections again.

'I think by next week we'll be able to install the new brew kettle,' she informed him. 'Would you mind if I had Thomas come for a few days so he can watch? I know you're strict about his schooling, but I think he'll benefit greatly.'

'He's going to be your apprentice, so of course he may come.' Taking her hand into his, he gave it a kiss. 'There's one more thing I want show you.'

'What is it?'

'Another improvement.'

He led her back upstairs to the main gaming floor, then to the staircase that led to the higher floors. On the way there, she recognised a few of the employees from the club, as they carried paint buckets, ladders, and tools up the stairs. While any other employer who'd lost their business would have left his workers out on the street, Ransom ensured every single one of them had temporary work, either in his other companies or helping with the rebuild.

'Are we going to the house?' she asked. 'I thought you said we wouldn't be able to start construction for at least a year?'

Persephone had loved their home on the rooftop, but they couldn't move back in until the construction on The Underworld was done. So they'd finally gone on that honeymoon he'd promised they could have anytime. They'd started in Paris, then made their way to the south of France. When they came back home to England after three weeks, Ransom had had another surprise for her. Since there was already construction being done on the lower floors of The Underworld, Ransom had decided to build a brand-new house—larger and even more grand, on the same spot as their previous home on the roof. For now, they'd found a temporary residence on Upper Brook Street, not far from Mabury Hall.

'No, we're not going to see the house. We're going to my office. I decided it needed some improvements and I wanted you to be the first to see them.'

They continued up until they reached his office. It was a miracle this entire floor and the roof had been untouched—otherwise, they would have lost all their records, as well as Persephone's notes on the brewery.

A smile touched his lips as he opened the door, and Persephone supposed it was for the same reason she too was grinning. This was, after all, where their journey began, on that winter night more than a year ago.

He gestured for her to enter first. 'After you.'

She stepped inside, excited to see what kind of changes he had made. To her surprise, it was exactly the same. He had the same flooring, the same desk, the same chair. Everything was the same as it had been before the fire except—

Oh.

She spun around to face him. 'Ransom, did you—'

'Do you like it?' He waved his hands at the empty walls and bare shelves behind the desk.

'I do!' She launched herself into his arms, and as he'd promised her, he caught her before she fell. Snaking her arms around his neck, she brought him down for a long, passionate kiss. 'Thank you.'

His green and brown eyes shone with what Persephone could only interpret as love. As Ransom had promised her, these last months he had begun to let go of the past. He spoke to her of his childhood and she listened patiently. Instead of locking up his feelings about his adoptive family or grandfather, he tried his hardest to express them. And while she knew there were bad days, she told him she loved him and they would get through this together.

Today, however, was one of the good days.

Releasing him, she took a quick glance around the room. 'Now that the walls and shelves are empty, you'll have to start a new collection.'

'I already have.' He strode behind his desk, picked up an object hiding on the top shelf, and handed it to her.

'My spectacles?' She chuckled. 'Why would you have these up there?'

'These are the spectacles you left with me that first night. I've kept them since then, hidden away, like the way I hid my obsession with you. But now—' he put them back in the middle most shelf, right in the centre '—I want to display it for everyone to see, though mostly for myself so I never forget the woman who brought me back my soul.'

She melted into his arms…and somehow wound up on her back, on top of the desk, with her skirts around her waist, and her husband making slow, sensuous love to her in the middle of the day.

'This…simply isn't fair,' she panted as soon as he finished. 'How do I always end up like this? You must be cheating somehow.'

'Cheating?' He raised his head to her. 'How am I cheating?'

'I don't know…but all you have to do is kiss me and touch me and I do whatever you ask.'

'You must be mistaken.' He brushed strands of damp stray hair from her face and neck. 'I told you, I never cheat.'

'You also said the house always wins,' she pointed out.

'Ah, but my queen, I think we can agree that in this game, we both win.'

* * * * *

If you enjoyed this story, be sure to read
Paulia Belgado's other great stories

May the Best Duke Win
Game of Courtship with the Earl

Get 3 FREE REWARDS!

We'll send you 2 FREE Books plus a FREE Mystery Gift.

FREE Value Over **$20**

Both the **Harlequin® Historical** and **Harlequin® Romance** series feature compelling novels filled with emotion and simmering romance.

YES! Please send me 2 FREE novels from the Harlequin Historical or Harlequin Romance series and my FREE Mystery Gift (gift is worth about $10 retail). After receiving them, if I don't wish to receive any more books, I can return the shipping statement marked "cancel." If I don't cancel, I will receive 6 brand-new Harlequin Historical books every month and be billed just $6.19 each in the U.S. or $6.74 each in Canada, a savings of at least 11% off the cover price, or 4 brand-new Harlequin Romance Larger-Print books every month and be billed just $6.09 each in the U.S. or $6.24 each in Canada, a savings of at least 13% off the cover price. It's quite a bargain! Shipping and handling is just 50¢ per book in the U.S. and $1.25 per book in Canada.* I understand that accepting the 2 free books and gift places me under no obligation to buy anything. I can always return a shipment and cancel at any time by calling the number below. The free books and gift are mine to keep no matter what I decide.

Choose one: ☐ **Harlequin Historical** (246/349 BPA GRNX) ☐ **Harlequin Romance Larger-Print** (119/319 BPA GRNX) ☐ **Or Try Both!** (246/349 & 119/319 BPA GRRD)

Name (please print)

Address   Apt. #

City   State/Province   Zip/Postal Code

Email: Please check this box ☐ if you would like to receive newsletters and promotional emails from Harlequin Enterprises ULC and its affiliates. You can unsubscribe anytime.

Mail to the Harlequin Reader Service:
IN U.S.A.: P.O. Box 1341, Buffalo, NY 14240-8531
IN CANADA: P.O. Box 603, Fort Erie, Ontario L2A 5X3

Want to try 2 free books from another series? Call 1-800-873-8635 or visit www.ReaderService.com.

HHHRLP23

Get 3 FREE REWARDS!

We'll send you 2 FREE Books <u>plus</u> a FREE Mystery Gift.

⭐ FREE Value Over $20

Both the **Romance** and **Suspense** collections feature compelling novels written by many of today's bestselling authors.

YES! Please send me 2 FREE novels from the Essential Romance or Essential Suspense Collection and my FREE gift (gift is worth about $10 retail). After receiving them, if I don't wish to receive any more books, I can return the shipping statement marked "cancel." If I don't cancel, I will receive 4 brand-new novels every month and be billed just $7.49 each in the U.S. or $7.74 each in Canada. That's a savings of at least 17% off the cover price. It's quite a bargain! Shipping and handling is just 50¢ per book in the U.S. and $1.25 per book in Canada.* I understand that accepting the 2 free books and gift places me under no obligation to buy anything. I can always return a shipment and cancel at any time by calling the number below. The free books and gift are mine to keep no matter what I decide.

Choose one: ☐ **Essential Romance** (194/394 BPA GRNM)   ☐ **Essential Suspense** (191/391 BPA GRNM)   ☐ **Or Try Both!** (194/394 & 191/391 BPA GRQZ)

Name (please print)

Address   Apt. #

City   State/Province   Zip/Postal Code

Email: Please check this box ☐ if you would like to receive newsletters and promotional emails from Harlequin Enterprises ULC and its affiliates. You can unsubscribe anytime.

Mail to the **Harlequin Reader Service:**
IN U.S.A.: P.O. Box 1341, Buffalo, NY 14240-8531
IN CANADA: P.O. Box 603, Fort Erie, Ontario L2A 5X3

Want to try 2 free books from another series? Call 1-800-873-8635 or visit www.ReaderService.com.

STRS23

HARLEQUIN
PLUS

Try the best multimedia subscription service for romance readers like you!

Read, Watch and Play.

Experience the easiest way to get the romance content you crave.

Start your **FREE TRIAL** at
<u>www.harlequinplus.com/freetrial</u>.